Lilies for Lauren

Lilies for Lauren

In Bloom Series Book 3

KASEY KENNEDY

Lilies for Lauren
In Bloom Series, Book 3

ISBN-13: 978-1-958942-08-6 (paperback)
ISBN-13: 978-1-958942-09-3 (hardcover)
ISBN-13: 978-1-958942-07-9 (e-book)

Cover and interior design by Alt 19 Creative

Author Website:
www.kasey-kennedy.com

Published by:

CHAPTER ONE

*L*AUREN LARGENT SET her wine glass on the coffee table, watching the burgundy liquid sway back and forth as she settled on the loveseat. She smiled as she glanced at the women surrounding her. They were an eclectic group, three young women and their seventy-year-old boss who owned the In Bloom Florist Shop in Bloomington, Illinois. It was the first week of January and they were having their year-end/New Year holiday party. Anna Lee had invited them to her home to eat a delicious potluck dinner and relax while enjoying each other's company outside of work.

Her boss, Anna Lee Foster, laughed at the extra-large, flip-board-size piece of paper that Paige was affixing to the front of a framed landscape print hanging above Anna Lee's couch.

Lauren smiled as Paige teetered on the soft cushions, her pink and white striped socks clashing with the blue plaid couch.

"Well, I wanted to share some best practices for our vision boards," Paige said, hopping down and pointing to the list.

<u>VISION BOARD GUIDELINES</u>
- ☐ Be Aspirational
- ☐ Be Intentional
- ☐ Be Specific
- ☐ Be Positive

Nica, Paige's roommate and another coworker, laughed and said, "That is the most Paige thing you've done in a while, Paige."

"Tease me all you want. I don't care," Paige returned. "I am so excited that we decided to include this activity in Anna Lee's holiday party! I make a vision board every year, and I think they pay off."

"Did you have 'get engaged' on your board last year?" Lauren asked.

"No, I didn't. After my breakup with Caleb the prior Christmas, I had no intentions of dating anyone, let alone getting engaged." Paige looked down at her left hand and wiggled her fingers. The light bounced off the beautiful green stone.

"Well, maybe that board didn't work so well," Anna Lee chimed in. "But for the better. I can't wait to see what you put on this year's board."

"I have a few ideas." Paige passed out legal pads to everyone. "I find it best to start with a blank piece of paper and just brainstorm ideas. Go wild. Shoot for the moon. If you dream it, write it down. I'm going to set a timer for eight minutes for this initial exercise." Paige started tapping on her phone.

"So, anything we can think of, we write down?" Lauren asked. She was a pro at creating goals and attacking them, but this was the first time she was doing a vision board.

"Yes," Paige replied. "Oh, wait. I have another paper to hang up. This list has some categories to help with brainstorming. You don't have to include any or all of these, but it helps me to get started."

Paige climbed up on the loveseat next to Lauren and taped a second piece of flip chart paper to another framed picture on Anna Lee's wall.

<u>AREAS TO CONSIDER:</u>
- ☐ HEALTH
- ☐ FINANCIAL
- ☐ EDUCATION
- ☐ RELATIONSHIPS
- ☐ HOME
- ☐ SPIRITUAL
- ☐ TRAVEL

Paige stepped off the loveseat and bumped into the coffee table. Lauren lunged for her glass of wine. *Whew, that was close. She glanced at the beige carpet underneath her feet and was thankful the wine didn't spill.*

Paige continued. "This is a starting list; you may come up with ideas not related to these categories, and that's okay."

Nica was sitting cross-legged at the coffee table. "What about hobbies?"

Paige nodded her head. "You can use that as another category."

Anna Lee jumped up from the couch. "Hold on. I have a box of colored pens that would be fun for this." She walked to a small chest of drawers near the front window and pulled a shoebox out of one of the drawers. "Here." She put the shoebox on the coffee table and took off the lid. There were hundreds of pens. "If you find one that doesn't write, drop it on the lid. I know a place that recycles them."

Lauren put her Montblanc ballpoint pen back in her purse and searched in Anna Lee's shoebox. She found a dark green one and tested it on the legal pad to make sure it worked.

"All right, ladies," Paige cheered. "Eight minutes. And go!"

Lauren looked at the blank sheet of paper in front of her. Where to begin? She already had her plans laid out for this year. She'd graduate in May and start her MBA program in the fall. The only unknown on her list was which grad school she'd go to. She had been accepted at her top three schools—The University of Chicago, which would mean being close to home—and there were advantages and disadvantages with that—Stanford, and Harvard. There were a few other schools she'd been accepted to, but those were the "just in case" schools. She was thankful that her parents had footed the bill for all application fees. She'd worried they would balk at her request to apply to ten MBA programs.

She had lots of vision board-worthy desires for when she was out of grad school—married by twenty-six, two kids before thirty, and a corporate CEO position before thirty-five. But a one-year vision board? There were only a few she could think of: a good roommate for grad school; a date to take to graduation so her parents didn't try to set her up with one of their law practice partners; and a fun trip over summer break—she was planning to go to Greece, and she would like to have a travel buddy. She had hoped to talk Paige into going, but now that Paige was recently engaged, she had a feeling it wouldn't work out. She'd know more once they started sharing their vision boards for the year.

Lauren had spent over two months in Europe the previous summer, traveling by train to a long list of desired destinations. She hadn't made it to Greece and really wanted to see the beautiful beaches and Instagram-worthy landscapes.

Two minutes into the brainstorm exercise, Anna Lee declared she was done. "I'm seventy years old, I know my limits," she said, leaving for the kitchen to get a refill on her wine. Her orange and white tabby cat, Salty, followed.

Lauren smiled at Anna Lee's comment and looked back at her own blank list. This was harder than she'd expected. She could put down the things she thought she was supposed to do—volunteer, work out more, and do something artistic, but that seemed like cheating. Paige had made it clear that this list was for the things that Lauren really wanted, her deepest dreams. Once she identified these things and became intentional about them, she could start to manifest them. Lauren struggled with that concept. Her parents had taught her that if you wanted something, you had to work hard at it. You created a plan, and you executed that plan. You worked harder than everyone else who wanted the same thing.

She'd taken that advice well. Being the only child of two over-achieving parents had made her an overachieving daughter. She loved to win. She loved to prove to her parents that she could do what she set out to do. She valued their praise and their attention. It wasn't always easy to get; they both worked sixty hours a week and were involved with all the right organizations and groups.

Lauren glanced at the timer that Paige had set in the middle of the coffee table. There were only two minutes remaining, and she was still looking at a blank page. She quickly scribbled "volunteer", "start a yoga practice", "trip to Greece", "decide on grad school", "graduate with a 4.0 GPA", and "begin research of Fortune 500 companies". There was no time like now to begin to narrow down the list of organizations she'd apply to once she was finished with school.

There was no need to put down "find a boyfriend" or "start a relationship". There was no time for that.

The buzzer went off, and Paige clapped her hands. "Okay, time's up. Does anyone want to share their list?"

Lauren shifted in her seat; she didn't have very many things written down.

Nica volunteered to go first and shared her list. Lauren thought it was sweet that she included Grady in her plans. They weren't sure whether Grady was her boyfriend or fiancé; Nica was sporting a ring but was non-committal about whether wedding bells were in their future or not.

Anna Lee went next. "The main thing on my list is to ensure that John's daughter, Deana, has a beautiful wedding this April. I feel blessed that his family has accepted our relationship. His girls are just the sweetest bunch! I'm going to go all out for Deana's wedding. It will be all hands on deck for that wedding. That's it. That's my vision."

"That is a wonderful vision, Anna Lee," Paige praised. "What about for your relationship with John, anything you'd like to see there?"

Anna Lee ran her hand down Salty's back, the cat was standing at her feet, looking for attention. "Well, I guess I could add that we both stay healthy enough to enjoy a full year together. That our relationship continues to grow and blossom."

"That's beautiful. Add it to your list." Paige turned her focus to Lauren. "Lauren, do you want to share?"

Lauren read off the items that she'd written down on her list. Then she asked Paige to read hers.

"Complete my internship with high marks, graduate in May, find a job after graduation. And..." She paused, taking a quick sip of her white wine. "Plan a wedding."

"Did you set a date?" Nica asked.

"Not yet. I know we just got engaged a week ago, but I don't want to have a long engagement and Trevor agrees. I love the fall, so maybe this fall. Or maybe sooner..." She smiled, her eyes glowing.

Lauren reached over and squeezed Paige's hand. "Oh, Paige. We are here for you. Whatever you need. It may be hard for you to do much planning while you're in New York, but we'll do whatever you need."

Anna Lee stood and raised her glass. "Ladies, let's have a toast." Everyone stood around the coffee table, glasses in hand. "To a beautiful year ahead, full of new growth, new adventures, lots of wedding bells, and good friends."

"*Salud!*" Nica said.

"Hear, hear!" Lauren chimed in.

Paige smiled as she clinked their glasses. "Cheers!"

Salty jumped up on the coffee table and meowed.

Lauren took a sip of her wine. She sighed inwardly, feeling the cozy glow melt any lingering tension. She was surrounded by ladies that cared about her and that she cared deeply about. The high expectations of her parents were forgotten for a moment, and she could just be herself. If only she could carry this feeling with her everywhere.

SUNDAY MORNING, LAUREN woke to the sound of her phone ringing. Ugh, she preferred to be up well before this weekly check-in with her parents. Preferably with a couple cups of coffee in her and a piece of paper with her talking points bulleted out. The bullet points made sure she didn't stray too far from what her parents wanted from her—the highlights of her weekly successes and the list of planned accomplishments for the coming week.

She stood up quickly and did a couple of jumping jacks to get her blood pumping before answering the phone.

"Good morning!" she said into the phone. She never knew if it would be her mother or father talking first or if they'd be together on the speaker phone; that was much more efficient, though not as intimate.

"Lauren!" It was Dad. "Good morning. You sound a little sleepy. Late night?" he asked, sounding disappointed.

"No. Not a late night. Guess I just forgot to set my alarm when I went to bed." She crossed her bedroom and made a beeline for the coffee pot in the kitchen. She was definitely putting an extra scoop of coffee into this morning's pot! "Must have needed the extra sleep today. How's Mom?"

She propped the phone on her shoulder as she scooped coffee into the filter. She knew her dad hated it when she put the phone on speaker and busied about. He got irritated at having to listen to the noise.

"She's good. She'll be here in just a few moments. She's heating muffins."

Great. I'll get to listen to them eat. "Nice," Lauren replied. She quickly hit the mute button while she ran water into the pot and poured it into the machine.

"Are you ready for the semester to start tomorrow?" Bob Largent asked. "Oh, your mother's here now."

Lauren quickly unmuted. "Hi, Mom!"

"Lauren," Nicole answered. "Answer your father, dear."

Lauren hit the start button on the coffee pot and wished she had her talking points in front of her. "Yes, I'm ready. I can't believe it's the last semester of undergrad. I'm prepared and ready to start."

"Good, good," Bob said. Lauren could picture him nodding his head in approval. "We have high expectations, honey."

As if I didn't know that! "I know. I won't disappoint you."

"Have you decided where you're going to go to grad school yet?" Nicole asked. Lauren heard the extra emphasis on 'yet'.

This is why she needed her notes. She was mentally putting together a list of pros and cons for all the schools she had been accepted to. She needed that list to be able to decide and then defend that decision with her parents.

"No, not yet. I'm working on it. I should have a better idea in a couple weeks."

She stared out the windows of her living room. Glancing up, she could see the rotunda above the McLean County Museum of History building across the street. She loved her apartment's location, charm, and twelve foot ceilings. It was in a former pencil factory in downtown Bloomington.

After searching for an apartment with her mom for several hours—her parents were paying for it and wanted to see it before she signed a lease—when she'd walked into this apartment, she'd known it was the one. And she was happy that her mother agreed.

It was a newly rehabbed building, and Lauren was the first to rent her apartment, so it was pristine. The hallway led into a small, fashionable kitchen. Spotless white cabinets hung on the wall. Underneath, a cream and brown speckled granite counter rested on top of dark brown floor cabinets. A bar-height counter served as a table for the tiny space. Her mother had chosen three solid wood bar chairs, along with the rest of the apartment's furniture, from her favorite high-end furniture store. Lauren was grateful that she had been allowed to shop with her mom and help pick *anything*.

Lauren listened to her parents debate their top picks for Lauren's graduate school. Her mother was partial to Stanford, and her dad was hoping she'd choose Harvard. They were disappointed that Lauren wasn't pursuing law like they had, but they'd come around.

She grabbed a plain white coffee mug out of the cabinet and set it next to the coffee pot. It wouldn't be long now before she'd be able to fill up on caffeine.

She murmured her agreement to her dad's repeated reasons for why Harvard would be best for her—the alumni connections being his top selling point. She could pretty much recite both of her parents' reasons for their preferred school; it had been the most common topic of conversation for the last three months, ever since the acceptance letters started coming in.

"Don't you agree, Lauren?" her mom asked.

Lauren realized she had drifted away from the conversation.

"Oh, I'm sorry, Mom. A large delivery truck drove by and drowned you out. What did you say again?"

A little white lie. Better than admitting she had been daydreaming.

"I can call your landlord and demand that they put thicker windows in that apartment," her dad said. He'd declared that he wouldn't have let Lauren take this apartment if he'd been with them when they found it. He did not like a century-old building being turned into apartments. He was sure there would be asbestos or other air quality hazards lurking.

"No, it's okay, Dad. The windows are fine. I just had one opened a little bit."

"What? The weather channel said it snowed there last night. Why do you have the window open?"

Lauren knew they were worried that she'd take up smoking while at college.

Thinking on her drowsy feet, she said. "I was doing some yoga earlier and got a little warm."

Would someone get warm doing yoga? She wasn't sure.

"Oh, that sounds wonderful," Nicole said. "I told you I love my Vinyasa Yoga class. I'm glad to hear you are taking it up. Did you hire an instructor? Join a class?"

"Um, no. YouTube video."

"Oh." Her mother sounded disappointed. Why get something for free when you could pay for a higher quality?

The coffee was finally brewed. Lauren poured a cup and waited thirty seconds before taking her first sip. *Ah, heaven.*

She glanced at the clock on the stove. They'd been on the phone for ten minutes. This wouldn't last much longer.

As if on cue, her dad said, "Well, dears. We need to hustle if we're going to get to brunch on time."

"Sure, Dad. I hope you both have an excellent week. I'll talk to you next Sunday."

"Have an excellent first week of classes, dear," she mom said. "Call us if you need any help."

"Of course." Lauren hung up after the goodbyes. She knew her parents meant well, but she also knew they didn't expect her to need any help. They had important jobs to do, and they expected her to treat school like a job and execute well. Full stop.

She set her phone on the counter and took her coffee cup to the leather couch in her living room. Sitting down, she thought about what she wanted to accomplish today. It was the last day before the semester began and she had a long list. But first she wanted to enjoy a cup or two of coffee. She'd give herself thirty minutes to relax before she tackled the list. She knew her goals for this semester—get straight A's, add a volunteer experience to her résumé, and finally make that decision on grad school. She just needed to work on how to get there.

CHAPTER TWO

AWK SPRINGER BLEW the whistle that hung around his neck, halting the basketball drill of the eleven and twelve-year-olds on the court.

"Listen up, Cardinals!" he shouted as the dribbles began to fade. "Great job today. I saw heart and hustle, my two favorite things, from all of you. Now, you know what's next. Drop those basketballs and run five laps. Go!"

He chuckled as he listened to the groans. No matter how many times he told them they had to run during practice so they could hustle during the games, they didn't like the laps at the end of practice.

"Hustle, hustle!" he called as he made his way to the sideline where the metal cart for basketballs stood. He pushed it back onto the court and began gathering the balls as he watched the boys running around the court.

"Jeffrey! Run! Move those legs!"

"Aw, Mr. Springer! I worked extra hard today."

"I know you did, kid. I saw you. I still need your hustle to end the practice. Show me you mean it!"

Hawk smiled to see Jeffrey kick it into a faster gear. "There you go! Nice!"

Once all the basketballs were on the cart, he pushed it to the storage room near the front desk. The community center space was always bustling with activity. After he coached this group of boys, a girls' volleyball clinic was scheduled to take over the gym.

Hawk closed the door to the storage room and heard his name being called. He scanned the large space for the location of the voice. Spotting Sharon Tuttle by the front desk, he met her eyes and waved. She was the program director for the community center and managed all the volunteers and coaches. She was also a friend of his from grade school and they'd stayed close over the years. She was the one that had recruited him to coach one of the boys' basketball teams at the center.

They'd tried dating once, just after college, but it didn't work out. Hawk smiled recalling how the entire time he'd felt as if someone would jump out at them and yell, "Surprise, you're on hidden camera!" At the end of the date, they'd both decided they were much better off being just friends.

He glanced around the gym at his basketball team. This was a fun group of kids. It had taken a few weeks, but they'd finally begun to leave their problems at the door and let Hawk coach and mold them on the floor. There were a couple of exceptionally talented kids in this group.

Sharon jogged over to him and gave him a side hug. "Hey, Hawk. How's it going?"

"Great! How about you?"

"Same. I'm excited about today's clinic. Want to stick around and help?"

"Thanks for the invite, but I can't. I promised my brother I'd help him replace the brakes on his car."

"You are a true jack-of-all-trades. Is there anything you can't do?" Sharon asked, watching the boys that were still running laps.

"Fall for the right woman, obviously."

"Obviously," she barked. "One of these days, Hawk, you're going to find the right lady. One that will put up with your special blend of b.s."

Hawk threw his head back and laughed heartily. "You know it."

"Yes, I do. Hey, that kid over there in the gray sweatshirt. Seems like he was headed to juvie last fall. What's his story?"

"Can't believe you remember that. Yeah, he was. But he got into a new foster situation that seems to be great for him. His attitude has changed, and he's more focused than he was last summer."

She nodded. "Darius, right?"

"That's right."

"I'm sure you've had a hand in his improvement, Hawk. You're one of the good ones."

"Right. Don't you forget it." He laughed again as he watched Darius walk toward the bleachers and grab his coat.

As the kid got closer, Hawk yelled. "Hey, Darius! Need a ride home?"

Darius sauntered over to them. "No, Mr. Springer. I got a ride. Hello," he said to Sharon.

"Oh, Darius, this is my friend, Sharon Tuttle. She's also the program director here."

Darius stuck out his hand. "Nice to meet you, Miss Tuttle."

She took his hand. "My pleasure, Darius. How are you liking basketball?"

"Love it. This guy's a good coach."

Hawk warmed at the praise. It wasn't that long ago that he'd had to fight for Darius' attention. He hadn't been sure the kid was going to turn around and it was heartwarming to see it happen.

"You're a good kid, Darius. Keep up the hard work. See you next Sunday?"

"Yeah, sure. See ya." Darius left.

Sharon checked her watch. "You're good for these kids, Hawk."

"They're good for me, too."

"Have you thought any more about fostering?" Sharon had been the one to talk to Hawk about the requirements and application process. He had been toying with the idea for months now.

Knowing the need for more quality foster homes and remembering how a concerned adult had pulled him from the brink of wrong decisions when he needed it most, had made Hawk ask her about the foster system.

At twenty-nine, Hawk felt his "biological clock" ticking. He hadn't found the right woman yet, and he yearned for kids. Coaching helped, but it wasn't the same as tucking someone into bed at night and reading them bedtime stories or taking them to a movie matinée or teaching them to ride a bike.

"I'm still thinking about it. I printed off the initial application like you suggested. It's sitting on my desk. I want to talk to all of my parents first." He smiled; it was complicated. His parents had divorced, both were remarried, and Hawk included his stepparents in everything. "I want to make sure I have their support. Being single and working full time, I would need it."

Hawk was a computer programmer at a large insurance company. He loved the problem solving, the creativity, and the team atmosphere at work. He'd started his position right out of college and was approaching his seventh anniversary in June. He couldn't imagine leaving a great company with good pay and benefits. He enjoyed what he did, and he was living where he'd grown up, with no plans to move away. He loved the small-town feel and mid-size city benefits of Bloomington/Normal.

"Yes, you would. Wish I knew the right woman to set you up with, Hawk, but you're a conundrum."

Didn't he know it. Dating was a conundrum for him. He always seemed to fall too hard and too fast. He was done looking. If he were to become a dad, it looked like he'd have to go it alone. Fostering seemed like a good way to test the waters. He decided to try it for a few years, and if being a single dad worked under those conditions, he'd see about adopting solo.

CHAPTER THREE

REVOR PULLED UP in front of Hawk's house and honked. Hawk grabbed his winter coat and keys and gave his Golden Labrador Retriever instructions and a pat on the head.

"I'll be gone a few hours, Goldie. Take a long nap, don't drink out of the toilet, and no barking at the neighbors. We'll go for a long walk when I get home."

Outside, he jogged down the length of his driveway. He glanced back at his quaint Cape Cod house and smiled to see Goldie's nose on the window. He knew Goldie would be sitting on the couch, keeping an eye on him and the neighborhood.

He hopped into the truck and slap-shook Trevor's outstretched hand. "How's it going, brother?" he asked his long-term friend.

"Great! Thanks for agreeing to run errands with me. I want to show Paige that I can pull this party together, and I don't want to miss anything."

Hawk chuckled. "You are over the moon for that lady. I'm here for it."

"Yes, I am. And in four short months, we'll be married and thinking about making babies."

"Paige agrees with your plan, right?"

"Yes, we've talked at length about it. We both have siblings who have young kids or are starting families, and we want our kids to be close to their cousins growing up. Tricia's boys are growing so fast, I can't keep up. Every week they are into something new."

"That's great, Trev."

Hawk thought about his own yearning for kids. The foster application was still sitting on his desk. It'd been there for weeks now. He worried that submitting it would set him up for disappointment if he didn't get approved. Would they approve a single man, as a foster parent?

"Hey. What just happened? Your mood shifted."

"It's nothing." It was everything. "I'm not going to drag you down before your party. Now, tell me about the group. Who's in the wedding? Any eligible bachelorettes?"

Trevor raised his eyebrows. "Wouldn't you like to know?"

"Seriously? Are you twelve?"

"No. Just kiddin'. All three bridesmaids are single, from what I understand. Of course, one is my sister Tricia, so you can just forget that."

"Yeah, that would be too weird."

"The other two are Paige's friends. Macey is a friend of hers from Pontiac. Lauren worked with Paige at the flower shop. She's a senior at ISU and is from Chicago. I've met both of them a few times, but don't know either very well. So, it's up to you to figure out if there's a connection. Just don't do anything to make my wedding awkward. Got it?"

"Loud and clear, Trev, loud and clear. Who am I paired up with for the ceremony?"

"Macey."

"And who are your other groomsmen?"

"Paige's brother Brian and Chase Bishop. You know Chase."

"Right." Hawk nodded. "I can't wait to meet everyone else. I'm here to support you—whatever you need. I'm happy you found the right person and somehow convinced that pretty bookworm to look your way."

"That I am. And look, one of these days, Hawk, the right lady is going to come along and fall madly in love with you. Be patient."

"Yeah, right. You've seen my dating history. It's been a freak show. The problem is, I fall fast, and I fall hard. Haven't learned the lesson to be patient."

LAUREN GLANCED AT her slim watch. She only had thirty minutes before she needed to be at the airport to pick up Paige. It was mid-February and Paige was back from New York for a small party to introduce the bridal party to one another. She and Trevor had decided they didn't want a long engagement. Paige would finish her internship in May, graduate from college, and they would marry in June.

Paige had called Lauren a week earlier to ask her to be in the bridal party and for the lift from the airport. Paige's flight would land less than an hour before the party started.

Lauren was looking forward to meeting the rest of the bridal party. At this point, she only knew Paige and Trevor. Paige was tight-lipped about the rest of the bridal party on the phone—she didn't want to give Lauren any misleading thoughts about the other members. The only hint she shared with Lauren was that one of the groomsmen was someone she'd wanted Lauren to meet for a long time.

Lauren pulled into the two-hour free parking lot in front of the terminal and parked. She sent a quick text message to Paige letting her know that she was waiting.

Five minutes later, she got a text from Paige saying that her flight had landed, but she needed to stop in the bathroom before she'd be out.

Lauren swapped out the playlist on her phone from classical to pop hits. She checked her makeup in the visor mirror and reapplied lip gloss. As she finished touching up her makeup, she popped the visor back up and saw Paige exit the building. She hopped out of the car and waved.

Paige waved back and rushed toward the car with a broad smile on her face.

"Oh my gosh, Lauren! I'm so glad to see you!" Paige squealed as she embraced her friend.

Lauren laughed as she hugged back. "Likewise. I've missed you. I can't wait to hear all about New York and the internship. Hop in."

Paige tossed her backpack in the back seat and settled into the car. "Are you busy tomorrow morning?"

"Nothing planned." Lauren backed out of the parking space.

"Let's go to breakfast, and I'll fill you in. Today I just want to focus on wedding planning. I'm so happy you're going to be in the wedding! I was worried that you would be off on a big trip again this June."

"Thank you for asking me. And no trips planned for June. I want to go to Greece at some point. I will be gearing up for grad school, though I haven't decided where I'm going yet."

"You haven't? That's not like you."

"I know. But let's save that conversation for tomorrow and focus on your wedding today. I was shocked when you said you want to get married in June."

Paige laughed softly. "You and everyone else. But I can't imagine a long engagement. I have half a mind to elope! I hate having a lot of attention on me, and I don't want a big affair. A simple wedding, with only our dearest family and friends—won't take too long to plan that."

"You are having Anna Lee do your flowers, right?"

"Of course! We're meeting her for lunch tomorrow to talk about it. I fly back to New York tomorrow night."

"We?"

"My mom, Trevor, and me. We're meeting at Anna Lee's house, since it's Sunday. Mom's driving down in the morning."

"So, your parents won't be at this get-together today?"

"No, it's just a meet and greet. Most of the bridal party doesn't know each other, so we wanted an informal 'get to know you' lunch. And we'll do a little planning, since we only have four months to pull this off."

"Yikes, I feel a panic attack coming on," Lauren laughed.

Paige chuckled. "I imagine you'll have a very long engagement, with a huge three-hundred-guest wedding."

Lauren rolled her eyes as she turned into Trevor's driveway. "Whoa. I hope not, but if my parents have a say, it might be."

Her left foot started tapping next to the brake. Being the daughter of two prominent Chicago lawyers practically required a three hundred-guest wedding. She imagined the months of planning every detail to perfection, with her mother making the final decision on everything. Her stomach flipped thinking about fighting her mom for control of her own wedding.

Paige stared at the house getting closer and sighed. "It won't be long until this is my home, too."

"Still hard to believe. You said not to bring anything, but I made a fruit salad anyway. I hope that's okay." She noticed several cars parked on the side of the drive and pulled behind the last one. "We're not the first ones here."

"I'm not surprised. I was cutting it close already, and with the twenty-minute flight delay..." She shrugged. "I'm thankful Trevor agreed to take care of all the food and set up and I just had to show up. Almost on time. And thank you for making a fruit salad, that was so thoughtful."

They exited the car, gathered their things, and walked toward the house.

"You still haven't told me who's in your wedding party," Lauren said, stepping onto the front porch.

"You'll see in just a few minutes. I bet we're the last to arrive."

There was no need to knock; Trevor threw the door open before they reached it. "You're here!" he shouted as he picked Paige up and spun her around. He set her back down with a grunt. "I didn't calculate your backpack when I made that move. How many books do you have in that thing?"

Paige smiled sweetly. "A few. Sorry about that. With the flights, I wanted to be prepared." She turned toward Lauren. "Trevor, you remember Lauren."

"Of course! Come on in, ladies, the rest of the gang is here!"

Lauren appreciated Trevor's enthusiasm. It was great to see a man so in love. She'd never experienced that before firsthand. Her parents were not outwardly affectionate toward her or toward each other. 'Emotions belong behind closed doors' was her mother's motto. As Lauren grew up, hugs became less frequent. She longed for the easy affection that Paige and Trevor shared. She hoped that her future husband would be able to show affection and teach her how to as well.

LAUREN FOLLOWED TREVOR and Paige inside. The front room was decorated with lavender and pale green streamers. There was a banquet table set up along the wall, filled with snack foods. Trevor pointed to it, and Lauren added her fruit salad to the spread.

"I'll get a serving spoon from the kitchen. You can put your coats in the study." Trevor pointed to a room across from the banquet table before hurrying toward the dining room, which Lauren assumed led to the kitchen.

Paige was hugging a tall blond guy who Lauren didn't recognize. Tapping her friend on the shoulder Lauren said, "Give me your coat and backpack and I'll put them in the study."

Paige handed over her backpack and shrugged out of her puffy coat. She mouthed a thank you to Lauren and went back to talking to the man.

Lauren wanted to unburden herself before being introduced to anyone. In the small study she found a pile of coats on a large wooden desk. She placed their coats on top and set Paige's backpack on the floor next to the desk.

Lauren took a moment to check her makeup in a small compact mirror she carried in her purse and stomped her feet to release her wool slacks from clinging to her knee-high socks. Satisfied that she was presentable, she walked back into the room where the guests were gathered.

Paige broke free of the conversation she was in and approached Lauren. "Let me introduce you to everyone. This is Tricia, Trevor's sister. Tricia, this is Lauren."

Lauren stuck her hand out to shake the tall brunette's. "Pleasure to meet you."

"Likewise. We're going to have to hustle to find dresses," Tricia said, turning back to Paige.

Paige nodded. "I know. I have a few ideas. Let me introduce Lauren to everyone, and we can chat about that." She turned to Lauren. "My friend Macey is getting food ready in the kitchen, so I'll introduce you to the guys next."

Paige introduced her to Chase Bishop, one of Trevor's friends. Lauren was excited to see that Chase, who would be walking down the aisle with her, was taller than her. At five foot eight inches tall, she wasn't always so lucky.

Paige glanced around. "Where's Hawk? I thought I saw him a minute ago. Let's try the kitchen. This way."

In the large country-style kitchen, they found a mess. A large tray of sliced beef had fallen and was upside down on the floor. A cute girl with short, curly blond hair had her hands in the air and hopped from foot to foot. "Oh, no," she groaned.

Trevor walked in from a side door with an empty cooler. "Found it," he said as he spotted the mess. "What happened?"

The other guy in the room shook his head. "It's my fault. I startled poor Macey."

"He snuck up on me," Macey said. "I was turning away from the stove, and he was right there."

"I didn't sneak intentionally," he said, chuckling. "Let me clean that up. I can run and get more, Trev, if I can borrow your truck."

"Hold on. Let's see if we need more. I bought enough food for a party of twenty, and there are only eight of us. We should be fine. I'll get the broom and dustpan."

Paige turned to Lauren. "Great timing." Turning back to the room, she continued. "Macey and Hawk, I'd like you to meet my friend Lauren. Lauren, you can figure out who's who. I'll give Trevor a hand."

Everyone laughed, and Macey jumped over the mess at her feet. "Hi, Lauren. I'm so excited to meet you! Paige has said such nice things about you. I'm going to dash off and pull off my shoes before I track beef juice through the house."

Lauren smiled and shook her head as Macey "dashed off". She turned to the man and inwardly sighed. *Oh dear, he is handsome.*

"Hi, I'm Lauren," she said, offering her hand.

One corner of his mouth perked up, and she longed to see a full smile on his face. He was at least six feet, with broad shoulders and a medium build. His face was full, almost perfectly rectangular, and he had a five-o'clock shadow. His eyes were wary, as if he already didn't trust her and she wondered if she were putting off her usual unapproachable vibe—that vibe she'd perfected to keep unwanted advances away. She was usually thrilled with the results, but not today. Today, she wanted this man to approach. Full on.

"Lauren. It's great to meet you. I'm Hawk Springer."

He seemed quietly confident, but distant. *His* "don't approach me" vibe was definitely turned on. Such a shame. Maybe he was attracted to Macey, and irritated that his sneaking up on her had been interrupted.

"The pleasure belongs to me." She was thankful she'd been forced to attend formal events with her parents. Approaching people, handling small talk, never bothered her. "You wouldn't happen to know where the beverages are, would you?" she asked.

He smiled again, that half smile. Why wouldn't he give up the whole thing for her? She sighed inwardly. She took a moment to study his eyes. They seemed to squint slightly, and it was hard to tell what color they were. She'd have to get closer, but not too close.

"Yes. Trev is filling another cooler, but there's a cooler with beers in the dining room. This way." He gestured for her to follow him.

In the dining room, her eyes swept the space. There was a very large table pushed up against the wall. There were no chairs, no decorations on the walls, and no other indication that this was a dining room.

"What would you like to drink?" Hawk asked, pointing toward the assorted bottles of booze, mixers and a large tub filled with soft drinks and cans of beer.

"What are my options?" she asked with a teasing lilt.

"I'm no bartender, but I can make a decent rum and Coke or tin and tonic. There's wine or I can grab you a can of something."

"Don't you mean gin and tonic?"

"I think they taste like tin; I like my name better."

Lauren smiled. This guy was funny and charming and handsome. A perfect trifecta. "I'll take a white wine, please."

He picked up a couple of bottles, and seemed to assess which was best for her. Holding out a bottle of Chardonnay, he raised an eyebrow.

"That'll be fine," she replied to the question in his eyes. She leaned toward him to get a napkin while he poured the wine. As she got close to him, she could smell his aftershave or cologne. He smelled like a bright day in the woods—not that she'd ever been to the woods, but he smelled the way she imagined it to be.

"So, how do you know Paige?" he asked as he handed the glass to her. Lauren noticed that he grabbed a craft beer for himself.

"We work together. Or I should say worked, before she went to New York. At a flower shop here in town, In Bloom." Was she rambling? It seemed she'd lost her power of conversation.

"Trevor told me you're a college student, too."

"Yes, and a senior like Paige. But she's an English major. I'm a business major."

"Business, huh?"

"What about you? What do you do?" Being a friend of Trevor's, she assumed he was late twenties, like Trevor.

"I'm a computer programmer. But that's not who I am. That's just how I make a living."

Lauren was confused. What you did made you who you were. Her parents were lawyers. She would be an executive. What else was there? "Interesting. Then who are you, Hawk Springer?" she asked, interested in the answer.

"A dog dad."

"A what?"

Hawk glanced down at his feet. Lauren's eyes followed his gaze down. He had on dress shoes and slacks. He wasn't too casual. She appreciated the effort.

He chuckled and met her eyes again. "I'm a dog dad. A big brother. A respectful son. A guy who loves the outdoors and hiking. Who volunteers. That's me."

Lauren paused. This guy defined himself by what he was *outside* of work. *That's crazy.* "What kind of volunteering do you do?"

His face lit up. "I coach a youth basketball team at the community center. I love it. Do you volunteer?"

"I haven't, but I'd like to. It would be great to do some this semester—I think it would help round out my résumé. You're interesting, Hawk Springer."

"You're thinking I'm pretty boring, right?"

"No, not boring. I mean, I'm sure hiking isn't boring."

"You don't know? You've never been?" he asked incredulously.

"Honestly? No. I'm a city girl."

"Where are you from?"

"Chicago."

"Chicago is a fairly green city," he said. "There are all sorts of forest preserves in and around the city. How have you never been on a hike?"

"It's just not something I've done."

"I'll have to take you sometime."

That was pretty forward of him considering they'd just met! She'd never go on a hike with a stranger, even if he was a friend of Trevor's. Well, she'd probably never go on a hike, period.

"That sounds…nice." She needed to change the subject fast. She tried to think of benign topics—sports? No, she didn't follow sports. Politics? Heck no. Not benign. The weather? Way too boring. She was out of ideas. "Well, I should mingle."

"See you around."

That was a given, but she didn't have to interact with him. Other than his rugged good looks, there seemed to be nothing at all interesting about him. He seemed too relaxed, not a go-getter like her.

CHAPTER FOUR

AWK WATCHED LAUREN walk toward the front room. Her cream-colored sweater looked softer than the underbelly fur on a kitten. She wore dark brown slacks and dark brown boots with chunky heels. She wasn't overly done up. He'd noticed simple gold hoop earrings and a delicate gold chain around her neck and a bangle watch. No rings. No over-the-top makeup. Elegant. Not what he was expecting from a college co-ed who was a good friend of Paige's. Paige was a sweet, down-to-earth, small-town gal. Lauren seemed like the exact opposite of all those things. Opposites attract, even in friendships, he supposed.

He turned back toward the kitchen to see if there was anything he could do to help now that he'd gotten Lauren, and himself, a drink. Trevor shooed him away and told him to go to the front room with the other guests. Trevor and Paige were going to introduce everyone and make a few announcements before they ate.

In the front room, he saw Lauren sitting on the loveseat with Chase, the one she would walk down the aisle with. He'd asked Trevor for the matchups while they were running errands. He didn't like the poke in his gut at the sight of the two of them on the couch. Why in the world should that bother him? They'd only just met, and Hawk didn't have a claim on her. He knew Chase

27

well, though, and Chase had a reputation for chasing the pretty ladies. Ha! He grinned at his own word choice. Chase wasn't the greatest-looking guy around—and Hawk didn't fancy himself as good-looking, either—but Chase had a way with the ladies. A charmer. The king of charm. He could talk to anyone about anything. He was probably pulling Lauren's deepest secrets out of her. They appeared to be old friends, not new acquaintances.

Hawk twisted his neck, trying to relieve the tension he felt. With Lauren occupied, he strolled over to where Macey and Tricia were talking. They were talking about kids; he'd met Tricia's two boys on a few occasions and Macey was talking about her twin nieces.

As he approached, Tricia brought him into the conversation. "So, Hawk, now that your wingman is getting married, when is it your turn?"

"You may find this hard to believe, but he stinks as a wingman. Or I stink with the ladies. Maybe both are true. What about you, Macey? Are you bummed at losing another single lady in your circle?"

"No. I'm thrilled for Paige. Besides, being in separate locations since high school, it's not like we get to go out together much anyway."

"Are you in a relationship?" Tricia asked. Hawk was glad she did because if he had been the one asking, it might have been seen as hitting on Macey. And even though she was cute, he didn't intend to ask her out.

"Not really. I didn't want to get serious about anyone. I'm leaving for a two-year teaching commitment in Baltimore. I don't know where I'll settle after that. I met a guy last year that I see occasionally. He was my date to Paige's brother's wedding last fall."

"Ah, a friend with benefits?" Tricia asked with a wink.

"Oh, no." Macey blushed. "Just an occasional date. Maybe it will lead to something long term, but not now."

"Will you invite him to Paige and Trevor's wedding?"

"Probably." Macey smiled. "What about you, Hawk? Will you bring a date to the wedding?"

Hawk reflexively glanced over to Lauren, wondering if she were listening. She didn't appear to be. "I'm not sure yet. I think it's a little difficult, standing up in a wedding and having a date that's not."

Tricia must have caught his glance because she jumped in. "And sometimes it's nice to be single at a wedding. Did you meet—"

She was cut off by Trevor's booming voice. "Okay, everyone. We'd like to make a few announcements." Everyone stopped talking and gave their attention to Trevor, who was holding Paige's hand as she stood by his side.

Paige jumped in. "First we need to get my brother, Brian, to join us." She picked up a cell phone that was lying next to the TV in the corner. She tapped a few times on her cell phone and pulled up a video chat window on the TV screen. A few seconds later, the image of her brother appeared on the screen.

"Hi, Brian!" Paige said, propping the phone up against the side of the TV. "I'll introduce you to everyone in just a moment. First, we want to thank all of you from the bottom of our hearts for supporting us today and for the wedding. It means the world to us to have you all beside us on our special day."

"And going forward," Trevor joined in. "We'll need the support from all of you to make our marriage as strong as it can be."

"Heck, yeah!" Tricia raised her glass, and everyone followed.

"Thanks, Trish," Trevor said as Paige began handing out gifts to everyone.

"We wanted to give everyone a little something to make this day memorable. You all mean so much to us and we are grateful that you've agreed to support us," Paige said as she handed out rectangular boxes wrapped in pale green paper. "When Trevor and I were talking about this day, we spent time talking about the words that sprang to mind when we were thinking about all of you, both our siblings that are here and our dear friends. So many words to describe what relationships are like with all of you."

She passed the last gift to Chase and turned to the screen. "Brian, your gift is in the mail. It will be anticlimactic when you get it if you watch everyone open theirs now. If you want the thrill of opening it without knowing what it is, you can drop off the video call now, and we'll call you back in a little bit."

He was shaking his head before she finished. "I'm good. I don't want to miss anything."

"Very well," Paige continued. She returned to Trevor's side and pulled an index card out of the back pocket of her pants. "Before you open your gifts, these are some of the words that we came up with.

"Fun. Great listeners. Loving. Loyal. Caring. Adventurous." She looked at Hawk and smiled. "Funky. Outrageous. Achievers." She looked up at Lauren and smiled. "And illuminating." She put extra emphasis on the last adjective.

Trevor chimed in. "On that note, go ahead and open your gifts."

Paige picked up a remote lying on the TV stand and hit a button. Music blared from the surround sound speakers. Hawk recognized the tune right away, "Shine a Light" by the Rolling Stones.

Hawk put his beer bottle on the side table and ripped open his gift, even as he glanced at Lauren. She was still on the couch next to Chase, and it was beginning to annoy him. He dropped the wrapping paper to the floor and looked at the gift in his hand, smiling as Paige's stress on the last descriptor made sense. He was holding a rechargeable, super bright, LED flashlight. The box had some weight to it. It looked high-quality and could be very useful in an emergency.

There were several laughs among the group. Tricia yelled to be heard over the music. "You two are the cheesiest."

Trevor laughed and shouted back, "And you love us for it."

Tricia rolled her eyes and nodded. Hawk felt a similar sentiment. He loved to see how relaxed and excited Trevor was with Paige by his side. Last year had been a challenge for Trevor and Tricia when they lost their dad to lung cancer. Hawk decided to call his dad and his stepdad on the way home, just to say hello.

Macey had pulled her gift out of the box and started using it as a microphone as she began singing along to the chorus of the Rolling Stones song. Hawk smiled and decided to join in. Shortly, everyone was using their flashlight as a microphone whether they knew the words or not. Everyone except Lauren.

LAUREN PUT THE gift box on the couch next to where she was sitting. It was a nice gift, and she'd appreciate it in the apartment if the lights ever went out again. With spring storms coming, she wouldn't be surprised if it were needed soon. She stood and went to the dining room to survey the beverage choices again. She didn't recognize the song playing, though it seemed everyone else did, so she didn't feel the need to attempt to lip-sync with the group. She noticed a couple in the group that should have been lip-syncing instead of singing at the top of their voices. But not Hawk; she heard his deep voice keeping the melody nicely.

She thought about another glass of wine, but she had to drive home and didn't want to overdo it. Besides, she needed to keep her wits about her, especially with Chase's not-so-innocent flirting. She wished she were getting the same attention from Hawk. Wait. What? Why would she want attention from Hawk? They were as compatible as fire and water. Sure, he was very attractive, but would he share any of her interests? Would he be willing to pick up and move with her if she were offered a position in another city? Another state? Another country? That was her dream—to be able to lead a large division or organization that had a global reach.

Hawk seemed like a homebody from her brief interaction with him. A "dog dad"? Who says that?

She finally decided on a diet ginger ale. Before getting a new drink, she took her wine glass into the kitchen. There was a pan soaking in the sink, so she put the empty glass on the counter next to it. Turning to join the others again, she was startled to see Hawk standing in the doorway.

"Not a Stones fan?" he asked.

"Is that who it is?" she returned.

The left side of his mouth lifted. That slow, easy, almost-smirk.

"Yeah," he said. "What kind of music do you listen to?"

"All kinds."

He laughed, a low, rumbly sound. "Have a favorite?"

"Not really. I listen to a lot of classical when I'm studying. It's hard to concentrate when there are lyrics." She had never admitted that to anyone. Her peers were into energetic pop music. Sometimes she felt like she couldn't think with all the noise.

"Makes sense."

"What about you?" she asked, really wanting to know.

"All kinds," he said, repeating her words.

"And your favorite?" She could play his game. At least they were talking.

"Classic." He paused. "Classic country. Bluegrass. Folk. Music where you can understand what's being sung."

"Oh. Interesting."

"You hate music."

"I never said that."

"What *do* you like, Ms. Lauren?"

She wondered why he called her that. So formal. So distant. He must not like her. He was just toying with her. She didn't need to put up with this. She could go back to Chase and enjoy the attention.

"I like learning and leading. I like to travel. I like my friendships."

"Movies or TV shows?"

"Movies."

"Cooking or take-out?"

"Hmm. Is this 'twenty questions'?"

"Something like that. Play along."

She looked at the floor, considering. "I would like to be a better cook. But living alone, it's usually take-out. What about you?"

"Same."

Paige interrupted their conversation. "Hey, we're going to talk about a few tactical things for the wedding; would you guys join us, please?"

"Of course," Lauren answered immediately.

She heard Hawk agree as well. They headed toward the front room and assumed their earlier places. Lauren sat next to Chase on the couch and Hawk stood in the doorway across from her. She tried to avoid meeting his eyes while Trevor and Paige outlined their vision of the wedding and shared a few key dates.

Lauren thought about her desired trip to Greece. She might not make it this year, after all. She didn't know where she would be moving at the end of the summer, and she'd be tied up here until the wedding, at least. She glanced at Hawk and felt a tingling in her chest, an excitement she couldn't explain. He'd be at the wedding. Their paths would likely cross a few times before then. For the first time in a long time, she was curious about what was right in front of her and not fixated on something months and years down the road.

CHAPTER FIVE

*L*AUREN AND PAIGE met at Max's Coffee Shop for breakfast the next day. Lauren asked to meet early, so she could be home in time to talk to her parents.

They settled into a booth and rehashed the party. Paige was thrilled with how well it had gone. She was thankful they could do a video call and include her brother, Brian.

Lauren asked Paige about the internship and enjoyed the stories about Paige's experiences exploring the city of New York. Paige said she was looking forward to spring when she'd be able to explore even more on foot.

After they'd finished eating and were waiting on their checks, Paige asked Lauren what she thought about Chase. Paige had noticed that they'd spent a lot of time talking at the party.

"He was very nice. Unassuming, easy to talk to." Lauren twisted the empty coffee cup in her hand.

"And Hawk?" Paige asked in a teasing tone.

"Nice. Handsome."

"Ah. Yes. He's the one I've been wanting to set you up with for months. I think you'd be adorable together. He's the sweetest guy. Always there when his friends need him. He's a rock. Solid."

Lauren heard "boring" and "settled" behind Paige's words. "Other than being handsome, I didn't think he had a lot going for him. He seems to be content in a nonmanagerial position. Not very upwardly mobile."

Paige's brow furrowed. "From what I understand, he's good at his job and earns lots of praise from his leaders. Like I said, he's steady. Not everyone wants to be in management. I don't!" She laughed and shifted gears. "I think a woman would be truly blessed to have Hawk by her side. He's a bit of a teddy bear, but he would be a grizzly if anyone messed with his partner. I love men that are strong like that. Don't you?"

Lauren considered. Of course, she loved strong men. Her dad was strong, tough, a no-nonsense negotiator who knew how to fight hard to get what his clients deserved and then some. He was ambitious and determined, and you knew that when you first met him. He didn't hide that strength behind a soft exterior. She thought that's what she wanted in a man, too. Hawk didn't seem to fit the definition of masculinity that she admired.

That was her head speaking, but when she considered how her body had reacted to Hawk Springer, the racing heartbeat and the warm cheeks, it was a whole different realm of emotions and physical responses. Even thinking about him now and imagining the way his mouth tilted to the side in a half smile, like you really had to earn his whole smile, caused her heart to beat a little faster. She wasn't used to this kind of attraction to a man. If she were interested in someone, she might feel heightened curiosity, but never this rapid heart rate and accelerated breathing.

Her meandering thoughts brought up an image of resting her head on Hawk's chest. She had the sensation of his arms wrapping around her and his woodsy scent surrounding her. She sighed without realizing it. It was a comforting feeling, not boring.

"Lauren?" Paige repeated twice. "Don't you?"

Lauren couldn't recall the exact question. Something about strength. "Yes, sure. But I don't think Hawk is the right person for me. I've always dreamed about dating a natural leader. Someone who's ambitious, can take charge, and who wants to achieve a long list of accomplishments."

"Like you," Paige responded.

"Yes, like me. That's not bad, is it?"

"Not at all. I love setting goals and going after them. You know that. I know you do, too. Just like when we did the vision boards. You had some great ideas for that. How is that coming along for you?"

Lauren was relieved that Paige was off the Hawk subject. "Good. Making progress on most items. Still need to decide on an MBA program, but the rest are on track."

"What about volunteering? I remember you had that on your vision board. Any luck there?" Paige thanked the server as the checks were put on the table.

"Oh, right. No, nothing there. But that might have to wait until fall, after I start grad school, with graduation and your wedding in June."

Paige tilted her head. "Don't you think it will be even harder to find time for volunteering once you start grad school? The work will be intense, and you'll be in a new place, making new friends. Sounds like enough of a challenge."

Lauren took her wallet out of her purse and slid the debit card out. She knew her parents wouldn't blink at the expense. They never did. "Maybe, but I don't really have the time now between school and work."

"Well, maybe something will come along. I hate to rush off, but I need to get back to Trevor's place. My mom is going to meet us there and ride with us to Anna Lee's to plan our flowers for the wedding. I'm so excited that Anna Lee will be designing the arrangements." She squeaked a little. Lauren couldn't blame her.

"Anna Lee is the best in town. And I'm not just saying that because I work there."

They exited the restaurant and went their separate ways.

Lauren drove home so she could take the call with her parents without any distractions. After the call, she planned to go to the campus library to study for a few hours before going to the grocery store. She wanted to be well-prepared for the week ahead. It helped ease the Sunday night anxiety.

HAWK KNEW HE was pushing his athletes a little harder than usual during Sunday's practice, but he couldn't help it. He was distracted, thinking about meeting Lauren the day before. She was very pretty, smart, and put-together. And it irritated him whenever he thought of her spending so much time talking to Chase and not him.

He usually had no trouble keeping a lady's attention. He was told that his caring eyes and quiet demeanor drew people in. People liked talking about themselves, and Hawk prided himself on his listening skills.

But it didn't seem to work on Lauren. After their initial conversation, she seemed to be actively disinterested. It was too bad because he could easily imagine dating her. He'd love to take her hiking. He couldn't remember the last time he'd met someone that had never hiked before. How strange. He pictured a pretty, easy hike, a romantic picnic lunch, and a lot of easy conversation. Alas, it didn't seem that was going to be possible with Miss Lauren Largent.

He blew his whistle to stop the free throw drill and told the players to huddle up. "We have our first tournament of the season next Saturday. It's here, and we're up against several strong teams, but I know our team is stronger. You have shown heart and desire to win. I'm looking forward to seeing what you've got when it comes to real competition, not a practice game with your teammates. Be here one hour before the game to warm up. I'll have the starting lineup at that time. Now, hands in." He waited for all the boys to put their hands together in a circle. "Go team. On three. One. Two. Three!"

"Go team!" They all shouted.

"All right, ten laps to finish up today. Let's go!"

He blew the whistle over the groans. He smiled to himself as he picked up a couple of loose balls from the floor. He walked to the cart near the storage room and plopped the balls on the top rack, then rolled the cart to the middle of the court.

Once the court was cleaned up, he cheered on the kids that were tiring and waved to Sharon. She met him in the middle of the court and watched the young men running.

"What's up, Hawkster?" she asked.

"Not much. Our first tournament is next Saturday. I think they're ready."

"Is the tourney here?"

"It is."

"Cool. I may stop by." She smiled and waved at Darius when he shouted hello to her. "Hey, how was that wedding-prep party yesterday? Meet anyone interesting?"

Hawk thought of Lauren. Interesting was a good word. "Yes."

"Care to expand?"

"Not really. I met someone, but it's not going to work out."

"Oh?"

"She didn't seem to find me charming." To say the least.

"What? A female that was able to resist your charms?" she teased.

"Hey, now. You managed to resist my charms."

"You forget that I knew you before you had any charm."

He laughed. "All right, smart aleck. That may have been true when we met in third grade, but I've been able to turn up the charm in the years since."

"Sure, sure. And that charm went far on our first and only date."

"Your beauty had me tongue-tied, Miss Sharon."

She scoffed. "Oh please. In all seriousness, tell me about this lady you met. The one that didn't fall for your charms upon first meeting you."

"College senior. A classic beauty. Sophisticated."

"Ah. There's your problem."

The side of his mouth turned up. Sharon always gave it to him straight. "You may be right. She may be too much of a jet-setter for me."

Sharon laughed. "If I remember correctly, you're terrified of flying. So, yeah, that probably wouldn't work. You need to get her out of your mind pronto." She looked at her watch. "Hey, I got to run. Catch ya next Saturday." She hurried off.

His basketball team was finishing their laps. He hadn't paid enough attention to whether they'd completed all ten laps, but he wasn't going to worry about it. Sharon had got him thinking. He did hate to fly, would rather go to the dentist for a root canal than get on a plane. If Lauren was the jet-setter he imagined she was, that was just one more reason to forget her.

If only his heart would let him.

CHAPTER SIX

I T HAD BEEN three weeks since Trevor and Paige's bridal party get-together. Lauren was neck-deep in studies and still hadn't decided where to go to grad school, but she had developed a scoring system that she was evaluating each school with.

Her weekly call with her parents had put her in a grumpy mood. They couldn't understand why she hadn't decided yet. She announced that she was working through her analysis and would have more to report next week.

After throwing a load of laundry into her in-unit machine, she stepped into the kitchen and began preparing a protein smoothie.

She almost missed the phone ringing because of the whirring of the blender. She glanced at the screen; unknown number. Nope. Not falling for that.

The ringing stopped and started right up again. Unknown number again. Odd. Maybe she should answer it. She took the blender cup off and tapped it on the counter before removing the lid. The ringing stopped and restarted AGAIN.

With a soft grunt, she answered. "Hello?"

"Lauren! Hi. It's Hawk. Trevor's friend."

Oh, interesting. Though it had been weeks since they'd met, she thought of him often. His warm eyes and lopsided grin flashed into her mind at the oddest moments. She looked forward to seeing him again but was surprised to hear from him.

"Hi. Of course. How are you?" She pulled a stainless-steel straw out of the drawer and popped it into her breakfast-in-a-cup.

"Good. Sorry for all the calls, thanks for answering."

"How many times were you going to call before just leaving a voice mail?" She hoped he picked up her teasing tone.

"I didn't have a set number; I was going by the feel. I got your number from Trevor, who got it from Paige. Hope you don't mind."

"No, not at all." She bit back the confession that she'd fallen asleep the night before with an image of him in her mind. "What's up? Is this wedding-related?" Gosh, she hoped not.

"No. Actually, I have a proposal for you." He paused and cleared his throat.

A proposal? For her?

"Yes?"

"At the party, we talked about volunteering, and I remember you saying that you might have some time for that this semester."

She *had* said that. Why did she say that? This was her last semester of undergrad. She was determined to get straight A's. She had a job. She had parents with high expectations. She had already gotten accepted to all the grad schools she'd wanted; she didn't need to pad her applications. The only reason would be an altruistic one. People talked about how volunteering filled something in them. Her parents always talked about giving back, but to them that meant cutting a check, not volunteering their valuable time.

But she *had* put it on the darn vision board.

"I remember."

"Well, the community center where I volunteer has a spring fundraiser every year. There's a formal dinner, a silent auction, and some other fundraising activities. I volunteered to organize the formal event this year, and I need some help. With your business degree and organization skills and my charm, I think we can knock this out of the park. I'm competitive, and I'd love to surpass last year's dollar amount raised. What do you think?"

He paused, and Lauren imagined his eyebrows raised and that sweet half-grin of his as he waited for her response.

She hadn't thought of him as competitive. It was interesting new information.

"Sounds like I'd be doing all the hard work, and you'd get all the credit? Is this how it would play out?"

He laughed, a low throaty sound that Lauren felt in her toes. She was going to have to figure out how to make him do that all the time.

"No. I'm not expecting you to do all the hard work. I'm dedicated to the success of this event. I could just use some help."

She took a small sip of her shake. "Tell me more about this community center."

"It's an amazing place. They have a teen lounge that is open after school and weekends. It's a safe place for kids to just hang out, play games, and have some fun. They also have all sorts of programming for the community—exercise classes, sports teams—basketball, volleyball, tennis, baseball—they have craft classes for kids and adults. They have day trips, to Springfield, Lincoln, even Chicago. There's a lot to do."

Lauren could hear his pride and enthusiasm for the place. "I could help, but you should know I've never done anything like this."

"I'm confident that you can and will succeed at anything you attempt, Lauren. It's a great cause, and if you're looking to build your résumé, this would be a great thing to add."

"Why do you do it?"

"Do what?"

"Volunteer."

"For the kids. They need a place like the community center, so they stay out of trouble. Stay off the streets. Stay away from making bad decisions." As he spoke, his words came faster, his passion apparent.

"It sounds like you speak from experience." She took her protein shake and sat on the couch; her feet up next to her. She pulled an all-white cashmere throw over her legs. She was still in her pajama shorts and T-shirt, and the shake was giving her a chill. And she wouldn't mind if this call took a while.

"I do. Joining the community center when I was a kid saved me from making some terrible decisions. I needed the outlet for my energy and found mentors who took me under their wing." He paused. "My parents split up, and it hit me like a ton of bricks."

"How old were you when your parents split?"

"Thirteen."

"Wow."

Lauren thought about how different their backgrounds were.

"Too heavy for a Sunday morning?" he asked.

"Sundays are perfect for tough conversations." She thought back on the earlier call with her parents. "During the week you have school or work, Saturdays are for errands and fun, and Sundays are a good time to reset and take stock. Taking stock can lead to tough conversations."

"Spoken like you have some experience with that."

"Sundays are my weekly check-in with my parents."

"Ah." Hawk chuckled softly. "Have you had that conversation already today? It's only ten a.m."

"I have."

"And how did it go?"

Lauren wasn't certain, but he seemed genuinely interested. She sighed. "It was fine. They're on my case a bit about grad school. I haven't chosen a school yet. They don't like open loops."

"Open loops?" he asked.

"Unmade decisions. They are two type A personalities that make decisions and bulldoze forward."

"I got the impression you're a type A, too."

"I am, but I don't want to rush into this decision."

"Sounds wise."

"Hey, I don't mean to bore you with my troubles. That's not why you called."

"You're absolutely not boring me." She heard his low, throaty laugh again. "So, am I rushing you into a decision if I ask again about helping out for this fundraising event?"

Lauren smiled. "Sometimes you don't need deep analysis to make a decision. I'd be happy to help you out."

"Great! What are you doing next Saturday? I have a meeting with the director to get the low-down about the dos and don'ts. Would you be able to meet with us?"

Lauren grabbed her tablet and opened it to her schedule. "What time? I work in the morning."

"Three p.m. It may take a couple hours. Could I take you to dinner afterwards? To say thanks for helping and maybe to continue brainstorming."

Lauren hesitated. Her schedule was open. She didn't have a date or anything; she rarely did. He hadn't made it sound like a date—more like a business meeting. "Sure. That would be fine."

"Fantastic! Should I pick you up, or do you want to meet there?"

"Let's meet there." She wanted to have her own means of transportation.

"Okay. I'll text you the address of the community center. See you there on Saturday at three p.m."

Lauren appreciated his going over the details again. She added the appointment into her calendar and would add the address once he sent it. It would be good to report to her parents next week that she was volunteering—and it would be nice to see Hawk again.

HAWK HUNG UP the phone and smiled. Success. He really hadn't been sure she'd agree, but she had. He looked at the fund-raising task list he had started on his computer. Eliciting Lauren's help was step one in a list of a thousand things. They would need more help, more volunteers, but he really wanted Lauren by his side. He wanted to get to know her better, and what better way to do that than to work together? There wouldn't be the pressure of always being on your best behavior or saying what you think the other person wants to hear like there was with dating.

Volunteering together would get tough. They would see each other under stress and pressure, and they would have lots of time to get to know each other. The good, the bad, and the not-so-great.

He pushed back from his computer desk and stood to stretch. Before calling Lauren, he'd spent a couple of hours thinking through a tricky coding problem he had at work. He'd had a breakthrough and the thrill of that had propelled him into making the call to Lauren.

Seeing him stand, Goldie, got out of her bed and stretched, her tail wagging. She trotted over to Hawk and put her nose in his hand.

"You want to go for a walk, Goldie?" Hawk asked, knowing the answer.

He put on his tennis shoes, drank a glass of water, and grabbed the dog leash.

Outside, they turned north and started walking. Hawk thought about the conversation with Lauren. He was thrilled she'd said yes. It would be great to get to know her better, and he was confident that she would be a strong partner for this fundraiser.

Goldie tugged on the leash. She'd spotted a squirrel and wanted to take off after it. Hawk redirected her.

They walked on, and Hawk surveyed the outdoor work being done. People were taking advantage of the sunshine and upper-fifties temperature. It made him think about his own yard and he planned to sow grass seed when he got home. Goldie was creating a few bare patches with her paws.

He didn't mind the work to fix things or clean up after her; he appreciated the companionship the dog had brought. He thought about having a family in the future and knew he'd always want to have a dog around, too. He remembered several nights after his parents' divorce when he'd cried into the fur of the family dog. That dog, Mooch, had kept all his secrets and was there to lick away his tears. So far, Goldie had not had to dry his eyes, but if this fundraiser went sideways, it might be needed.

CHAPTER SEVEN

*L*AUREN KNEW THE Saturday morning shift at In Bloom would be busy and she was appreciative of the fast pace that came with a hard deadline. They had a large wedding to prepare for with twenty-five centerpieces, eight bridal bouquets, and a score of corsages and boutonnières to make.

Anna Lee had them all around the worktable, laughing and creating. On mornings like this, Lauren especially missed Paige. She knew Paige was where she wanted to be, and her internship was already almost halfway over. Lauren was sure Paige would like to be here, closer to her fiancé, but like Lauren, Paige was goal-oriented and getting the experience in a publishing house in New York would be a boon to her career.

Tilly asked everyone what their plans were for the rest of the weekend.

Nica spoke up and said she was helping her boyfriend Grady with a home improvement project. They were retiling one of his bathrooms.

"What about you, Lauren?" Tilly asked, reaching for a handful of roses from the center of the table.

"I'm meeting someone this afternoon about planning a fund-raiser for the community center."

"Oh, that sounds wonderful, Lauren," Anna Lee said, joining the conversation. "Let me know if I can help in any way."

"I will. I don't know much about it. I've never done anything like this before."

"You'll do great!" Tilly enthused. "Whatever you're doing, you are always great."

"I appreciate the vote of confidence," Lauren said. "I think I'm going to need it." She thought she might need it more for working alongside Hawk than for the actual fundraiser.

Anna Lee nodded emphatically. "I agree. How'd you get involved in the community center?"

"It came up at the get-together for Paige and Trevor's wedding party. One of the groomsmen volunteers there. He called me last weekend and asked if I'd be willing to help. I had told him at the party that I was sort of looking for a volunteer activity. I had it on my vision board at the party."

She looked down at the ribbon she was wrapping around a handful of flowers. Salty was lying on the table and swatting at it as she unrolled it from the spool. Anna Lee brought Salty to work with her everyday. He rode in a animal safe backpack that Anna Lee wore while she drove her red scooter to work.

"Vision board?" Tilly asked.

"Oh," Nica chimed in. "You weren't there. We made them at the holiday party at Anna Lee's." Turning to Lauren, she continued, "I remember you talking about that, Lauren. Were you being intentional about seeking out the opportunity? Were you manifesting it?" she asked with her megawatt smile.

Lauren smiled. "Actually, no. Hawk brought it up."

"Hawk? Who's that?"

"One of Trevor's friends." Lauren was unsure how much to share about Hawk with her coworkers.

Trying to divert attention from herself, she asked if anyone had worked on a fundraiser before. Anna Lee and Tilly had, so

Lauren asked them a bunch of questions about their experiences. She knew that you needed to interview the experts to learn, so she was absorbing everything she could.

Anna Lee rolled her shoulders and stood up. "Time for a coffee refill. I'll be right back."

Once she left the workroom, Tilly leaned over and nudged Lauren. "So, this Hawk. How cute is he?"

Lauren shook her head and rolled her eyes playfully. "He's very handsome, in the outdoorsy, rugged-type way."

Tilly shimmied her shoulders. "Sounds scrumptious. Are you interested?"

Lauren paused. Hawk was very attractive and kind. But they were worlds apart. Plus, she'd be leaving in less than six months for grad school. There was no point in starting to date anyone now. But the thought of giving Tilly or anyone the go-ahead to pursue Hawk caused her breath to catch.

"I don't think so, but—"

Anna Lee walked in with her coffee cup in one hand and the pot in the other. "Anyone else need a refill?"

Lauren used the distraction to divert the conversation back to Nica's tiling project. It was better than having to talk about Hawk anymore.

HAWK PULLED INTO the community center parking lot at two p.m., an hour before Lauren was scheduled to arrive. He'd gone home to let Goldie out after the basketball tournament in the morning and wanted to catch up with Sharon before Lauren got there.

Sharon had assisted with last year's fundraiser, and he wanted to get some insights from her before he and Lauren met with the director. In exchange for the insights, he agreed to help Sharon with volleyball practice on Sunday.

A few minutes before three, Hawk walked to the front door to wait for Lauren. He had no doubt that she would be there on time. As expected, she walked in four minutes before the hour. Hawk smiled as he approached her.

"Ah," she said, "You *do* have a full smile."

He wrinkled his brow. "You doubted that?"

"I didn't get the pleasure of seeing it at Trevor and Paige's party." She shrugged out of her light jacket. "Who are we meeting with?"

"Ellen. The director."

"A woman. Nice."

"Yes, she runs the whole place."

Hawk led the way to the few offices behind the reception area. He knocked on the door and gestured for Lauren to walk in first when he heard the command to enter.

"Ellen, this is Lauren Largent. She's volunteered to help me pull this year's event together."

"Pleased to meet you. May I call you Lauren?" Ellen asked, pushing aside a few files from her desk, and indicating that they should sit.

"Yes, please do," Lauren said, sitting. She pulled a pen and a leatherbound notebook from her tote bag.

They spent the next thirty minutes getting the lowdown on all the key aspects of the fundraiser from Ellen. Ellen appreciated their willingness to pitch in and execute and promised to be a sounding board for any ideas or questions they had going forward.

After the meeting, Hawk showed Lauren around the community center. He was disappointed when he couldn't find Sharon; he wanted to introduce them.

Once the tour was complete, Hawk looked at his watch. "It's only four; too early for dinner?"

Lauren tilted her head. "Yes. I'm not hungry yet. Could we go to a coffee shop and work on our next steps?"

"Sure. That sounds great."

He followed her to the parking lot and walked her to her car, a pale blue Mini Cooper. "Nice wheels," he said as they approached.

Lauren turned and gave him a big smile. "Thanks. She's a lot of fun. Where should we meet?"

"I got an idea. Follow me. I'm in the black Jeep Wrangler over there."

"Lead the way."

Hawk left her and jumped in his Jeep. For a moment he thought about driving to his house. He could make coffee there, and Goldie would love to be let out and run in the backyard. But he didn't want to creep Lauren out. She didn't know him well enough to trust him yet.

Instead, he drove to Max's Coffee Shop, knowing they'd be able to get a table and not be rushed at this time of the day.

Lauren pulled in next to him and got out of her car with a smile on her face. "I love this place."

"I do, too. I think I might get a piece of pie with our coffee. I don't think it will ruin my dinner."

Inside, they were seated and got to work. Hawk pulled out a tablet and started a to-do list—he didn't want Lauren to think he saw her as a secretary or notetaker.

After an hour brainstorming their list and assigning owners to the first several tasks, Hawk asked Lauren if she would be willing to meet up the next day to compile a list of possible business donors for the silent auction they were planning for the fundraising dinner.

"Sure. It would be better for me if we met in the afternoon."

"Parental call in the morning, right?"

"You remembered. Yes. And I'll get my homework out of the way, so that won't be nagging at me when we meet."

He nodded. "That works for me, too. I coach basketball in the morning and will help a friend coach volleyball at noon."

Lifting her coffee cup, she motioned to their server that she needed more. Hawk took a moment to study her profile. Her nose was perfectly straight, and her lips were plump but not too plump. She was a natural beauty. Today her hair was wavier than he'd seen it before. Had she taken the time to curl it? Did that mean she'd put in extra time on her appearance today because she was meeting him? He hoped so.

"How about meeting at my house? We can spread out and not feel guilty for hogging a table in a restaurant for a couple hours."

Lauren studied him, her eyes assessing. Had he suggested it too soon?

"You have a house?" she asked.

"Yes."

"Rent or own?"

He hadn't anticipated all the questions. Smiling, he said, "Own."

"That's smart. And sure, I can meet you there. What's the address?" She picked up her phone and he gave her the address. "Is three o'clock all right?" she asked.

"Certainly."

"Do you mind if I skip dinner? If we're meeting tomorrow, I want to get a jumpstart on my homework tonight."

Hawk was disappointed but he could understand her need to complete schoolwork. "I don't mind. I'm looking forward to working with you on this, and I really appreciate your agreeing to help."

She smiled. "I'm looking forward to it, too."

CHAPTER EIGHT

LAUREN PULLED INTO Hawk's driveway at three p.m. on the dot. She'd used the map to see how long it would take and left her apartment with time to stop for coffee along the way. She'd texted Hawk around noon, saying she'd make a coffee run, and he'd given her his order.

She leaned over to lift the drink carrier off the floor. With her large coffee, Hawk's large coffee, and the puppy-chino he'd requested, she'd needed the carrier. She kicked open her door, put the carrier in her left hand, and grabbed her tote bag with the right.

Stepping out, she took a good look at the house at 310 Whirlwind Drive, a one-and-a-half story Cape Cod-style home. The symmetrical house featured a dark wood front door in the middle, flanked by a porch-light and a window on either side, with smaller windows in the dormers on the second floor. The house reminded her of a face, the upper windows its eyes, the lower windows its cheeks, and the door its mouth. It was a happy, welcoming face.

The door opened before she stepped onto the first of three steps leading to the door. Hawk beamed at her, keeping one hand on the collar of the pretty golden-yellow dog near his knee. Holding the dog caused him to lean way over to his right side, while his left hand lifted in a wave. The sight of him warmed her insides;

he appeared as friendly as his house. "Hi! Come on in! Can I grab the coffee carrier?"

"Looks like you have your hands full already." Lauren hesitated a moment. Unfamiliar with dogs, or any pets, for that matter, she worried that Hawk's dog would jump up on her. She was thankful she'd worn jeans and a sweatshirt, she didn't want Hawk to think that she was dressing to impress.

Hawk pulled back the dog, which was wagging its tail like it didn't know how to stop. She stepped into the tiny entryway, taking a step forward into a living room. There was a large light brown couch along the window with a hefty wooden coffee table in front of it. A coffee cup and a pile of books sat on top of the table. On the far wall was a display of board games used as artwork. Lauren thought it looked kitschy, but welcoming, like this was a home meant to be lived in, not photographed.

Hawk shut the door behind her and turned the dog loose. The dog ran up to her and nudged her knee, letting out a soft bark.

"She wants you to know she's there. Her name is Goldie Hawk. Goldie for short."

"Goldie Hawk?" Lauren raised an eyebrow.

"Yes. A play on the actress' name and mine."

"I see. I'm surprised she didn't jump on me. I thought all dogs did."

"She's trained. If you sit on the floor, though, she's going to be all over you, and you won't be able to count all the kisses. Follow me in here, and you can put everything down on the table. I'll give you the nickel tour."

She followed him through the living room to the open dining and kitchen area at the back of the house. The dining "room" contained a large round table in a dark wood similar to the coffee table and two built-in corner hutches with glass doors. To the right of the dining area was the kitchen. It seemed to have been remodeled; the white cabinets and steel gray counters were contemporary. The work area was a small u-shape. Appliances lined the far wall, a sink faced a window looking out to the backyard, and a counter defined the boundaries of the kitchen and dining areas.

On the dining room side of the counter was a single door that led to the backyard. Lauren glanced outside. Growing up in a condo in the city and living in apartments both on and off campus while in college, she'd never had a yard. It seemed so quaint and so freeing.

She set her tote bag and the drink carrier on the dining table.

"Dining area, kitchen. Here are the stairs." He stepped past the counter into the kitchen area and pointed to a set of stairs on his left. "This leads upstairs. Past the stairs are a full bath and a small study off a short hallway."

"What's upstairs?"

"Two bedrooms. Well, my bedroom and an office. Came in handy with COVID. Even now, I work from home a couple days a week."

"That's nice."

"It is. Would you like to see the upstairs?"

Lauren hesitated. She was interested, but it seemed like the upstairs was his private space. "No, that's okay." She glanced back at the dining table and finally leaned over to pet Goldie, who'd not left her side. "Hi, doggy."

"Goldie."

"Oh, right. Hi, Goldie, it's very nice to meet you."

At that, the dog held up a paw to shake. Lauren laughed and leaned over to shake the proffered paw. "Smart dog," she said, looking up at Hawk.

She finally noticed that he'd recently showered; his hair was still damp, and the ends curled slightly. She remembered he had mentioned that he coached on Sunday mornings. He was wearing an ISU T-shirt and jeans. "Did you go to ISU?"

"I did. Close to home."

It suddenly felt warm and tight in the space. She turned toward the dining table and drink carrier. "Right. I got your coffee and the puppy coffee you asked for."

She heard Hawk open a cabinet behind her. "Here, Goldie."

She turned. He had a large bowl in one hand and was reaching out with the other. Handing him the dog's beverage, she watched him pour it out into the bowl.

"That's safe for them?"

"Yes, it's just whipped cream. Goldie will have a little extra energy, and I'll let her out to run in the backyard."

"It's fenced?" Lauren asked, removing the lid from her mochaccino. She tossed it into the garbage can in the kitchen.

"It is. Here, I'll show you, then we can get started."

He opened the door to the backyard and stepped out, leaving the door open. A few seconds later, Goldie finished her treat and followed them out. Hawk picked up a ball lying on the concrete patio and tossed it across the yard for her to chase.

It wasn't a large yard, but there was a nice sitting area, a grill, and toward the back of the yard, a fire pit surrounded by a couple of large, two-person swings. To the right, there was a single-car garage, and a gate led from the fenced yard to the driveway.

"It's nice," Lauren said, surveying the yard.

"Thanks. I love it here. The neighborhood is great; mostly young families."

"Right, the house doesn't really scream 'bachelor pad'. Most of the guys I know wouldn't want to bother caring for a house or a yard."

"Most of the guys you know are still in college and chasing girls."

"Well, sure. But aren't you chasing girls?"

Eek. Why did she say that? Sounded like more than mere curiosity. Almost like she was interested, which she wasn't, for the record.

"I date, I don't chase. Speaking of Chase, you seemed to hit it off with Trevor's friend at the party."

Was he jealous?

"He was super nice, easy to talk to. Conversational." All the things she hadn't seen in Hawk the first time she'd met him.

Goldie approached Hawk for the fourth time and dropped the ball again. "We're done, girl. You can stay out; we're going in." He turned back toward the house and gestured for Lauren to go in.

Back in the dining room, Hawk left the door to the yard open, and the cool breeze caused a chill to race down Lauren's back. She was thankful she had a sweatshirt on, but she wasn't sure it would be enough with the door open. She wrapped her arms around her stomach as she sat down, then pulled her tablet from her tote.

"You cold?" Hawk must have noticed her discomfort.

"A little."

"Hold on." He walked past the fridge and grabbed a flannel off a hook. "Here," he said, bringing her the warm jacket.

"Thank you." She wrapped the flannel around her shoulders and caught a whiff of "eau-de-Hawk", that familiar woodsy scent. She wondered how weird it would be to ask him what type of cologne he wore. Maybe she would get a bottle for her dad for his birthday. No—he wouldn't want to try something new. "So, where do we start?"

Hawk sat in the chair across from her, and she was a little disappointed at the distance.

"How about if you search local businesses, and we'll create a list of those we want to contact for gift baskets? I'll create a spreadsheet and add them."

"What if we start by brainstorming the businesses we're familiar with that might participate, before we do a broad search?" she asked in reply.

"Great idea."

They spent the next hour brainstorming. Goldie eventually came in and curled up on the couch in the living room. It made Lauren happy to be able to look over and see the dog snoozing away.

Hawk stood up abruptly "I need to move. Do you want to take a walk with Goldie and me?"

Lauren was thankful she hadn't worn the boots she'd considered.

"Sure," she replied, rising.

"You can wear that flannel, or I could get you a heavier jacket."

"This is fine," she said, slipping her arms into the sleeves.

Hawk let her hold the leash, and she loved the responsibility and the way Goldie frequently looked back to make sure she was following.

"She loves to be out and about, doesn't she?" Lauren asked Hawk twenty minutes into their walk.

"She does. There are a few houses where people greet her if they are out. She's always looking for that extra attention."

Lauren laughed. "I bet you don't mind it, either."

"I'm a single guy who lives alone. No, I don't mind it either."

Lauren ignored that comment. "I could see myself with a dog someday."

"Have you ever had one before?"

"No, my parents wouldn't allow any pets. They both work a ton of hours and don't want any distractions."

"And you were an only child?"

"I was. Still am." She smiled at him.

"With no pets, that must have been lonely."

She looked away. That was a painful subject she didn't want to share with him. "It was fine. I was always involved in extra activities. 'A bored kid gets in trouble', was a constant refrain from my parents. So, they didn't let me get bored, and they didn't allow nonstop television or video games."

"And that is why you're so brilliant," he said with a nudge to her arm.

"I'm not brilliant. I think I'm fairly smart, but I'm stubborn. I'll study harder than the next person. I'll study as hard as I need to."

Lauren was relieved to see his house come into view. She didn't like the conversation turning to her and her upbringing.

"At the party, you said you were figuring out grad school. Have you made a decision?"

Talking about the future didn't bother her as much. "No. I've knocked a few schools off the list, but no final decision."

"What's playing into your decision criteria?"

Hmm, she liked that he asked that. "Location, alumni support."

"What about friends or family, people you know in the area, is that important to you?"

Lauren thought about it. The only location where she did know people was in Chicago, at home. But she yearned to see new places. Staying in the same state for undergrad was a concession she'd made to herself to justify a more expensive grad school. But the closer she came to making that decision, the more hesitant she felt—more so than she'd expected—when faced with the decision to go to one of the coasts, where she didn't know anyone. The feeling surprised her; she'd never had a problem making acquaintances.

For the first time in her life, thinking about leaving her friends—Anna Lee, Tilly, Nica, and Paige, too, when she returned from New York—gave her pause. For the first time, giving up something that had become precious felt like too big a sacrifice for anything she could gain.

"Yes, it is," she finally answered. "Well, it is now. It wasn't important to me in the past. I don't know why that's changing, but it is. Maybe I didn't have the kind of relationships in high school that I've formed here in college, but I'm having a hard time thinking about leaving my friends to go to grad school. Maybe that's why I'm having such difficulty choosing a school."

"Maybe it is." Hawk walked up the front steps to his house and unlocked the door. Turning back to her, he said, "Sounds like 'relationships' is something else to add to your criteria list."

She followed him inside. "I think you're right."

She thought about adding Hawk to that list of considerations, but that didn't make a lot of sense. They were just partnering for the fundraiser. Once that was over in May, she wouldn't need to work with him as closely. She really wouldn't need to see him again except at Paige's wedding. For some reason, that thought made her very sad.

CHAPTER NINE

HAWK STARTED MAKING phone calls to local businesses asking for contributions to their silent auction as soon as he got home from work on Wednesday. Well, as soon as he'd taken Goldie for a walk to tire her out. He took note of the dark clouds as he reentered the house and checked the weather app on his phone for the forecast. Chance of snow the next three days. Ugh, he was ready for winter to be over. He was itching to take Goldie to new hiking trails on the weekends and spend hours walking and exploring.

In the foyer, he shook off his coat and hung it and the leash behind the door. He grabbed a beer out of the fridge and sat at the dining table, ready to work.

Opening the list on his tablet, he scrolled past the fifteen businesses he'd already contacted. He'd had about a fifty percent success rate in getting businesses to commit. He wondered how Lauren was coming along with her list and decided to text her to check in.

> **HAWK:** Hey, I hope your week is going well. Any luck with the biz's on your list?

When she didn't reply right away, he called Adam's Autobody and had to leave a message for the owner. That was the downside to calling in the evening. He might get hold of *someone*, but it usually wasn't the right person. He left a message for a call back and gave the person on the other end of the call his cell phone number.

Once he hung up, he checked for a text, smiling when he saw Lauren's reply.

> **LAUREN:** Hi, Hawk. Happy to report I have twenty-five yeses!

Yikes! She was way ahead of him. He reminded himself that she didn't have a full-time job and could make some calls during normal business hours, unlike him. That soothed him, but his competitive side still sat up and took note.

> **HAWK:** Fantastic! I'm gonna have to step up my game. How are classes going this week?

He had made a note on the tablet about his call with the autobody company and was searching for a phone number for the next business when he heard the chirp for Lauren's reply.

> **LAUREN:** Under control. How's my favorite dog, Goldie?

Hawk chuckled. He knew Lauren was smitten with Goldie. He leaned over the table and snapped a picture of the lab lying on the couch, fast asleep. He sent the picture to Lauren along with his message.

> **HAWK:** She's worried you won't come to see her again.

> **LAUREN:** LOL. It doesn't look like she's
> worried about a thing.

Hawk debated how to respond. Lauren hadn't taken his bait about visiting Goldie, and of course, him. He was going to have to be more persistent.

> **HAWK:** We should get together to regroup
> on our donation efforts. You could see Goldie
> if you came by here. How about Friday
> evening?

He watched as the three dots popped on his screen indicating she was typing. They disappeared, started again, then disappeared again. He started to get nervous. Finally, she responded.

> **LAUREN:** We should. Friday is fine. I can pick
> up takeout on the way.

He really needed to come up with a couple of easy dishes that he could pull off to impress a woman. But there was no chance of that happening by Friday.

> **HAWK:** Sounds good. Let's check in during
> the day on Friday to firm the plans.

He dialed the next business on his list and whistled while the phone rang. That effort was a resounding success; they agreed to donate a hundred-dollar gift card to the silent auction. Hawk threw leftover pork fried rice in the microwave and got a glass of water for dinner. While the rice was heating, he glanced at his personal to-do list and saw a reminder to submit the foster application. He'd put that off long enough. He was in a great mood after the text conversation with Lauren, and it propelled him to complete the application. He'd do that right after he ate.

Sitting back in his chair, he jotted a few more notes down on his list. He needed to clear out his upstairs office and move all his equipment into the study on the first floor. If he were going to become a foster parent, he'd need a bedroom for the kid. He would need to shop for a bedroom set, mattress, and box-spring.

He followed a social media influencer who was a foster parent, and she had several videos about things she kept ready for kids—toothbrushes, shampoos, snacks, books, etc. He planned to watch more of those videos, take notes, and create shopping lists. He couldn't plan and prepare for every scenario, but he wanted to be sure to have a plan for the basics for whatever child might be sent his way.

He knew he wasn't prepared to take on a newborn and was glad the application asked about ages he would be most comfortable with. He thought school age would be best since he worked full-time, so he marked down ages five and up. Plus, he couldn't imagine obtaining and maintaining all the gear babies required—a crib, car seats, diapers, bottles, oh my.

He filled out a question that asked about after school care and he was glad he'd talked to his mom about that already. She worked part-time in the mornings and she would be able to help out until he was off work.

He didn't think Lauren would be interested in dating him, but that was okay. Even if they didn't forge a relationship and she left in a few months as she planned, he'd be able to do something he felt passionate about, help a troubled kid when they needed a level-headed adult the most.

Once the application was submitted, he felt like marking the occasion with something special. He went to his favorite online sporting goods website and looked at the fancy mountain bike he'd saved in his shopping cart months ago. It felt good clicking "submit" on that order.

The online-shopping thrill was short-lived, so he called up Trevor and asked him to meet for a drink, he had to share the news with someone and it was too soon to share with Lauren.

AFTER TEXTING WITH Hawk, Lauren pulled up her list of talking points for her parents, so she'd be prepared come Sunday. She typed in the progress she'd made in garnering support for the fundraiser. She was looking forward to meeting with Hawk on Friday because she got a sense that she had more contributions secured than he had. She wanted to try to double the number of contributions from twenty-five to fifty by Friday. She worked at In Bloom on Thursday, and she would talk to Anna Lee about donating a floral arrangement.

Standing up, she did a couple of jumping jacks to get her energy level up. She had to read and take notes on two chapters from her business law class before she could unwind for the evening.

Glancing at the bottle of wine on the counter, she shook her head. She grabbed a stickable note pad and jotted down "take to Hawk's Fri" on the note, peeled it off, and stuck it on the bottle.

"There," she said aloud. "Can't open that bottle before Friday." She walked around the counter and filled the tea kettle with water. She would make a cup of tea to help power through her studies tonight.

As the water heated, she thought about the text exchange with Hawk. Though she couldn't hear his voice, she could imagine him saying those words out loud. It was strange that after just a couple of meetings she could hear his voice in her head. She felt warmth spread through her limbs, and she hadn't even gotten to the cup of tea yet, the memory of his voice brought a sense of comfort. She was not a New-Age type, but if she had to classify Hawk as a natural element, she'd say he was earth. Definitely a rock like Paige called him. Steady. Firm. Stable. He was the type of person she could see herself turning to when she was feeling out of sorts.

Then there was the woodsy smell that she associated with him. She'd stopped at the mall after class on Tuesday and found a candle that had a similar scent—not the same, but similar enough. She was burning the candle now and loved the reminders of him that it elicited when she caught the scent.

The kettle whistled, and she turned off the burner. She reached into a drawer for the clear acrylic tea bag holder, noticed that she was running low, and decided to stop at the store and stock up on Thursday. Winter was not letting go of Central Illinois just yet, and she loved the feeling of coziness the tea gave her when she could sit on the couch, look outside at the snow or sleet or rain, and appreciate being inside.

Curling under the throw blanket on the couch with tea mug in hand, she started to play the what-if game. What if she'd met Hawk a few years from now, when she was ready for a serious relationship? What if Hawk were willing to move to a metropolitan city where she could thrive in a large corporation? What if their kids had his dark hair and her blue eyes? Wow. That went too far, too fast.

Time to pull out the business law textbook and focus on where she was going, not where she was. Where Hawk was. Where Hawk seemed to be perfectly content.

CHAPTER TEN

*L*AUREN WALKED IN the front door of In Bloom after visiting the beauty shop across the street, where she'd successfully solicited another donation for the community center fundraiser.

She looked for Salty before heading to the back office to hang up her coat. She found the orange tabby lying on top of the register counter, completely content, taking up half the space. She stopped to rub his head and listen to his purr. "Maybe someday I'll be able to bring Goldie over to meet you, Salty. Would you like that? Do you like dogs?" she asked the cat, though he didn't oblige her with an answer.

Anna Lee walked into the retail space with a coffee cup in hand. "Hello, Lauren. Did you come in the front door, or did you sneak past me in the back?"

Lauren smiled at Anna Lee. "I came in the front. I stopped across the street to ask for a donation to the fundraiser I told you about. They have a silent auction, so we're asking businesses for donations that can be used to generate bids in the auction. Would you be able to donate either a floral arrangement or a gift card or something from the retail space?"

Anna Lee was nodding before Lauren finished. "Surely! I'd be pleased to help. What do you think would work best?"

"We're getting a lot of gift certificates, so I was thinking it might be nice to have some other items—things people can take home with them at the end of the night. Then they won't have to add another action item to their list."

"A floral arrangement it is! When is this shindig? I'll put it on my calendar and start thinking about the design." Anna Lee shooed Salty off the register and pulled out a wall calendar from underneath it.

"May twentieth," Lauren replied. "It's a Saturday. The fundraiser begins at six p.m. I could stop and pick it up on the way. I have to be there at three to help set up. Will that work?"

Anna Lee flipped to May and circled the date. She scribbled something in the calendar block, but Lauren could not make it out. "That works," Anna Lee said, putting the calendar back under the register.

"Marvelous! When I pick it up, let me know what the retail value is so we know how to start the bidding."

"You got it, my dear. Now, for this afternoon. I'm going to have you and Tilly make bouquets for the retail space. The usual. New baby, anniversary, birthday-type arrangements. Getting low on stock—I think we should have ten of each going into the weekend. I'm going to work here in the retail space. Besides helping any customers that walk in, I need to reorganize the spring garden display. I'll be bombarded soon with people wanting to pretty up their yards. Everyone is getting spring fever, and their temperatures are a risin'.'"

Lauren glanced out the window, where big white fluffy snowflakes were falling. "Do you promise that spring is coming? I'm beginning to have my doubts."

Anna Lee cackled. "Yes, have patience. Tilly's already in the back, setting up. Why don't you join her?"

"Definitely."

Lauren dropped her coat and tote bag in the office and joined Tilly in the workspace, where she was using a list on a clipboard—obviously written by Anna Lee—to pull ceramic and glass vases, wicker baskets, and plastic buckets off the stock shelves.

"Hey, Tilly. How can I help set up?" Lauren asked, tying an apron around her waist.

"Oh, hey, Lovey. Hold on." She shuffled papers on the clipboard. "Here's the list of flowers needed. Would you mind pulling these?"

"Not at all." Lauren pulled roses, lilies, tulips, and dahlias from the walk-in refrigerated storage room, then returned to the workroom, where she set out what they needed in a logical, neat fashion. She reviewed the list of arrangements that Anna Lee wanted and discussed a process with Tilly. She was thankful that they were both experienced in working for Anna Lee. It didn't take them long to decide how to divvy up the tasks at hand.

"How's school going for you, Tilly?" she asked.

"Good. I have a big project coming up for my psychology class that needs some extra focus. I'll feel better once I have that wrapped up."

"Oh, what's the project on?" Lauren tied a green ribbon around a clear glass vase filled with pink tulips and stepped back to admire her work.

"'Nature versus Nurture and the Adopted Adult', that's the name of my paper." Tilly spun her flower arrangement around, looking for gaps in coverage.

"Sounds interesting. Was that a topic of choice or assigned?" Lauren asked.

"Choice. My mom was adopted, and her story has always fascinated me."

"Wow. That is very interesting. Good luck with your paper. Let me know if you want me to read it when you're done. A fresh set of eyes, you know."

"That would be immensely helpful. Thanks for the offer. Hey, how is that fundraiser coming along? Any updates on the handsome partner?"

Of course, Tilly went there. She was always looking for the relationship aspects of everyone's lives: "What kind of relationship are you in?" "How's it going?" "Could it be better?" She was a sponge when it came to stories of human dynamics.

"I think we're off to a great start. We're gathering donations for both a silent and a live auction. I suspect I might be ahead of Hawk as far as the number of donations goes. We're meeting tomorrow night to check in with our progress and strategize what to do next."

"Wouldn't it be funny if he brought you in to help and you surpassed him with the achievements? But I wouldn't be surprised. You always seem to achieve what you set out to do. I could learn a lot from you. I always get distracted by shiny new objects or ideas. On to the next thing! That seems to be my life's motto." Tilly sighed, and Lauren sensed the hurt behind Tilly's always bubbly persona. A good reminder that people often held back their truest selves until you really got to know them. She wondered how much of Hawk's personality he was still holding back.

"Hey, Tilly, you're doing great. Don't get discouraged. It's easy to get enamored with new stuff. Setting a priority list helps me. That way I can say 'not now' instead of 'never'. Then I can park it lower on my priority list and get back to it when I have more time. It helps me stay focused on the top priorities."

Like which grad school to commit to. She needed to put "pursue relationships" at the bottom of her list, not toward the top where thoughts of Hawk kept interrupting her top priorities.

THURSDAY NIGHT, HAWK beeped the horn on his Jeep outside Trevor's house. He waited patiently, and Trevor walked out of the front door sixty seconds later.

Climbing into the Jeep, Trevor said, "Can't wait until we can ride with the top off," patting the hard-sided cover on the Jeep.

"You and me both," Hawk replied. "Thanks for agreeing to shop with me. I promise it won't be too painful, and then I'll treat you to dinner."

"Not a problem. Like I said on the phone, I need to shop, too. Soon I'll have the floors in the two guest bedrooms refinished and I'll need furniture. I was thinking of hiring Paige's friend Nica to refurbish something for me, but it might be too much to ask now that she's dating."

"Refinishing is a great idea, but I need something fast. Sharon told me that once I submit my application to foster and complete the background check, medical exam, training, and interviews, it could be literally days later that I'm getting a call."

Hawk took a deep breath, He didn't want to get ahead of himself, but his mind was racing with the possibilities.

"Wow. You are serious then. That's awesome, man. I'm glad you're doing this. I still think there's time for the traditional path. You know—girl, date, marry, kids."

"That path seems to be falling into place for you, but I'm not having much luck there. I feel like a pro player looking to get sent down to the minors. Three strikes, you're out and all that. Heck, I haven't made it to three strikes, if strikes were dates, with a girl in years."

"No prospects in sight?"

"Nope." Hawk thought of Lauren. He wished she were a prospect, but she had other plans for her life. Grad school, travel. She was upwardly, globally mobile, and he was committed to Central Illinois. This was where his friends were, his brother, his parents, and stepparents.

"Well, blast it. Do what you want to do, and if there's any way I can support you, let me know." Trevor paused for a moment. "Just don't ask me to babysit. My nephews wear me out."

Hawk laughed. "Fine." He turned up the radio to listen to the sports highlights for spring training baseball games.

Ten minutes later, they pulled into the row of furniture stores on the east side of town. He hoped he'd be able to find something here, and fast. After a full workday and an hour-long basketball-coaching session, he was hungry.

He found just what he was looking for in fifteen minutes with the assistance of Gaby, the sales rep. She happily took his debit card, swiped it, and promised delivery in nine days.

At dinner, Hawk asked Trevor about wedding updates. Trevor said that they'd decided on Lattimer Greens Park as the venue. They'd ordered invitations and Paige had found her dress. Her mother had made a trip to New York for dress shopping. Paige would be home in a couple of weeks for additional planning, and they would make the decision on tuxedos while she was home.

Hawk congratulated him on their progress. "I can see why Paige and Lauren are such good friends. Both are organized and motivated and achievement oriented."

Trevor's eyes lit up. "You are right. And how did you discern that much about Lauren at our party?"

"Actually, I asked her to help me with the community center spring fundraiser. We've talked on the phone and met a couple of times to plan."

"Interesting." Trevor cut a piece off his steak. "And yet you don't see her as a potential prospect?"

"No. She's got plans, and they don't include sticking around here."

"Huh," Trevor replied, chewing. "When Paige is home, maybe we can do something fun together. Paige could feel her out."

"Don't ask Paige to do that."

"Don't you want to see Lauren in a relaxed setting to get to know her better? And not when you're working on a project."

"Well, sure. But I don't know how that would help. The gap between us is just too wide."

Hawk hoped Trevor would let it go. Sure, Lauren was beautiful and smart, but she was meant for a life that was radically different from his. He wondered what her thoughts on kids were. Was she even interested, or did she feel they would get in the way of her career? He wanted to ask, but that wasn't a friendly get-to-know you conversation. That was a "we've been dating for a little while and we should see if our hopes and dreams align" conversation. Maybe this was why he seemed to scare the women away so fast in a relationship.

Trevor was talking about how, at first, he'd worried that he and Paige were too different for it to work, but he'd pushed through those concerns, and now they were engaged to be married in a few months. Courtships didn't need to be long and drawn out.

Hawk heard him, but his experience was vastly different. He'd had multiple serious relationships; at least they were all serious in his mind. But inevitably the relationship would end, and he would be left scratching his head, wondering what went wrong. If that happened in a relationship with someone that seemed compatible from the beginning, then there was no chance a relationship with someone like Lauren would fare any better. From the get-go they were very different: different backgrounds, different ambitions, different desires. It seemed to him that a relationship with Lauren was doomed before it could even start. So while his heart said yes, his mind said no.

CHAPTER ELEVEN

*L*AUREN CHECKED THE Friday evening weather report on her phone. High chance of an ice storm later in the evening. Springtime in Illinois was so fickle—high in the sixties one day, an ice storm or snow storm the next. She thought about canceling her plans with Hawk. They were supposed to reconnect on status and start a a media marketing plan for the fundraiser tonight, but looking at the weather report, the smart thing to do would be to postpone. It was the end of a tough school week, and she would prefer to curl up on the couch with a bowl of fried noodles and a Ted Lasso marathon on the TV. She loved that the owner of the soccer team on the show was a woman. Seeing a powerful, smart, and beautiful woman leader was Lauren's elixir. However, she wanted to far exceed all expectations for this fundraiser, and to do that, they needed to put in the effort.

After a quick salad at home, she gathered her things and threw an extra stocking hat in her bag, just in case. She'd put some effort into curling her hair—for herself, not for Hawk—so she didn't want to put the hat on if it weren't needed.

She glanced at the wine bottle that she'd earmarked for tonight and decided not to take it. If it did sleet or ice tonight, she should be fully alert for driving.

Before leaving her apartment, she pulled down the blinds covering the high windows of the living room. She didn't like coming home after dark and feeling exposed to anyone in the building across the street. She sent Hawk a quick text saying she was on her way and should arrive in fifteen minutes.

Fourteen minutes later she pulled into Hawk's driveway. She grabbed her bag, glancing at the house as she got out of her car. She noticed Goldie's face gazing out the window and waved to the pup, smiling as she approached the house.

The door opened before she stepped onto the porch and her heart quickened and cheeks flushed at seeing Hawk. It had been five days since she'd seen him, and she was surprised at her physical reaction. They were just working together on a project. There was nothing going on between them, but while her mind understood that it seemed her body did not.

In a weird way, seeing him standing there smiling broadly at her, made her feel giddy like Christmas morning, her mind and body full of anticipation for pleasant surprises.

"Good evening," Hawk said as he bowed his head slightly and waved her in.

The over-the-top formality made her laugh. "Good evening, Mr. Hawk."

In the foyer, she turned to greet Goldie. "Hi, Goldie girl," she said, giving the dog scratches behind her ears. "I missed you," she whispered softly, hoping Hawk wouldn't hear.

"She missed you, too," Hawk said.

Lauren stood and spun quickly, embarrassment flooding her system. "I was hoping you didn't hear that."

"Hey, she's a great dog. I'm not surprised you missed her. She's missable. Let me take your coat. How were the roads? Looks like it's misting."

Lauren held her tote bag between her knees, shimmied out of her jacket, and handed it to Hawk. She looked over his attire and wondered if he'd just worked out. The back of his hair was damp, and the ends curled. He had on black sweatpants and a gray pullover. He looked comfortable and warm. As she turned toward the dining room, she noticed several stacks of file folders on the table—their solid bright colors made them hard to miss. She strolled over and tossed her tote bag on a chair.

To answer his question about the roads, she said, "Just started. Roads were fine."

"They said it might freeze."

"I heard that too, but not until later. I'll keep an eye on things." She noticed music playing softly and thought she recognized the singer. "Is this Neil Young?" she asked.

Hawk walked past her into the kitchen. "It is. I'm impressed."

"I thought so." She gestured to the variety of folders. "Is there a method to this madness?"

He laughed as he began to gather everything but two green folders into a pile. "Why, yes, there is. Blue folders are work-related. Green folders are related to the community center. And the yellow ones are different personal things."

Lauren glanced down. She didn't want to pry, but she was curious about the yellow folders. She noticed folders labeled "Mortgage", "Jeep", and "Home Improvement". She wondered what kind of home improvement he was working on.

"You're more organized than I originally thought."

"Hmm." He gave her a puzzled look. "I can't decide if that's a compliment or a put-down."

"Please take it as a compliment."

"Have a seat. Can I get you something to drink?"

"What are you drinking?" she asked. Goldie nudged her leg, and Lauren sat down to pet her.

"I was thinking about making coffee."

"Coffee sounds good. Do you have cream or milk?"

"Both." He busied himself in the kitchen. "How was your week?"

"A little rough. I have a couple of mid-term tests this week, so a lot of studying. And I worked a couple days, so it was busy."

"Do you work tomorrow?"

"No, I'm off. Hope to catch up on some sleep tomorrow."

Goldie lay down and put her chin on Lauren's foot. She smiled as she leaned over to pet the dog.

"Would you be interested in driving around with me in the afternoon to collect some of the donations? I told a bunch of businesses that I would stop by tomorrow."

"Sure. That would work. I picked up a few things this week."

"Even with the busy week? You are a go-getter!"

"Well, I don't work a full-time job like you, so it was easy to make a couple stops between classes and work."

Hawk grabbed a small container of cream from the fridge. "Is this okay? I have skim milk, too."

"Skim milk would be great."

He brought both to the table and returned to the kitchen for coffee cups which he set on the counter by the coffee pot. She liked watching him work. He moved like a man comfortable in his own skin, in his own home.

"How long have you lived here?" she asked.

"It'll be a year in May. It took me a while to save up a down payment once I started working." He leaned back against the kitchen counter and put his hands on the counter's edge behind him.

"Have you always lived in the area?"

"Yes. Grew up here. No desire to go anywhere else."

That was such a foreign concept to Lauren. She always wanted to go somewhere else. She couldn't wait to fill her passport. "Do you ever travel?" she asked.

"Sure. I love to get outdoors. Hike. Camp. My brother and I

usually take a road trip every fall and go to new parks. Some of our favorites are in Colorado and Tennessee."

"Road trip?"

"Yes, sometimes we take my Jeep, but for the long trips it can be a little rough. Last fall we rented a small RV. It was a gas guzzler, but it was easier than pitching a tent every night."

Lauren had never been camping. She couldn't imagine "roughing it". "Interesting. I've never been."

"Camping? Or on a road trip?"

The coffee pot beeped.

"Neither," she admitted.

"Oh, you are missing out, my friend." He filled the coffee mugs and brought them to the table, smiling as he looked down and saw Goldie at her feet. "Camping is an experience. You really have to do it at least once in your life. Sleeping in nature. A campfire at night, telling ghost stories, roasting marshmallows, making s'mores, and watching the stars. It's pure bliss."

"We may have different definitions of bliss."

He threw his head back and laughed. She was beginning to love the sound of both his laughs, this loud, boisterous one and the low rumbly one. He shook his head as he sat down with a half grin on his face. "You might be right, but I'd love to prove you wrong. What about road trips? Haven't you done that with your family? Trip to Florida for Spring Break? Disney?"

"Oh, we've been there. But we always fly. My parents don't take a lot of time off work, and when they do they want to *be* there. Like *now*. You know? Driving for hours in the car is a waste of time for them."

"That's too bad. There are so many great things to see when you travel the highways, byways, and back roads. Even here in Illinois, Route 66, for example. There's the Dixie Truck Stop in McLean, the oldest truck stop in Illinois. There's a Paul Bunyon statue in Atlanta. Both of those are a short drive from here. In Collinsville, which is near St. Louis, there's the world's largest catsup bottle. There's so much Americana to see on Route 66. Did you know it starts in Chicago and ends in Santa Monica, California?"

"No."

"Your education is lacking. My mind is racing with all the mini-road trips we need to take as soon as the weather cooperates." He leaned forward, his eyes widened, and the half smile teased upon his face. "Oh, and though it's not on Route 66, but the Superman statue in Metropolis is not to be missed."

"Metropolis is in the movies."

"No! It's a real town in Southern Illinois!"

Lauren smiled as she shook her head. "You are full of interesting information. Now, one thing at a time. Let's focus on the event for the center."

Hawk opened a folder and started reviewing a few ideas he had for the marketing plan. Lauren listened and added a few ideas of her own, but in the back of her mind, images of a long car ride with Hawk kept forming. Stopping for soft drinks, ice cream, getting gas. Laughing and listening to music. Pointing out thirty-foot-high statues and other oddities. Her parents always said road trips were nightmares. But right now, she couldn't imagine anything she'd rather do.

After an hour of planning, Hawk stood. "I have to move a bit. Let's take a break."

Lauren stood and stretched. "Good idea. I'm going to check the weather. If the rain and sleet have started, I should head out."

She pulled her phone out of her tote. She had a text message from Paige, saying she'd be back in two weeks to do bridesmaid dress shopping and wanting to see if Lauren was available. Lauren checked her work schedule and replied that she could. Paige sent back several heart emojis.

Hawk was in the kitchen, rinsing out their coffee cups and the now-empty coffee pot. "What's the weather app say?"

"Hm. Says it should start in an hour. I'm good."

"Good."

"Hey, back to the vacation topic. Have you ever traveled outside the US?" she asked.

"Nope. Not a fan of flying."

"Have you ever flown?"

"Nope."

"So, you're afraid of flying."

"No, no," he said slowly, with an emphatic shake of his head. He smiled and shrugged his shoulders. "Well, maybe a little bit. But hey, there's so many amazing places to see within driving distance. Once I hit everything that I want to see within a twenty-hour drive, I'll think about flying."

Wow. He'd never flown. She couldn't imagine limiting her travel to a car. She'd already been to Europe three times and was itching to go back. She dreamed of someday traveling to every continent. She could only think about all the places that you *couldn't* get to in a car.

"That could take a lifetime," she finally said.

"I hope so. Much better than getting into a death trap that I can't control." He turned from the sink. "Do you want to go over the plan one more time?"

"No. I'd better head home before the ice." She tossed her notepad, phone, and tablet back into her tote bag. "Thank you for the productive evening. I think we accomplished what we wanted to."

"You're right. I hope you had a little fun, too. I did."

Lauren stood and looked down at the dog, still at her feet. "I did. Goldie here puts a smile on my face."

Hawk walked nearer. "I hope I do, too."

"Oh, you do. You do."

"Hey, that sounds like a put-down."

Lauren laughed. "I didn't mean for it to sound like that. You do make me laugh." She walked through the living room to the coat rack behind the front door. She grabbed her down jacket, setting her tote bag on the little bench by the door.

Hawk approached her, Goldie following behind. "Sit, Goldie," he said, and the dog obeyed. Turning to Lauren, he said, "Drive safe."

She zipped her jacket and pulled her stocking hat out of the tote bag. Now that she was leaving, she didn't care what happened to her hair. It could get as staticky as if she'd put her finger into a socket; she wouldn't care. She'd rather be warm than cute.

Turning toward Hawk, she hoisted her tote on her shoulder. "I will!" she said cheerfully.

"Hold up." He reached toward her face, and she suppressed a gasp as his fingers brushed her cheek. "You've got hair shooting out of your cap at a weird angle," he said, pushing a strand of hair behind her ear. His movement displaced the hat, so he pulled it down over her ear, where it belonged. "Stay warm."

The gesture was sweet and comforting, she wanted to lean her face closer to his steady hand. His touch was so gentle and caring. She blinked a couple of times, replaying the moment in her mind. Her heart fluttered like hummingbirds had taken up residence.

Sweet, comforting, steady, gentle, and caring—all words she would now use to describe Hawk, as she'd gotten to know him better. She finally squeaked out a "Thanks. I'd better be going." She leaned forward and rubbed Goldie's ear. Goldie thumped her tail on the ground and seemed to smile at Lauren. "Be a good girl." Lauren walked outside.

Hawk stood in the doorway, watching her walk to her car. Once she got into the small car and started it, she looked back up at the house. Hawk still stood in the doorway. She lifted her hand to wave, and he waved back. She could see Goldie's tail wagging as if the dog were waving at her, too. She felt sad at having to leave the cozy house with the friendly pup and the handsome man. She projected forward about seven years. Some day she would have a loving husband and perhaps a pet to come home to. She looked forward to that day but knew it wasn't right to rush things along.

CHAPTER TWELVE

AFTER SHE GOT home from Hawk's, she had extra adrenaline from the three cups of coffee she'd consumed at his house. She got out her dust rag and organic essential oil-based spray and dusted the whole apartment. Technically, her living room and bedroom were the only rooms that needed to be dusted. Once that was complete, she scrubbed the kitchen and the bathroom. Since the apartment was small, it only took her thirty minutes to have it sparkling.

She wasn't one to keep extra knickknacks. She liked everything neat and tidy. Since she was a teenager, she'd lived by the motto "a place for everything and everything in its place". She had the means to shop as a hobby, but she would rather put the effort into studying either class work, leadership skills, or where to travel next.

Her mom was a classic beauty and a professional partner in her law firm. She dressed very well and elegantly. Simple colors—black, white, beige, and navy blue.

Lauren had taken her fashion sense from her mother and never wore bright colors or bold graphics. She leaned toward whites, beiges, and tans; black washed her out too much. She loved high-quality linen and silk materials for her clothes except when she was working at In Bloom. That work required denim jeans and long-sleeved cotton T-shirts. She'd had a reaction to a flower once that made her arms break out in hives, so she tried to keep them covered.

Once the apartment smelled like a lemonade factory, she glanced around for what else she could do to fill her time. She was too amped up to sit and read, so she decided to take a hot shower to unwind.

In the shower, she lathered on lavender body wash. Once she got out, she covered her body with lavender body cream and dressed in long cotton pajamas.

She made a cup of chamomile tea and sat on the couch, searching for a cute, sweet romance on the Hallmark channel. She found one and sank onto the couch to enjoy it, pulling the cashmere throw over her legs and settling in.

Halfway through the movie, she found herself mentally putting Hawk's face on the male main character in the movie. When he held the car door open for the female lead, she pictured Hawk holding the door for her. When he popped out from behind a store aisle wearing a silly clown hat, she pictured Hawk doing the same.

Once the movie was over, she finally felt ready for sleep. She drank a glass of water before turning the lights off in the kitchen and going to bed.

In her bedroom, she turned the usual seven a.m. alarm off. She wanted to sleep in, and Hawk wasn't picking her up until eleven. She was confident she'd be awake in time to get ready before he arrived.

Crawling into bed, she fluffed her pillow and rolled over to face the wall of windows. The shades were drawn, but there was a slight glow from the streetlights shining behind them. She found the soft light comforting and she fell asleep with the image of Hawk building a campfire. For the first time in her life, she thought she might like to try camping. Someday.

HAWK PARKED HIS Jeep and looked for a place to pay for parking. Finding a sign showing how to text and pay, he followed those instructions and proceeded to the front door of Lauren's building.

He stepped into the lobby and found a doorman. His lip twitched at the sight—he hadn't realized there was an apartment building in town with a doorman. Approaching the desk, he asked for Lauren.

The man in the navy blazer picked up the phone. A minute later, he set the phone back in its cradle and told Hawk that she would be down in just a few moments. Gesturing to the metal and leather chairs lining the lobby, he suggested Hawk take a seat.

Before he sat down, Hawk looked around the posh lobby. It featured a black and white marble floor and an extra high ceiling, perhaps twelve to fourteen feet tall. The walls were painted an elegant deep gray color in a faint textured pattern. Framed black and white prints decorated the wall, depicting some of the oldest buildings in Bloomington/Normal. Examining them, he read the date when each had been built. Included was a photograph of the David Davis Mansion, built in 1872; another picture showed the Vrooman Mansion, built in 1869. The Old Bloomington High School, built in 1917, was in a third frame. The final print showed the Normal Theater, built in 1937. Hawk made a mental note to check out what was playing there in the next couple of weeks. Might be fun to take Lauren to a movie there.

While he waited, a postal carrier walked in the front door and dropped a stack of mail and several packages on the front desk. The female postal worker and the doorman chatted for a minute, and she left.

The elevator door dinged, and Hawk glanced over. Lauren walked out talking to a man that looked to be closer to her age than his, probably a college or graduate student.

He took in every detail. She was wearing khaki-colored pants, tan shoes with a pointy toe, a tan and white striped jacket, and a white sweater underneath. She carried a large beige leather tote bag but no additional purse. She held a pair of brown sunglasses in her hand.

It wasn't like they were dating, but his stomach clenched anyway, like he was bracing for a punch. He stood quickly, waiting for Lauren to notice him. When she did, her face brightened, and Hawk no longer cared about the guy she'd walked out with. She said, "See you!" to the other guy and Hawk was pleased when he slunk away.

"Good morning. How are you?" he asked as she approached. He felt the urge to shake her hand; a hug would be inappropriate. He held out his hand and wanted to shout "Hoorah!" when she put her soft hand in his. He did not want to let go.

"Well. How about yourself?" She tilted her head and her eyes dropped to their hands; he was still holding on.

He smirked and let go. "I'm wonderful. Ready for a busy day?"

"I am." He noted some hesitation in her voice. "Let's do this."

He led her out the front door and turned right toward his Jeep. "Secure building with a door person. That's got to make you feel safe."

"It helps."

"Do you have a lot of friends in the building?" He thought about the guy that had walked out with her.

"No. I wouldn't say that. People sort of keep to themselves."

That was good. If that guy was special to her, she probably would have mentioned it.

"Here we are," he said, opening the door for her. She managed to get in with ease. He closed the door and walked around to the driver's side.

Climbing in himself, he saw that she was glancing around the vehicle. "Have you ridden in a Jeep before?" he asked.

"No. It's a first."

"It can be a little rugged. But it's a lot of fun."

He settled in and reached to the floor behind his seat for his tablet. Flipping the cover open, he pulled up a list. "Here are the businesses that said we could stop by today. I spent some time studying the map, so I listed them in what I think is the most efficient order to save us some time and gas. If you could be the copilot and tell me what's next, that would be great. I have a pretty good idea where everything is, but we'll use the GPS if I don't. Ready?"

"I'm ready." She spoke softly, and Hawk worried that she was uncomfortable being in the enclosed space with him. She buckled her seatbelt and laid the tablet on her lap. He started the engine and checked for traffic.

"What's the first stop?" he asked.

"Kinton's Car Repair. On Empire," she said.

"And what do they have for us?"

"A certificate for an oil change and tire rotation."

"Excellent. So, no problems getting home last night I take it. Were the roads icy?"

"No."

"That's good. Did you do anything fun?"

"Watched a little TV before bed."

Hawk didn't pride himself on his conversational skills, but this didn't seem to be going well. She seemed withdrawn and quiet.

"Nice. Are you feeling all right? You seem a little off."

She sighed and hesitated before answering. "I'm all right. Just a little groggy. I was able to sleep in, but maybe I overslept."

"Sometimes I think rolling over and going back to sleep will feel great, but then I do, and I feel like I can't shake the sleep off me."

"Yes, that's how I feel. I sleep in so rarely. It always seems luxurious and then this happens."

"Would a coffee help?"

"Yes, definitely. I didn't have enough time to make any at home."

Hawk scanned for a drive-through and found one on the next block. He swung in and ordered for them, then pulled up to the curb and put the Jeep in neutral.

Taking the coffees from the barista, he handed Lauren's to her. "Here you go. To put a little more pep in your step."

She smiled. "Thank you. I need it."

She took a drink, put her head back on the headrest, and sighed. "Yes, caffeine!"

Hawk chuckled. "I hope that does the trick."

"I hope I'm not being a bore. I'll try to keep up my side of the conversation."

"I can't imagine ever being bored in your company." He pulled onto the street, and they were at Kinton's four minutes later. "I'll get this one. Keep drinking your coffee."

He ran into the shop and came out with an envelope containing the certificate.

In the Jeep, he handed it to Lauren. "Here. One down, twenty-two to go."

They drove around, taking turns entering the retail and service businesses, picking up donated goods and certificates. After the caffeine kicked in the conversation picked up, but it was still superficial; there wasn't enough time between stops for long stories or deep conversations.

Hawk pulled into his driveway a couple of hours later. "I'm hungry. What about you?" he asked as he got out of the Jeep, pulling several bags and boxes from the back seat. Lauren was doing the same on her side.

"I could eat."

"Once we unload, I'll pull something together for lunch."

Inside the house, they dropped the packages on the dining table. Hawk took Goldie outside and Lauren followed the pair.

"Can I toss the ball for her?" she asked.

"Go for it. You'll make a friend for life if you do."

Lauren smiled at Hawk and started telling Goldie what a good girl she was for running down that "silly, yellow ball" so fast.

Hawk watched as he reflected on the morning. Lauren had been cool at first, but once the caffeine kicked in, she'd come to life. She came up with several more businesses they could solicit donations from as they drove around, and she entered them into the tablet. She'd suggested that they divide up the list this afternoon, so she would have more to work on in the coming week. Of course, she had contacted everyone on her original list already. *Overachiever*, Hawk thought as he watched her. He went in to start putting lunch together.

After ten minutes, Lauren came in with Goldie. Lauren said she'd organize the items they'd picked up and clear off the dining table so they could eat.

She double-checked the items against the list to make sure everything was accounted for. When she got to the middle of the table, she opened the Target bag and said, "We didn't stop at Target. Did someone use this bag...?" her voice trailed off.

"Oh, no. That's mine. I stopped and shopped before I picked you up," he said over his shoulder as he heated sliced beef on the stove.

Lauren laughed. "Um, I didn't picture you as a Scooby-Doo kind of man." She pulled a comforter out of the bag with the lovable pup on it.

Hawk laughed. "Well, you still don't know me enough so how can you say that? But that's not for my bed." He turned back to the stove. "I'm getting the guest room ready."

"You have younger guests?" she asked. "Nieces and nephews?"

"No, not yet. But you never know."

"I thought you said you were using the guest room as an office."

"I was. I consolidated my office into the study down here, so I'd have a spare bedroom." He didn't want to bring up the foster dream to Lauren. She would probably find it either outrageous or terrifying. Neither would be good. With his track record of scaring women off *without* the prospect of foster car, he couldn't imagine how fast Lauren would run.

"If I were designing a spare bedroom, I think I'd go for more neutral colors," she said in a teasing tone.

Hawk loved that she was teasing him. She was letting her guard down, little by little. If she kept letting him past that cold, professional exterior, he might find out who the real Lauren Largent was.

CHAPTER THIRTEEN

AWK COACHED THE kids' basketball team after work on Monday and picked up Chinese takeout on his way home. He didn't mind eating late and he didn't mind eating alone, but he wanted something delicious and filling.

He put the bag of food on the counter and grabbed Goldie's leash. They went on a quick walk around the block. When they got back to the house, Hawk let Goldie out in the backyard and turned on the back patio lights.

He plated up beef and broccoli, beef fried rice and three pot-stickers, covered the plate with a paper towel, and heated it up in the microwave for two minutes. Grabbing a glass of water, he sat at the dining table, ready to eat and browse through his personal email on his tablet.

He deleted forty-seven spam emails and got excited when he saw an email from the Illinois Department of Children and Family Services. He hoped that the email was a response to his application.

It was.

He skimmed the email quickly, and a smile spread across his face. He pushed the now empty plate away and began re-reading the email. Ms. Anita Ryan was pleased to inform him that his initial application had been approved. He would need to submit the names and contact numbers for three references. They would run a background check and schedule a home visit. She stressed that the home visit should show that he had adequate room for a child or children.

The email further informed him that he needed to schedule a medical evaluation and have the doctor fill out the attached form.

Ms. Ryan explained the training that he would need to attend and informed him that the next class cohort would start on the tenth of April.

Hawk printed out the form for the doctor and the training schedule.

He replied to Ms. Ryan to tell her that he was thrilled to hear from her, and that he would be on top of the additional tasks. He said he would make himself available for a home inspection at any time.

It was too late to call the doctor's office to make an appointment, so he wrote a reminder on his planner for the following day.

He stood and called Goldie inside, having her stand just inside the door while he wiped off her muddy paws.

"Are you ready to be a big sister if we get a placement, Goldie?" The dog seemed to give him a serious look and offered a paw. Hawk took the paw and said, "I'll take that as a yes."

He grabbed a dog treat out of the metal canister on the counter. The canister was labeled "flour", but Hawk didn't see a need for that much flour. He kept a small bag in the freezer, just in case.

He glanced at his watch. It was almost eight p.m. He called his mom to tell her about the application. She was thrilled and offered to support him in any way she could, including babysitting.

"I'm so proud of where you are today, Hawk. You gave me some concern when you were a teenager." Marilyn Stein paused. "I know I gave you some concern, too, at that time."

"Right," he answered. "We managed to pull ourselves out of some pretty dark places. But look at us now."

"Yes, look at us now. I can't wait to tell Rodney that you were approved. Keep me updated on the process. I can't believe you could be caring for a young person soon."

"Hey, it won't be in the next couple of weeks. I still have to go through training and complete a few tasks. Maybe I won't pass the training."

"Yeah, right. You will pass." She sighed. "Maybe someday you'll even have kids of your own. I'll be here to support you and any kids you get. But I hope you haven't given up on the idea of eventually having your own, married or not."

Why did Lauren's face pop into his mind? If he were being honest with himself, he could imagine dating her and maybe asking her to marry him someday. But right now, they were on different paths. She would be going off to grad school in the fall, and hopefully, he'd be taking care of a kid soon. He hadn't even told her about the dream.

"Someday, Mom," he finally answered, "I hope to marry, but not right now."

"No prospects?"

"Hey, look at the time. I need to make a couple more calls before it gets too late. I'll talk to you soon!"

His mother laughed softly. "Talk to you soon, Bug." And she hung up.

He smiled, thinking about the nickname. He always thought it was hilarious that his parents named him Hawk and then called him "Bug". Maybe "Bird" was too cutesy even for them.

Next, he called his dad and his brother. He was going to need all the support he could get on this journey. After finishing the calls, he started to wind down for bed. He longed to make one more phone call. To Lauren. But they didn't have that type of relationship.

He got ready in the bathroom and walked upstairs. Before going into his own bedroom, he glanced into the spare bedroom.

It was still bare now, but the furniture was scheduled to arrive on Saturday. He'd painted the walls a soothing beige on Sunday. It was a nice neutral color, and the Scooby-Doo bedding would go nicely. He thought about Lauren's comments on the bedding and decided he would get another neutral set. If a teenager were placed in his care, they would *not* want a Scooby-Doo comforter.

Thinking of Lauren made him smile again. Goldie followed him into his room and curled up on her bed in the corner. Hawk knew she'd be up on his bed before the night was over, but he liked pretending he was a disciplined dog dad.

LAUREN WAS HAPPY to be home after her classes and a short shift at In Bloom on Tuesday. She placed her backpack on the bar stool and went into her bedroom to change. She pulled on yoga pants and an over-sized sweatshirt, swept her hair up into a ponytail, and washed the makeup off her face. She planned to go to the on-site gym before dinner to work out, but she had a couple of hours to make phone calls for the fundraiser before then.

She took her backpack to her bedroom and put it on the chair at her desk. Taking out the schoolbooks and notebooks and her laptop, she plugged the laptop into the charger on the desk, grabbed the file folder labeled "Comm. Ctr Fundraiser", and carried it, along with her tablet, to the living room.

Lauren placed the needed items on the glass coffee table and went into the kitchen for a beverage and a snack. She sliced up an apple, put a tablespoon of peanut butter on a plate, and brewed an extra-large cup of Earl Grey tea. Returning to the living room, she placed them on the coffee table and sat down on the couch.

She reached for the tablet and her phone. She had twenty

new businesses on her list, and she was determined to call all of them today.

Ninety minutes later, the calls were made, the snack was eaten, and she'd refilled the tea three times.

Mission accomplished, she thought as she checked off the last business on the list, AnnaBelle's Chocolates. They had agreed to put together a large picnic basket filled with everything needed for a romantic picnic—a wool blanket, a thermos, a bottle of wine, a package of chocolate-covered strawberries, a box of chocolate-covered hazelnuts, s'more fixings, and other miscellaneous treats. She marked on her calendar that she would need to pick it up the day before the auction because of the fresh food.

The thought of a romantic picnic made her think of Hawk. He'd talked about picnics when they were discussing road trips and camping.

She stood and stretched. She was looking forward to her workout; time on the exercise bike while reading her business law textbook would be beneficial for her mind and her body.

She gathered what she needed—the law book and a large bottle of water. She left her apartment, looping her key chain around her wrist and headed for the elevator. She was still amazed that a building with only three floors had an elevator, but being on the third floor, she was always grateful when she came in with multiple grocery bags. She'd learned to plan accordingly and never went on super-big shopping trips.

In the lobby, the doorman, Bill, was holding the door open for a package delivery person with a hand truck full of packages. She wondered if there would be any for her; she'd check on the way back upstairs.

During her workout, she was able to read two chapters of the law textbook. She'd read them again after dinner and take copious notes. She put the textbook on a shelf while she ran through a few exercises with hand weights. Workout completed, she stopped in the lobby and chatted with Bill for a moment. There was a package for her; she'd ordered a few office-type supplies that she hoped would last her until the end of the semester.

The thought of the end of the semester, the end of her undergraduate program, graduation, and leaving for her as-of-yet still unspecified grad school, made her wistful for the first time. Normally, she was eager to get on to the next rung in her ladder to success, but the thought of leaving Bloomington/Normal—and Hawk—was rather unpleasant.

CHAPTER FOURTEEN

*L*AUREN HAD A Wednesday afternoon shift at In Bloom, where she helped Anna Lee prepare arrangements for a funeral that evening.

At home, she dropped her mail on the island and changed into her workout clothes quickly. She wanted to get her workout in and shower before making a salad with grilled chicken for dinner.

She grabbed her headphones and keys, and headed down to the lobby, catching the elevator with her neighbor, Brant. They exchanged a few pleasantries on the ride down, and he hurried across the lobby.

She turned toward the workout room. With only eight units in her building, she didn't usually run into others in the gym. She assumed that others who used the gym must go in the mornings before work or school. She liked to work out in the early evening, then she could shower and really relax in the evening. While she studied, of course.

After the workout, she showered and put on pajamas. It was only six-thirty, but she had no plans to go back out. She buzzed about the kitchen, chopping lettuce and vegetables for a salad while she heated some frozen chicken in a skillet.

Once the salad was ready, she slid her bowl across the counter and pulled silverware out of the drawer. She grabbed a glass and filled it with water before sitting down on the barstool. She remembered the dining table at Hawk's house and thought that when she eventually had her own house, she'd like a large round table like Hawk's. Lauren liked the friendly feel of the round table. Her parents had a beautiful formal dining room set that sat twelve easily, and it was nice for big holiday meals when her aunts, uncles, and cousins were over, but they were expected to be prim and proper even during those holiday celebrations, and she wasn't filled with warm memories. She imagined that holidays with a round table would feel very different.

Almost like she'd summoned Hawk telepathically, her phone buzzed on the counter. Seeing his name and 'text message' filled her with a glow. She hadn't seen or heard from him in four days.

> **HAWK:** What's happening?

> **LAUREN:** Eating dinner.

> **HAWK:** Didn't mean to interrupt. Are you out?

> **LAUREN:** No. Home.

She almost told him she was in her pajamas, but that might be a little too bold.

> **HAWK:** Did you make enough for company? I'm starved.

She shook her head. Now, that was a bold statement.

> **LAUREN:** Sorry, no.

> **HAWK:** Fine. Fine. Wanted to check in—how are you doing on the new list?

Lauren smiled as she took a bite of her salad, making sure she had a chunk of chicken on it; she needed the protein after her workout.

> **LAUREN:** Done. Got commitment from all of them.

> **HAWK:** What? Wow! Fantastic! You rock!! Should we plan for more pickups this Saturday?

> **LAUREN:** I work at In Bloom 8-1. Available in the afternoon…

> **HAWK:** That works.

> **LAUREN:** I have notes on which are expecting pickups and when. I'll email them to you.

> **HAWK:** Perfect. Just like you. You think of everything. Are you sure you're not a professional event planner?

He'd called her perfect. That was sweet. She'd never been called anything like that before. She'd never gone out with anyone long enough to earn a pet name or to get a lot of compliments. And her parents only complimented her on the really big things, like graduation or awards. They expected day-to-day activities to be executed with perfection, anything less was not acceptable.

LAUREN: I'm not.

HAWK: Well, you're just amazing. Keep it up. Send me that email. I'll pick you up on Sat at 2 p.m. Your apt.

That was the other thing Lauren liked about him. He was direct. He didn't disguise his feelings, he didn't wait for her to make plans, and he didn't hide things from her, as far as she could tell.

Plus, working with him on the weekends made them so much more enjoyable, especially with Paige away in New York.

LAUREN: Sounds good. Night, Hawk.

Hmm, typing that made her think of the Edward Hopper painting *Nighthawks* at the Art Institute of Chicago, a painting of a late-night diner and the four people inside; a couple, a single man, and the server. She loved visiting that painting when she could. It made her yearn for a life as one of a couple, going out for coffee after a theater production. It seemed so sophisticated and grown up.

HAWK: Good night, Mizzzzz Lauren. Sweet dreams.

She thought she might have sweet dreams tonight. Hawk wasn't going anywhere anytime soon. They'd be partnered together for the next two months. The fundraiser for the community center was one week after graduation. She wasn't sure how long she'd be around after that. Her lease was up the end of June, but she could extend it until the end of July or August, she just had to be out by September first.

There was no hurry to get to the East Coast or the West Coast, wherever she decided to attend grad school. Besides, she had a lot of reasons to stick around for the summer; Paige would be back, and Lauren could keep working with Anna Lee and the ladies at In Bloom. And then there was Hawk. There were so many reasons to stick around.

CHAPTER FIFTEEN

THE SATURDAY MORNING shift at In Bloom was usually one of the busiest. They were normally preparing dozens of centerpieces, bouquets, and other wedding arrangements. And today was no exception; they had a tight schedule and were working with hurried hands. It was a good thing Nica and Tilly were there with Lauren and Anna Lee. If anyone had been off or out sick that morning, they would have had a hard time making their deadline.

There was less conversation than usual, since they were in a rush, but Tilly did manage to ask how things were going with Hawk and the fundraiser.

"Great. We're getting a lot of generous donations. If you are all around, please consider buying a dinner ticket. The tickets are forty-five dollars, but the food will be great, and the proceeds go to a great cause. We will have so many items available in both a silent auction and a live auction during dessert. I think Hawk is going to be the auctioneer, so that will be fun and interesting."

"Will you be the Vanna White," Nica asked, "walking around in a beautiful dress, holding up the items for auction?"

"Well, no one's asked me to yet." She glanced at Nica. "I hope they don't."

"Oh, you would be a beautiful model, Lovey," Tilly said. She'd recently taken to calling everyone "Lovey" and no one knew why.

"Thank you for the vote of confidence." Lauren got distracted by the boutonnière she was working on. Sometimes the small pieces were harder than the larger ones. You had to be so precise; since there wasn't a lot to look at, you had to make sure what was there was perfect.

Perfect. What Hawk had called her the other night. It made her cheeks flush thinking about it. She wished the conversation had been in person or speaking over the phone. As it was a text exchange, she couldn't get any underlying meaning from his tone of voice or inflections.

Anna Lee stood up and rolled her shoulders back. "Who's ready for a donut? And coffee!" There was a chorus of "Me!" and Anna Lee left the workroom.

"So, tell us, Lauren. What are the plans for graduation?" Nica asked.

"Yes, do tell. I'm so jelly. I won't graduate for two more years. Yuck!" Tilly added.

"Well, the different schools have different days and times to graduate. Paige's graduation is Friday night. That's May twelfth, and mine is Saturday, the thirteenth. We've talked about having a combined party, but nothing is solidified yet."

"And when is Paige's bridal shower?" Tilly asked.

"The Saturday before, which is the sixth," Nica responded. Since they'd been roommates before Paige left for New York, Nica was almost as close to Paige as Lauren was.

"Oooh," Tilly said, clapping her hands. "That is going to be so much fun!"

Anna Lee walked in carrying a box of donuts and a coffee pot. "What's going to be fun?" Salty, the cat, strutted into the room behind her. He jumped up on the worktable and seemed to plead with everyone for a bite of a donut.

"Paige's bridal shower!" Tilly exclaimed.

Anna Lee smiled broadly as she put the donuts down. There was a short stack of napkins on top. "Yes, I'm looking forward to that myself. We're making the centerpieces and they will be unique!" She drew out the *u* sound dramatically.

"Just like Paigey," Tilly said.

Anna Lee retorted, "Just like all of us. We're all unique. That makes us special."

"I wish we were toasting that sentiment," Nica said.

"Well, we can toast that at Paige's shower." Lauren walked over to the donuts. She didn't normally indulge in sweets, but today it felt like a treat. Plus, she'd need energy for the afternoon with Hawk.

SHE DIDN'T HAVE time to take a shower after her shift at In Bloom, but she quickly freshened up and put a few curls in her hair. She applied a shiny, but not sticky, pale-pink lip balm.

She took the stairs down to the first floor five minutes before the scheduled pick-up time. She'd be driving around with Hawk all afternoon, so the extra steps felt good. She chatted with the weekend daytime door person, a friendly lady named Rosetta.

Hawk walked in right at two, and Lauren smiled at the sight of him. He said hello and came over to help her pull her coat on.

As they started toward the front door, Rosetta called out to Lauren. When Lauren turned around, Rosetta was fanning herself with a folder and pointing at Hawk's back. Lauren nodded and laughed.

On the sidewalk, Hawk led the way to his Jeep. "Do you have indoor parking with your apartment?" he asked as they approached his vehicle. He clicked the fob to unlock it.

"Yes. There's a door to the garage to the right of the front desk. It's convenient."

"That's wonderful. Especially in the winter, and I bet it's safer than parking on the street."

He opened Lauren's door, waiting for her to sit before shutting it. Then he ran around to his side and climbed in.

"Thanks for agreeing to meet in the afternoon. I appreciate it," Lauren said as she buckled her seat belt.

"Not a problem. It worked well for me, too. I had some furniture delivered."

"Oh?"

"Yes, for the guest bedroom. Remember I said I was getting it fixed up?"

"Right. Yes. With the Scooby-Doo bedding." She turned to him and raised her eyebrows.

"Yep. That's the room. Hey, I also bought some neutral bedding like you suggested."

"Instead of? Or in addition to?"

"In addition to. Want to give guests an option. Now, for our task at hand, I created an order list based on the store hours for the businesses we're hitting today. Three of them close at three, so we have to get moving. Ready to navigate again?"

"Certainly." Lauren picked up his tablet and gave him the address of the first business. "How was your week?" she asked as he started to drive.

"Interesting. And busy. How was school and work for you?"

Lauren got the feeling maybe he didn't want to talk about his week. Surely, he didn't expect this to be a one-sided conversation.

"Good. Busy like yours. And it's only going to ramp up from here."

"How so?"

"Well, Paige is back next weekend to go shopping for the bridesmaid dresses. We'll do some wedding planning then. And there's the fundraiser work. Graduation. Paige's wedding in June. Wow, it's a lot."

"You're right. At least they are fun and exciting activities. What do you do to unwind?" He downshifted as he turned onto Veteran's Parkway.

"With school and work, there isn't a lot of downtime. But when I do have some, I read, watch movies, or watch Rick Steves' shows about traveling through Europe."

"Have you ever been?"

Lauren smiled. She knew he hadn't been. "Yes, a few times. My parents took me to Paris when I was a kid, and I fell in love with traveling and Europe at the same time. Oh, the croissants and the Nutella crepes. Yum! Plus, the history and architecture. The people. There's so much to love! As soon as I come home from a trip, I'm thinking about my next one."

"Really? And what is the next trip on your agenda?"

"Greece. I'm hoping to go this summer."

"Who will you go with?"

"Probably no one."

"You travel alone? Is that safe?"

"I do. And mostly. Sometimes I join a package tour, so I'm traveling in a group. But with people I don't know, so I consider that 'alone'. Being single, it's not always easy to find someone willing and able to travel to Europe with me. I still travel with my parents at times, but I don't want to be constrained by their schedule." Lauren looked down at her hands. Working at In Bloom this morning had done some damage to her week-old French manicure. She'd have to go to the salon tomorrow.

"Wow. That's brave. And I've never even been on an airplane."

"Would you consider it?" She didn't want to appear too bold, but a girl had to ask.

"Well, I guess I'd need to have a strong reason."

She let his words hang there. She wanted to follow up with "Could I be a strong enough reason?" but she didn't. That was too forward. They weren't even dating. She finally said, "I see."

Hawk pulled into the shopping center that housed the first two businesses on their pick-up list. He went into The Book Bonanza and came out with a stack of books on Bloomington/Normal history, and Lauren went into Doherty Ice Cream Shoppe and came out with a gift card for an ice cream cake. Back at the Jeep, they put the items into a collapsible tote that Hawk had stashed in the backseat.

"Where to now?" he asked, restarting the Jeep.

"Market Street," she answered. She held the tablet between her knees as she put her seat belt on. "What is your favorite vacation memory or location?"

"Ah, great question. They are tied together. The summer before my parents divorced, we took a family vacation to Gatlinburg, Tennessee. We camped, we hiked, we saw live music—great folk and bluegrass music. It was amazing. Guess it really left its mark on me, because I can't get enough of doing those things now. It was the best. One night," he continued, "we popped popcorn on an open fire—"

"Huh? How?" she interrupted.

He laughed, that low throaty laugh that she loved. "In a cast iron kettle. With a lid. And you put a grill grate over the fire. Easy. Anyway," he continued after she nodded, "my brother and I got into a little popcorn food fight. Made a mess. We didn't worry about it. Went to bed. My dad woke us up in the middle of the night. A family of albino skunks were having the time of their lives eating the popcorn."

"Albino skunks?"

"Well, that's what we called them. Not sure it's the right term. They were white with black stripes. I should look it up sometime."

"Did you get sprayed?"

"No. We kept our distance. Just peeked at them from our tent. My parents were happy that it was just skunks, and not bears, that visited our campsite."

"I would be too. Sounds like great memories."

"They are. And, like I said, I still love doing all those things today. Camping, hiking, watching live music. It's the best."

"I like live music. I go to musical theater with my mom all the time. We've seen so many Broadway shows in Chicago performances. *The Phantom of the Opera, Cats, Wicked, The Lion King.* Have you ever been to one?"

"No. Maybe one day. Have you been to see a musician live? Like a single musician? Guy and a guitar?"

"My mom took me to see Prince at the United Center when I was ten. She was a big fan. I remember it being loud, and the fans were almost hysterical. Well, maybe just my mom."

"Wow! I bet that was a show. But that's a completely different experience than what I'm talking about. I'm talking about a small venue. Maybe a hundred people there. One guy, one guitar, and a good sound system. That's my favorite way to see live music."

"I've never done anything like that."

"Well, that's got to change. The very next opportunity, we're going. What are you doing next Saturday?" He turned to her, winked, and smiled—a full smile. She got those so rarely.

"Dress shopping next Saturday with Paige, remember?"

"Oh, right. Well, that won't go late, right? Maybe we can figure something out. I'll talk to Trevor, and we'll see who's playing locally. I want to take you to see someone really good. So, you can catch the live music bug."

She pointed out the turn for the next stop and thought about his suggestion. It kind of sounded like a date, but it kind of didn't. She wished she were better at interpreting his intentions.

CHAPTER SIXTEEN

NORMALLY, TUESDAY FLEW by for Hawk. It was one of his work-from-home days, and he found he could concentrate on coding and work for hours without a break. He would walk Goldie around noon and grab a quick bite to eat, but other than that, he was sitting at his desk, working away.

Having moved all his office furniture and equipment into the small study on the first floor so he'd have the second bedroom for a kid, he was enjoying the change in view. Upstairs, his view was of the back and side yard. Here on the first floor, he had a view of the street and the opposite side yard. He worried at first that the street view and the cars driving by would be distracting, but it was so boring that it wasn't a problem at all.

But today, the hours dragged. The case worker for the Department of Child Services was coming to inspect his house for possible foster placement. He was the most nervous he'd been in ages.

He'd read all the requirements and rules for the home inspection and believed he would pass without any major issues, but he worried that a particularly picky case worker would find some reason to block his application.

The doorbell rang promptly at 5:30 p.m. He'd quit his workday at five and had been pacing for the last thirty minutes. Goldie was restless too, and Hawk wished there had been time to take her for a walk, but he'd been too worried that the case worker would arrive before they were back, so he put Goldie in the backyard and promised her a long walk after the case worker left.

He opened the front door to his case worker, Anita Ryan. She was wearing a long trench coat, appropriate for the rainy day. She smiled at Hawk as he asked her to come in.

"Nice to meet you in person," she said as she walked in. "Sorry for the dripping water."

"Not a problem at all. Let me take your coat." He held out a hand as she shrugged out of the long coat. "I'll hang it here on the back of the door."

"Wonderful," she replied. "I'll get started. I don't want to be in your way longer than I need to. I have a checklist of things I'm looking for, and I'll leave a copy with you when I'm finished."

Hawk nodded and felt his pulse throbbing through his veins. He was going to need a long walk once this was over. Rain or no rain.

Ms. Ryan continued, "Does this house have a basement?"

"It does."

"Let's start there."

Hawk led the way to the basement and answered her questions about locks on doors, smoke detectors, and carbon monoxide detectors.

In the first-floor bathroom, she checked for water pressure and temperature in the sink, shower, and bathtub.

In the designated child's room upstairs, she measured the floor space, checked that the window opened, and that the light fixtures worked. She asked Hawk about toys, books, and games, as she did not see any in the room. Hawk felt chagrined and told her that he would start looking for and buying appropriate equipment as soon as he could. He was irritated with himself for not having done that prior to her visit but reminded himself that he'd been focused on the fundraiser, and Lauren, the last few weeks.

When she was finished inside the house, she looked at the backyard. She liked the fenced-in yard and gate. After looking in the garage, she told him to secure the hazardous chemicals in a locked cabinet. Finally, she examined the Jeep and checked that the seat belts worked and that there was room for car seats. She'd wrinkled her nose when she saw the Jeep, concerned it might not have enough room. Hawk made a mental note to consider a new vehicle. He would miss his ride but understood the concerns she'd pointed out.

Once Ms. Ryan was finished, she tore off carbon copies of the pages of her report. She had found a few things that Hawk needed to remediate before a child could be placed in his home, such as putting an additional carbon monoxide detector in the basement and removing the lock from the door handle in the bathroom. She suggested a hook and eye latch higher on the door to prevent a child from locking themselves in the bathroom.

Closing the door behind Ms. Ryan, Hawk took a deep breath. *That went pretty well,* he told himself. *A few things I need to address, and I'll get right on them.*

He was thankful the rain had stopped. He grabbed the leash, a baseball cap for himself, and his keys, and met Goldie in the backyard. He snapped Goldie's leash on her collar, and they left the yard by the fence gate. Hawk was amped up, so the walk was a mix of walking and jogging. When he passed by the Daniels home, he noticed a man getting out of the car. He thought about asking if Mrs. Daniels wanted to come out to see Goldie but decided against it. He'd wait until the weather was a little bit better. Sunnier, warmer days had to be on the way.

On the rest of the way home, he thought about where he would be able to get kid stuff—some basic toys and games to get started with. When he got home, he'd post a plea on the departmental online chat board. That way the plea would be contained to co-workers and could not spread too broadly. He'd already talked about the idea with several coworkers, so they would not be shocked. If he posted this request on social media, he was sure the uproar would be greater, and he risked Lauren hearing about this before he had a chance to tell her.

CHAPTER SEVENTEEN

*L*AUREN WAS EXCITED to be meeting Paige, Macey, and Tricia at the bridal shop after her shift at In Bloom on Saturday.

She rushed home to take a quick shower and change before meeting the girls. She made a protein shake and drank it in the bathroom as she put her makeup on and dried her hair. Once her products and tools were put away, she wiped down the sink and counter with bathroom cleaner.

She dressed in a peach sweater and a tan linen jumpsuit, slid on tan flats, and grabbed her purse, jacket, and cell phone before heading out. She thought about Hawk's dog, Goldie, and was thankful that she wasn't leaving a pet behind. Between school, work, and normal social activities, she was gone too much to care for a pet.

She arrived at the bridal store five minutes late. She hated to be late. She rushed inside and found Paige and Macey waiting.

"Hi, Lauren!" Paige said, approaching and giving her a warm hug.

"I'm so sorry I'm late," she said in return. "Hi, Macey."

"Hi! We're still waiting on Tricia, so you're not the last to arrive," Macey said.

"Yes, she called and said that Waylon had an upset stomach," Paige chimed in. "She thinks he ate too much cheese at lunch. She just dropped them off at Trevor's and should be here in ten minutes. We can get started. I'll alert our sales assistant."

Paige walked to the reception area and came back with their sales associate, who told them all to search the racks for two to four dresses they each loved. She directed them to a hanging cart with Paige's name written on an oval chalkboard on both sides.

They started roaming the racks and pulling dresses. Tricia showed up a few minutes later; Lauren heard her booming voice greet Paige from several aisles over. Smiling to herself, she pulled a floor-length, halter-top chiffon dress from the rack. She loved how classy and romantic it was. A large bow tied across the lower back and its ends trailed down to the back of the knee. She hoped the others would like it, as well. She could imagine reusing it at other formal events in the future.

Fifteen minutes later, she found another dress she liked, though not as well as the first. She took the two dresses to Paige's rack and joined the others. There was a nice mix of long and short skirt lengths, low and high-cut necklines, and short sleeves or sleeveless.

"This is so exciting," Paige said. "I'm not sure if I told you all; I want pale green dresses. I know different dresses in the same color is trending, but I would really prefer matching dresses. I know, I know. Don't come after me." She giggled. "If we really can't come to an agreement, I'm open to different dress styles."

"How do you want to do this?" Lauren asked, ready to move things along and make decisions.

"I was thinking each of you could take a dress you picked out and try them on at the same time. Then come out and we'll talk about what we like about each. How does that sound?"

"Peachy," Tricia said, grabbing a dress off the rack. Lauren noticed it had a thigh-high slit in the front.

Macey grabbed a pretty dress with a cape, and Lauren grabbed her favorite of the two she'd picked out.

They were all out of the dressing rooms a few minutes later. Tricia was already on the little platform showing off her dress when Lauren exited her changing room. She had to admit, Tricia's pick was stunning, and all three of them could pull off the slit.

Paige thought it was a little too risqué for her wedding; she reminded them that grandmothers would be in attendance, and everyone laughed.

Macey went next, and they oohed and aahed over her choice. Lauren was still feeling confident in her choice when she stepped up. She climbed onto the platform and twirled to see herself in the three-sided mirrors. This was her first time being in a wedding party and first time trying on a dress in a bridal shop. She daydreamed for a moment that she was trying on a white dress with a few more embellishments. That wasn't on the agenda for a good four to five more years, but it was fun to dream about.

Macey was a little concerned about the low-cut back on Lauren's dress but agreed that it was beautiful and would flatter all of them.

Paige clapped her hands and said, "I think this is the one!"

Tricia was nodding her head as Lauren stepped off the platform. "Done! Let's do it. Not that I'm trying to rush things along, but I did leave my sick kid with Trevor and Hawk, and I don't want to risk Trev never agreeing to babysit again."

"Oh," Paige squeaked, "don't worry about that. I can't wait to share babysitting duties for your little guys! I'll be back for good in less than five weeks."

"Hawk is helping?" Lauren asked.

"Yes," Tricia answered. "He said he needed the experience. Maybe his brother knocked someone up. I hope not, because his brother is still very immature."

Hawk had mentioned a brother to Lauren but hadn't said too much about him. She thought it was sweet that he'd volunteered to help babysit. He'd make a great uncle. Unfortunately, being an only child, she wouldn't get to be an aunt unless she married someone who had siblings. She thought about adding that to her "husband material" checklist.

The bridesmaids having picked out their dresses, the sales assistant took their measurements and was happy to ring them up.

Macey said she had to drive back to Rockford right away to work. Tricia needed to pick up her boys, and Paige was meeting Trevor to shop for wedding bands.

"Hey, Lauren. Trevor just texted me and said that he and Hawk want to go to a bar tonight to see some live music with a musician they love. Want to go with us?"

Hawk had talked to her about intimate live music and highly recommended it. It would be a new experience and a chance to spend some time with Hawk and their friends. "I'm in."

LAUREN WALKED INTO the bar and scanned the room for her friends. The small stage was to the left, the bar was along the wall to the right, and a few tables were scattered around a dance floor, measuring maybe ten feet by ten feet. Hawk spotted her first. He stood and waved, with that half smile on his face.

Walking toward them, she glanced around at the other people in the room and was thankful she'd decided on jeans and a pale pink sweater. She would have been overdressed if she'd worn the slacks, blouse, and blazer that she'd originally planned to wear.

As she approached their table, Paige stood and hugged her, Trevor shook her hand, and Hawk pulled out a chair for her. All the chairs were facing the stage and he placed hers directly in front of his. Trevor and Paige were sitting on the left side of the table, Trevor behind Paige. She and Hawk sat on the right.

She slipped off her jacket and hung it on the back of the chair. Sitting down, she turned to Hawk. "I'm surprised you're so close to the stage."

"We got here early."

The bar was crowded, and it was hard to hear above the music playing and the people talking.

Trevor leaned across the table. "Lauren, what do you want to drink? I'm going up for a round."

Lauren glanced around at what the others were drinking. Everyone had a beer. "I'll take a low-carb beer, like Paige is having," she said.

Trevor stood and picked up the empty cans and bottles. "Be right back."

Paige reached over and put her hand on Lauren's arm. "Thank you for finding the perfect bridesmaid dress today."

"I'm glad everyone liked that one," Lauren replied.

"I know." Paige nodded quickly, her auburn ponytail bobbing up and down. "They will be amazing."

Trevor returned with their drinks, and Paige made a toast to being together with good friends and seeing live music, ending with, "And only eleven weeks to go until I get to be Mrs. Morrison!"

Trevor leaned over and kissed Paige. It wasn't a sweet and innocent kiss—it was a passionate, "can't wait until we're married" kiss. Lauren wondered if the kiss was ever going to end.

Hawk must have wondered the same thing because he cleared his throat. "Get a room, you two."

The lovebirds broke apart and everyone laughed.

"I hope the music performance is just as entertaining," Lauren added.

Hawk leaned close to her and spoke softly, words meant just for her. "It will be. I promise."

The lights dimmed, and one guy with a guitar, just like Hawk had said, walked onto the stage. He wore a flannel shirt, jeans, boots, and a hat. Lauren felt comforted by his casual appearance—this wouldn't be an overdone stage performance.

As the musician began to play and sing, she was transported into his world. He sang songs about working hard, falling in love, getting into trouble, and everything in between. At one point, Trevor and Paige got up to dance to a slow song. Hawk nudged her and tilted his head toward the dance floor. She panicked for a moment. Slow dancing with Hawk seemed dangerous but exciting. She smiled and nodded slightly.

He took her hand and led her onto the floor. There, he pulled her very close. This was no eighth-grade dance, slow-dancing while arm's length apart. He held her right hand just a few inches from their bodies and her left hand in his, tucked between them. Lauren would only need to move her head a couple inches to rest it on his chest. She closed her eyes and breathed him in. There was that Eau-de-Hawk again. The woodsy scent made her feel safe and comfortable, like Hawk always did. He was gentle and caring and down-to-earth. She thought about some of the songs they'd heard. When the singer had sung about a young man fighting for what's right, she'd thought of Hawk. When he'd sung about a man getting crushed by his first love, she'd thought of Hawk, though she didn't know any details about his love life. She thought about asking when the time was right.

Hawk leaned forward, his mouth next to her ear. "What do you think?"

Was he asking about the musician, the dance, or being so near him? "I love it." The answer seemed to fit all possibilities.

He leaned back and held her gaze. A small grin played upon his lips. She noticed that he had a tiny scar just below his nose. This close, she finally saw that his eyes were blue. While her eyes were a uniform blue, his were hazy like the sky before a storm, with flashes of gold that looked like lightning. She wondered if his eyes changed color depending on his mood.

A few moments later, she realized that they were locked in a staring match, and it seemed as if the rest of the room had disappeared. The music sounded muffled and far away. The only thing she heard was the sound of Hawk's voice in her mind, replaying conversations they'd had before. The memory of his voice was stronger than the noises around her. She forgot about the necessary decision on grad school for a moment. She forgot about the pressure she constantly put on herself to be perfect. And she forgot that she would be moving away soon. She was only thinking about what could be. And for the first time in her life, she was thinking about falling in love.

THE NIGHT ENDED too early. Everyone was pulling on their coats, and Lauren took out her phone to summon a rideshare home.

"What are you doing?" Hawk asked, peering over her shoulder.

"Looking for a lift."

"No. Put that away. I'll take you home."

"But it's out of your way."

"Doesn't matter."

They followed Trevor and Paige outside and said their goodbyes.

"My Jeep is about three blocks away," he said. "Are you up for the walk?"

"Certainly." Lauren was thankful again that she'd worn sensible shoes.

Hawk guided her to the inside of the sidewalk which seemed strange to her at first, then she realized it was to protect her.

"So, tell me things," he said after half a block. "What did you think?"

All she could think about was the close dance and the times Hawk had leaned forward to speak in her ear. A few times, he'd rested his hand on her shoulder to indicate he was about to speak to her. One time, as he was telling her about the background on one of the songs, he'd let his hand rest on her shoulder while his thumb stroked the back of her neck ever so softly. She could barely hear his words over the buzzing in her body. "It was a great night. Fantastic performer. I had a marvelous time."

"Good." He paused. "Are you warm enough? It's chilly."

Lauren shivered, prompted by his words. "A bit. I'll be okay."

"Come closer." He put his arm across her shoulders, rubbing the upper part of her arm. She quickly felt warmer and appreciated the steadiness of his body as she leaned against it.

They passed a bagel vendor with a pushcart. "Bagels!" Lauren shouted.

Hawk gave his low rumbly laugh. "Hungry?"

"Yes!"

They made their bagel choices and Hawk paid. They walked the last block to his car and he opened her door and helped her into the Jeep, then jogged around the front. Climbing in, he started it up and turned to her. "Let's sit and eat these before we go."

Lauren had already pulled her bagel out and was using the bag as a place mat. She handed him his bagel. "I wholeheartedly agree."

Hawk chuckled and unwrapped his bagel. "I didn't picture you as the everything-bagel kind of gal."

"After an evening of drinking, they are the best." She bit into the bagel and sighed in relief. Less chance of getting sick, she thought.

They ate their bagels in silence except for the occasional moan of enjoyment. Hawk finished his, crinkled up the wrapper, and put the Jeep in drive.

They were in front of her building in ten minutes, and Lauren was sorry to see the evening end. She'd had more fun tonight than she'd had in years.

"Want to come in?" she asked, feeling daring.

"I'll see you in, then I have to go."

She felt bereft. He must not like her—she'd read the signs wrong.

"Oh," she said.

"Hey, don't take it the wrong way. I appreciate the invite. But I'm looking for something real. Something that takes time to grow. I don't want to rush things and get confused when I don't know where I am or what end is up. Come on, let's get you in."

Lauren thought about his words as she got out of the vehicle. She held her small cross-body bag close to her chest, wanting to hide behind it. She stumbled on a broken piece of sidewalk, but thankfully Hawk was there to steady her.

They walked through the front door and saw an unfamiliar night doorperson—Lauren was rarely out this late and didn't recognize him.

"Good evening," he said.

"Good evening," Lauren and Hawk said in return.

Hawk continued. "I'll be back down in just a few minutes."

Lauren wondered why he felt compelled to tell the doorman that.

They rode the elevator in silence. Lauren was trying to decide how she felt about his rejection. Her brain said it was smart and rational, but her heart screamed that it was a new kind of torture.

On the third floor, Lauren turned to the right, and he followed. They walked down a short hallway, and Lauren put her key in the lock on the door to the left.

"Want the tour?" she asked.

"Sure. Will be nice to be able to picture you at home when we talk on the phone."

She led him in and showed him the kitchen-living room combo. She led him into the bedroom and quickly pointed to the right. "Bathroom's in here. Need to use it before you go?"

"No, I'm good. Your place is great. Very elegant, like you."

Lauren was thankful she'd tidied the place before going out for the evening, though truth be told, she did keep it quite tidy all the time.

"Thank you. It's small and easy to take care of."

"I have a feeling if it was four times the size, you'd still keep it neat."

Hawk made his way back to the front door; Lauren followed behind.

He turned to her and smirked. Before she knew what was happening, he raised his thumb to her lip. "You have a little cream cheese on your lip." He brushed his thumb against her lip and put it in his mouth, leaving Lauren speechless.

"Good night, Lauren. Sleep well." He said. He leaned forward and kissed her cheek before turning and walking out of the apartment.

Stunned, she shut the door and leaned against it. She put her hand up to her cheek where he'd kissed her. This was too much to process. She was confused with a capital C. For one thing, she couldn't believe she'd invited him in. That was something you would do if you were interested in starting a romantic relationship, and why would she do that? She would be leaving in a few months. But the way she felt when he was near her was on a whole other wavelength. It was so far beyond what she was expecting in her life at this time that she didn't know how to process the emotions and physical reactions that erupted in her when he was close. She hoped a good night of sleep would clear her mind and reset her heart rate.

CHAPTER EIGHTEEN

*L*AUREN SURPRISED HERSELF by being awake, caffeinated, and ready to go before her parents' phone call on Sunday morning.

Her dad told her about a trial he had coming up. Though it was Sunday, he was going into the office around noon to continue his prep. Her mother was taking a tennis lesson in the afternoon and going for a mani-pedi afterwards.

Once they had updated Lauren on their plans, they asked about hers.

"Well, I have homework to focus on today. In the homestretch now, but I can't let up."

"That's right, kiddo," her dad replied. "You're within reach of that 4.0 average. We're so proud of you."

"Thanks, Dad. I, um…" She paused. She wanted to tell them about Hawk but wasn't sure how they'd react. "You remember when I told you about the volunteer work I was doing?"

"Yes," her mom answered. "How's that going?"

"It's great. I'm loving it. Learning a lot and having fun."

"That's great! That's what you should be doing."

"And," she started, "I'm really enjoying working with Hawk, my co-lead on this project."

"Oh?" her mom seemed to pick up on the nuance.

"Yes, he's great. I feel like I could be falling for him. In a romantic way." Gosh, this was so awkward. She'd never talked to her parents about a man, or boy, before.

"Lauren," her dad's voice was stern. "There's no time for that. You have to finish undergrad and get through grad school. You should hold off on relationships. They'll just get in the way of achieving your dreams."

Lauren felt a hot burn start in her stomach. Maybe she'd had too much caffeine. She needed to eat something solid.

Her mother came to her defense. "Robert, life is not all work and no play."

Interesting, that's not how they lived their lives. It was all work and just a dab of play.

"Well, I don't think it would turn serious. He seems rooted here."

"And you're not," her father pointed out. "You'll be off to Cambridge in the fall."

"What?" her mother exclaimed. "Lauren, did you decide on grad school and not tell me?"

She heard her dad laughing as she said, "No, Mom. I haven't decided yet."

Her mom sighed loudly. "It's April, Lauren. Time to make up your mind."

"I know. I will. Very soon." She jotted down on her paper, "research withdrawal penalties if commit to a school and change mind".

"We have to go, darling," Bob said. "Have a wonderful day. An excellent week. We'll talk next Sunday."

Lauren hung up and looked at the note she'd scribbled. She didn't know why this decision was so hard. Normally, she made decisions quickly, with sound reasoning. She wanted to say she'd made a grad school decision, so she'd stop being asked by her parents. But what would happen if she changed her mind in a couple of months? Making a decision meant sending in a large tuition check, and she didn't want her parents to waste their money.

She realized that Hawk was beginning to be a consideration in her decision. They'd had no conversations about a relationship, and she could be way off base with him, but she thought he was interested in her, and she was definitely attracted to him. She worried that they were too different, but maybe she needed to stop focusing on how different they were and start looking at what they had in common.

HAWK HAD ASKED Trevor for help on Sunday afternoon. He wanted to knock out all the issues the case worker had found and needed Trevor's second set of hands to hang locked cabinets higher up on the walls in the garage.

Trevor pulled into the driveway after dropping Paige off at the airport.

The garage door was open, and he strolled up the driveway. Hawk was sorting all the tools, cans, and miscellaneous garage junk when Trevor walked in.

"Hawkman!"

"Hey, Trev. Thanks for coming."

"Not a problem. Good to stay busy with Paige leaving. Again."

"Won't be long, and she'll be back here permanently."

"I know, I know." Trevor turned his ball cap around backwards. "On one hand, it doesn't seem much longer. On the other hand, I can't wait another day. Anyway, I'm glad you had some work that I could help with. What are we starting with?"

"Hanging three cabinets so I can store all chemicals and child hazards out of reach and in a locked space."

"Hmm. That's smart. I worry when Tricia's boys are over that they're going to get into something that I haven't thought about.

Maybe I should invest in some of these. As it is, I have to watch them like a Hawk!" He chuckled at his pun.

"You should do that anyway, even if you think your stuff is locked up."

"Yeah, yeah. So, all this came about from the foster parent application process?"

"Yes, after I submitted the app they did a home visit. This was one of the check marks against me."

"There couldn't have been many more. Your house is in good shape."

"True. Here, lift this cabinet so I can mark where to drill the holes." Hawk stood on the ladder as Trevor lifted the cabinet. "But I have a few things inside to do. Remove a lock, add a carbon dioxide monitor." He marked the spots to drill and Trevor put the cabinet down on the workbench.

"Need help with the other things?"

"No, I got it. Hey, while I'm thinking about it, do you think Tricia would have any clothes or toys the boys have outgrown? I need to stock up on some basics."

"I can ask her." Trevor handed Hawk the drill. "I imagine she does. Wow, that just made all this seem more real to me. You are going to be fostering kids. It's awesome, man. What does Lauren think of it?"

Hawk drilled pilot holes and motioned for Trevor to lift the cabinet into place again. "I haven't talked to her about it."

"What? Why not?"

"Well, she's not sticking around for long, so why let it get complicated? Kids are complicated."

"Maybe, but I saw the way she was looking at you last night, and I think she's open to complicated."

Hawk drilled the screws in place, contemplating what Trevor had said. He thought he'd seen that too, and she'd invited him up. But he knew she'd been at least tipsy, if not drunk, when they got back to her place. He was not the kind of guy to take advantage of that situation.

However much she might be attracted to him, she'd made it clear—she had long-range goals she was focused on. College. Grad school. Career. In that order. She hadn't even mentioned marriage or kids to him. Maybe they weren't even goals for her. He needed to get to know her a little better. They needed more time together to figure out where this was going, if anywhere.

After the last screw was in, he stepped down from the ladder. "One done, two more to go."

"Nice way to avoid the topic, Hawk."

"Not avoiding. Just trying to get the work done."

"Okay. Whatever you say."

Hawk needed to attack these action items. He wanted to send an email to Ms. Ryan tonight to say that he was done. He also needed to think about his next steps with Lauren.

WITH TREVOR'S HELP, Hawk corrected all the issues Ms. Ryan had found. He sat at his desk and wrote her an email letting her know they were done. He explained that he had scheduled his doctor appointment for Thursday, and he asked that she let him know if and when he was approved for training. As he understood it, there was a new round of training beginning the following week.

That task complete, he looked over his list of things to do this week and felt content. He was prepared for work. He was anticipating being approved as a foster parent soon. The only flaw, like a thread unraveling on a jacket, was not knowing where things stood with Lauren and where they might go.

He picked up his cell phone. Should he text or call? A text seemed safer, but now was the time to take some risks. He called.

The phone rang, and he thought about the first time he'd called her, when she hadn't had his name in her phone and ignored the call twice before finally answering it.

"Hello, Hawk," she said quietly when she answered.

"Good evening, Lauren. How are you doing tonight?"

"I'm okay. Winding down my evening. What about you?"

"Same. Feeling accomplished and ready for the work week."

"I don't feel accomplished," she stressed the word, "but I'm ready for the week."

"That's good. Any big tests or challenges this week?"

"Are you trying to sound like my parents?"

"Absolutely not," he said with a big smile on his face. She couldn't see it, but he hoped she heard it.

"Good. I've already had that run-in today."

"Didn't it go well?"

"It was fine. Same issues."

"Grad school?"

"Yeah."

"Why are you having a hard time making that decision?" he asked. Please let it have something to do with me.

"I don't know."

He didn't believe her.

"Anything I can do to help?"

He was going to push it.

"No. What about you?" she asked, changing the subject. "Any big challenges this week?"

He didn't want to bring up the foster application on the phone. "No. Pretty normal week."

"That's good."

It was now or never. Here was the time to ask her out. "Are you busy Saturday?" He hoped she didn't have to work.

"No. I'm off. Want to pick up more stuff for the fundraiser?"

"No, I think we've been working hard enough on that. I think this Saturday we need to have some fun. I looked at the weather, and it is supposed to be decent—high in the upper fifties. I thought it might be time to take you on a hike. There is a cool place west of Peoria called Jubilee College State Park. I thought we could take a ride over there and do a little hiking. The trails aren't overly treacherous, so they're good for a beginner."

"Really?"

"Yeah. Look it up online."

"I will."

"Do you need to look it up before you decide if you'll go?" He asked. She wasn't making this easy.

She laughed softly. "I'd like to go. What do I need to bring?"

He made a silent fist pump. Yes! "Nothing. Just yourself. Comfortable shoes. I suggest jeans, a T-shirt and a hoodie or jacket. Layers. I'll pick you up at nine. We don't want to get there too early; it will be chilly in the morning. And if you have any questions this week, don't hesitate to ask. I plan to take you to a late lunch, so eat a hearty breakfast."

"Yes, sir."

"Am I being bossy?"

"Yes, but in a good way."

"Whew. Well, good night, Lauren. Have a fantastic week. I'll see you Saturday."

"You too, Hawk. Good night."

He hung up and sat back in his chair, spinning it around so he could see Goldie. "She agreed to go hiking with me, Goldie girl. I'm going to tell her about fostering and see what she says. I'm going to be open and honest with her. I have to be. Now, who's up for one more walk before bed?"

Goldie wagged her tail, and Hawk stood to get the leash. He expected it was going to be a fantastic week all around.

CHAPTER NINETEEN

LAUREN JUMPED OUT of the Jeep, ready to go. She had a small knapsack with her that held a large bottle of water and a small gift for Hawk. She was waiting for the right moment to give it to him.

Hawk glanced down at her shoes. "You're hiking in those?"

"Yes. They're sturdy tennis shoes."

"They look awfully…clean." He winced. "I'll carry you over mud if I have to."

"Oh, you won't have to do that. I don't care if they get dirty." She did, but she wasn't telling him that. "Let's do this."

Hawk just shook his head and shouldered his backpack. Lauren didn't know what was in it, but it looked heavy. Maybe he was a Boy Scout and prepared for anything.

He walked across the parking lot. There were several other cars, but she didn't see any people. One car had an empty bike rack on the back. She wondered if they'd see bikes on the trail.

It wasn't fifty degrees yet, but it promised to be. Lauren was happy she had on a sweatshirt and a windbreaker.

Hawk found a trailhead (a term he had to explain to her) and a map. He traced a path and read the name to her. "Let's do this. We'll take Shorty's Trail and see how we're feeling after that."

"Sounds great."

They started walking, Lauren a few feet behind Hawk. She knew she should be taking in the beautiful view of the prairie land around her, but she enjoyed watching him move. He was comfortable in his own skin. And in his hiking boots. She fantasized briefly about being out here with him in warmer weather. Without the backpack and without the shirt and jacket. Maybe a pair of shorts instead of his cargo pants. And…

"Right?" he asked.

"I'm sorry. What did you say?" Busted.

"I said it's great to be out here without any crowds. It's so early in the season."

"Oh, right. It is."

Yes, they seemed to be alone. Completely alone. They had walked fifteen minutes by this time and hadn't seen another soul. A little cool. A little creepy.

They walked downhill for a bit and came upon a small creek running across the trail. It was perhaps three feet across.

"Here's where boots would have been a better choice," Hawk said. He paused to study the situation. "I'll jump across and reach back for your hand."

He jumped, and she winced as he landed in mud. He slid back toward the water a few inches. Ugh. This might not be pleasant.

"Ready for me?" she asked.

"Always," he said, and she warmed at the way his tone implied more than just this jump.

Leaning forward, she reached for his hand. He clasped hers and held steady. She sprang forward, hitting the muddy area hard. Hawk's firm grip held her, she didn't slide backward. Small win!

She looked up at the half grin on Hawk's face. "Did you see your shoes?" he asked.

She looked down. They were covered in mud. "Uh oh." She lifted her right foot and moved it forward. She loosened her left foot and put it on higher, drier ground as well. She might have to invest in hiking boots and thick wool socks.

"Maybe they'll dry as we walk," he said, turning to continue up the short hill. He didn't let go of her hand. She almost pulled it away but decided not to. If he wanted to lead the way and hold her hand, she was here for it.

They walked on in silence for a few moments. Rounding a corner, they came out of the tree coverage into a large open field with few grasses growing at this point in the season. The sun was shining, and the temperature rose five degrees as soon as they stepped out from the treeline.

Hawk turned toward her. "How about a little rest here in the sun?"

She looked around. "There's no bench or table."

"I've got a picnic blanket."

Ah, that's what was in the bulky backpack. He shrugged out of the backpack and unzipped one of the pockets, pulling out a large red and black plaid blanket. He dropped the backpack and laid the blanket out. "I've got a thermos of coffee and some snacks."

Sitting on the blanket, he patted the spot next to him. "Come on."

She spun around and sat abruptly—she didn't want to walk on the blanket with her muddy shoes, so she kept her feet on the grass.

Hawk poured coffee into two stainless steel cups, handing her one. "I've got powdered creamer and sugar. Want both?"

"No. Just the creamer, please." She placed the coffee cup against her knee to hold it in place and reached into her bag for the water bottle. Her eyes fell on the small present in the bag, and she thought *This is a good time to give it to him.* "Hawk, I have something for you." She pulled the small package wrapped in loose tissue paper out of her bag. "It's not much, so don't get too excited."

He took the package from her and raised his eyebrows with curiosity. "What's this for? It's not my birthday."

"It's a thank you for getting me involved in the fundraiser. I wanted to volunteer this year, and with your help, I've checked that off my list. And for this." She gestured with her hand and her eyes swept around them. "No one's ever taken me hiking before."

"Well, I'm glad I'm your first." He gulped and added, "Hike, that is. I don't think that's gift-worthy, but hey, I like gifts." His eyes danced as he began to unwrap the gift.

The tissue paper fell away, and he held up a small box. It held a Scooby-Doo alarm clock. He laughed and looked at Lauren.

"I thought it might go well with your guest bedding. Hopefully with the neutral bedding, too."

"It's fantastic! Where did you find this?"

"An eclectic boutique not far from my apartment building. I was walking by and saw that in the window. I had to get it for you." She lifted her shoulders to show him it wasn't a big deal.

"I love it. Thank you." He paused, holding her gaze. It felt as if an electrical storm was blowing in—the air seemed full of static. Lauren blinked, worried the charge would dissipate. It didn't. She felt leaden as Hawk slowly leaned forward, closing the gap between them. He rested his forehead against hers. "You amaze me, Lauren."

She didn't know how to respond. It was just an alarm clock. She started to say so when he tilted his head and leaned even closer. His deep blue eyes locked on hers. He raised an eyebrow, asking permission. She didn't want to break this spell. She didn't breathe. She didn't blink. She willed her heart to stop beating so loudly in her ears.

He closed the gap further and his lips brushed hers ever so softly. She heard a field mouse squeak nearby then realized that the noise had come from her throat. How embarrassing. What wasn't embarrassing was the way his lips gently brushed hers. To steady himself, she assumed, he rested a hand on her upper arm. It felt as though energy was passing from him through his touch and his lips. She closed her eyes. The intensity she saw in his was too much to process.

His lips pressed against hers again, and he pulled back. She sat with her eyes closed a moment more. The blood throbbing in her ears began to subside and she heard the chirps, caws, and chatter of the birds surrounding them.

"Thank you, again," he said.

"For?"

"The clock. It's adorable. Like you."

Right. The clock. "I'm glad you like it."

"I do." He sipped his coffee.

She shifted on the blanket and picked up the coffee. She'd forgotten it was there. They were sitting side by side, and she had to slide her eyes sideways to catch a glimpse of him. Maybe it was better that she couldn't see him now. "Are we not going to talk about it?"

"About...?"

"The kiss."

"Was it too soon? Too abrupt?"

"No," she said slowly. "It was nice. I am just not sure what it means."

He leaned forward and faced her, waiting until she looked at him. "It means I like you, Lauren. A lot. I think you're smart, driven, and beautiful. I'm not going to push you for anything."

"I'm moving away later this year."

"I know." He nodded slowly, and the lightning in his eyes flickered. "I'm bummed about that. But if it makes you happy, I'm happy."

"So..." she didn't want to say the words. "We shouldn't get serious."

"Some people would say that."

Did he mean that he would be willing to get serious even if she were leaving? That didn't make sense. That sounded like heartbreak to her.

She shifted her eyes to the land and grass and sky in front of her. The whole world was in front of her. Could a genuine love be next to her?

HE'D NEVER KICK himself for kissing her. He would remember that kiss for the rest of his life, whether he ever got another one with her or not.

But the kiss had made her a little quieter; not nervous or withdrawn, just quiet. They'd finished their coffee, then the trail they were on, and Hawk had decided it was time to move forward. He suggested they drive and explore.

In the car, she brought up the fundraiser. *She thinks this is a safe topic,* he thought to himself. He listened to her updates and ideas and responded appropriately and enthusiastically. She was avoiding delving into anything deeper, and he understood that.

Hitting the exchanges for East Peoria, he thought of a fun diversion. He took the exit ramp for Camp Street and followed it until he hit East Washington Street. After a few more quick turns, they stopped along the road.

"What are we doing here?" Lauren asked.

"Come see."

She followed him down the sidewalk and up onto the bridge. At the top, he paused and pointed. Below, on the concrete, was a Rolling Stones logo. She laughed when she saw it.

"Your artwork?"

"No," he answered. "I wish I could take credit for it. But it's pretty cool, huh?"

"I'm no art historian, but yes, it's pretty cool. How long has it been here?"

"No idea. I've heard it's been here since the late seventies or early eighties."

"But the colors are so bright."

"It's been touched up. Let's go down and take some pictures."

He led the way down to the concrete beside the bridge. They took pictures of each other by the logo and then sat together just under the logo and took a selfie with it in the background.

"How about ice cream?" Hawk asked.

"I like ice cream."

His lips twisted. "I mean would you like some ice cream now?"

"Sure!" Her eyes lit up and she gave him the biggest smile yet. He wanted to pull her toward him and wrap her in his arms.

"Come on." He reached for her hand. There seemed to be no hesitation when she put her hand in his. He liked how this felt. Walking hand in hand, side by side with Lauren. This was so new and felt so fragile. She reminded him of a feral kitten; one wrong move and she'd disappear.

He'd thought about bringing up the foster care potential to her today to let her know what his plans were. Maybe it was a cop out, but he told himself it was better to wait until he knew if his application was approved before telling her. What they had was so new and so tentative, that he worried telling her would send her scurrying away.

His timing was terrible; always had been. It was usually because he rushed into a relationship full steam ahead. He was usually the first to fall, and his falling caused the other to run.

But this time he was taking it slow. He was waiting to see how she felt. He wasn't rushing things with Lauren. She had her walls up, and it reminded him to keep his up. But the timing with the foster application was a new wrinkle.

She had reminded him that she planned to move away. She wasn't interested in a long-term relationship. With all of the goals in front of her, there was no way she would be interested in helping him take care of a kid and he wouldn't ask her to.

A couple of minutes later, they pulled into an ice-cream shop shaped like a giant ice-cream cone.

Lauren ordered a vanilla cone, and Hawk chose a swirl. They sat at a nearby picnic table. Hawk loved feeling the sun on his face as the ice cream cooled his parched mouth.

"Tomorrow's Easter. What are you doing?" he asked.

"Going home."

"Tonight, or tomorrow?"

"Early tomorrow. My aunt's family is coming in from Indianapolis for the weekend, so I lose my bedroom. I'll just drive up and back tomorrow."

"What time is dinner?

"One o'clock." A drip of ice cream ran down the back of her hand, and he handed her a napkin. "The nice thing about driving in is I don't have to help with cooking or set-up. Actually, mom hires a professional chef to come in and do most of it. What are you doing tomorrow?"

"Going to my dad's place for brunch with his family and then going to my mom's for a late lunch with her family."

"That's got to be hard, having to split your holidays across two places."

"It is. But eventually, it becomes your new normal, and you manage." He thought about future foster kids, how hard holidays would be for them. Though they might be coming from tough situations, don't all kids want to be with their families for the holidays? He was going to study hard in the classes on supporting kids if he managed to get approved.

She leaned toward him and rested her shoulder against his arm. "I hope you manage tomorrow well."

Her care and kindness filled him with confidence. She thought she was speaking to his wounds as a child of divorced parents, but he'd had a lot of years to learn to cope with that pain. Instead, she was filling him with the drive to succeed as a foster parent. He only hoped he'd eventually have her in his corner with that endeavor as well.

CHAPTER TWENTY

LAUREN'S COUSIN, DELIA, was the first to greet her when she arrived at her parents' apartment. Delia squealed, grabbing Lauren in a tight embrace.

Delia's product-enhanced red hair was up in a high ponytail, her makeup was flawless, and she wore a pale blue A-line shirtdress with a slim pink belt. Large resin easter egg earrings hung from her earlobes. "Oh, Lou, it has been way too long. I can't wait to catch up. Hurry, let's go hide in your bedroom before everyone else knows you're home."

Delia was the only one ever to call Lauren "Lou". Lauren liked it. It was nice to have a nickname.

Delia pulled Lauren's hand, and she dutifully followed. Her cousin was two years older than Lauren and never let her forget it.

In Lauren's bedroom with the twentieth-story view of Lake Michigan, she saw that Delia had made herself at home. Her suitcase was open on the floor, and several outfits were laid out on the bed. Lauren wondered where they would sit, but Delia quickly scooped up all the clothes and dumped them on top of the open suitcase.

"Okay, okay," Delia chattered. "Come here. Let's talk. How's school? No, don't tell me that. Are you dating anyone? That's the only important question. Once dinner starts, the—" She cleared her throat, "—grownups will dominate and direct the conversation. And we're leaving right after dinner. Spill."

Lauren smiled at her cousin. She loved Delia's energy and confidence; she was always the one to dominate and direct all their conversations. "I don't know."

"What do you mean you don't know? Are you seeing someone or not?"

"Well, there is this guy."

"Assumed that. Go on."

"We've been working together—"

"Okay."

"He kissed me yesterday."

"YES!" Delia shouted as she jumped up from the bed, dancing. "Yes, yes, yes. It's about time, Lou Lou! Tell me everything. First. How was the K. I. S. S.?"

Lauren felt her cheeks flush. "It was sweet. Gentle. We'd been hiking and were sitting on a picnic blanket, resting."

"Please tell me he pushed you down and rolled you around!"

"No." Lauren shook her head. "It was a very sweet first kiss."

"Oh, it was the first one. Aw, I'm dying here. Who is this guy? Are you in love? Lust? What?"

"Uh," Lauren groaned, not knowing how to answer. "He's very handsome. A little older—"

"How old?"

"Twenty-nine."

"Does he have a job?"

"Yes."

"How did you meet?"

"We're going to be in a wedding together in June. Mutual friends. I'm a bridesmaid, he's a groomsman."

Delia nodded slowly, watching every twitch on Lauren's face. This would be easier if the conversation were being held over the phone. Delia's scrutiny was hard to take. "So, you like him? Like *really* like him?"

Lauren smiled. Those words sounded wrong, but she understood the question. "I do, but it's not going to work out." She flopped backwards on the bed and covered her eyes. "I'm going to grad school this fall, and falling in love is not on my schedule."

Delia plopped down next to Lauren, resting her head on her hand. Lauren watched her from under her own arm. "Girl, no one falls in love 'on schedule'. It happens when it happens."

There was a knock at the door. Delia rolled her eyes at Lauren. "Come in!" she called.

Lauren's mom walked in. "Have you heard from—oh, you're home, Lauren. When did you get in? And why didn't you come say hello?"

Peevishly, Lauren would have liked to hear a hint of pain in her mom's voice to the last question. "Just got here a few minutes ago. Delia and I wanted to catch up for a few moments. We'll be out soon."

"Okay." Nicole turned to walk out. "You're going to wrinkle those pants even more lying like that."

Once the door closed, Lauren looked at her cousin and they burst out laughing. "Good thing it's my bedroom and I left some clothes here. I'll change."

She stood as Delia continued the questions. Lauren answered as best she could, but she wasn't sure what was happening with Hawk herself. She had more questions than Delia did.

EVERYONE WAS SEATED around the formal dining room table and her father was giving a toast. Her mother had been promoted at work in recognition of some big, huge accomplishment. Seemed to happen once a year.

Usually, Lauren was just as excited about these celebrations as her parents, but this time she felt more cynical than excited. Yes, her parents had achieved much in their careers. They excelled. It's what they did. It's what they expected her to do. But after the day with Hawk, she was beginning to have doubts. Would the world end if she didn't go to grad school this fall? What if she took a gap year and stayed in Bloomington/Normal getting to know Hawk better? Maybe in a year, he would consider moving with her to wherever she decided to go to grad school?

How would she broach this with her parents? Would they understand? They obviously understood love—they were devoted to each other. They were partners first and foremost. Partners in law firms, too. Lauren smiled at her own joke and got a quick glance from her mother. Darn, she'd missed what her dad had said.

He finished his toast, and everyone raised their glasses. Lauren toasted with lemonade because she had to drive back to school after lunch.

Delia winked at Lauren from across the table and stood up. "Congratulations, Aunt Nicole. So proud of you. I have an announcement, too. My online business has reached half a million in sales, and it's only April!" She raised her glass to the words of encouragement and applause from around the table. "Thank you. Thank you." As she started to sit down, she said, "Oh, and Lou Lou has a boyfriend."

Her parents' faces spun toward Lauren, and neither was smiling. Lauren knew she'd blushed bright red; it felt as though her whole face was on fire. She felt like kicking Delia under the table, but she refrained.

Lauren felt every set of eyes on her. This was news, big news. Every single person sitting around the table had heard for years how she wasn't going to get serious about anyone until she was out of grad school. It had been her personal motto for so long.

"What about grad school, Lauren?" Her father asked.

"Still going, Dad," she replied. "What about Delia's shop? Isn't that amazing? Here's another toast to Delia!" She picked up her glass to toast her cousin and prayed that the spotlight would swing back across the table. Luckily, it did. Delia's younger brother, David, asked what he could do to help build his sister's business. Lauren winked at Delia. She was thankful David was more interested in money than her love life.

Table chatter continued to focus on Delia and Nicole's accomplishments as the ham and sides were passed around. Lauren made small talk with her Aunt Debbie, who was sitting on her right. She tried not to turn to her left where she'd risk meeting her parents' disappointed expressions.

As soon as dinner was over, everyone adjourned to the living room, where Uncle Leon played the piano as after-dinner entertainment. Delia and Lauren sat on the loveseat and whispered about what Lauren's next move should be as far as Hawk was concerned. Delia advocated asking him out. "We're modern women; we don't need to wait to be asked," she'd said. Lauren was nervous about the idea. She was afraid of being turned down, but she finally relented to Delia's nagging and texted him. She told herself she couldn't ask to get together for the fundraiser; it had to be for a date.

LAUREN: Hi! Happy Easter!

HAWK: Aw, you're thinking about me. Sweet. Happy Easter.

LAUREN: Are you free Wed night? I'd like to take you to dinner.

HAWK: Why Ms. Lauren, are you asking me on a date?

Yikes. This was it. Would he turn her down?

> **LAUREN:** Yes.

> **HAWK:** I'm honored you asked. I can't Wed. Have something going on. Can we get together on Sat to do FR pickups?

FR must mean fundraiser. What did he have happening on Wednesday? She felt the heat rising up her neck. Delia gave her a look, but she smiled and shook off the feeling of failure.

> **LAUREN:** Saturday works.

> **HAWK:** I'll explain then.

Whew. Must not be a date. Must not be something he's hiding. That's a positive. She wished he'd give her a clue, at least. No. What she really wished for was that he would ask her out on a *date* for Saturday, not to work on the fundraiser together. Oh well, maybe it would turn into a date.

"Well?" Delia asked.

"He can't do Wednesday, and that's the only weeknight I'm available. We want to work together on Saturday for the fundraiser. I'm worried that I misread his signals yesterday."

"He kissed you!" Lauren's parents turned their heads at Delia's outburst. She lowered her voice. "You didn't misread. Give him a chance to explain. Stop worrying."

"I'm not—"

"Yes, you are. Stop."

Uncle Leon started playing a number from *Guys and Dolls*. Lauren leaned back on the loveseat, turning toward her uncle. She normally sang along with this number, but her mind was on Hawk. The song made her think about luck, and she thought it was luck that had brought her and Hawk together. But it was going to take more than luck to keep them together.

HAWK CLOSED THE foster care handbook and placed it on the coffee table. It was getting late, and his body was ready for bed.

Ms. Ryan had dropped the handbook off on Sunday morning, when she'd told him he'd passed the initial approval. She was impressed when he said he would make himself available for the training class that started the next day.

He stood and turned off the lamp that he'd been using to read by. The shades were already closed, and the front door was locked.

"Come on, Goldie. Bedtime," he said to the pup, who'd looked up when he stood but stayed on her warm blanket in the corner of the couch.

At these words, the dog hopped off the couch and stretched. Hawk smiled at her moves. He walked to the kitchen, straightening a few misplaced items on the way.

At the kitchen sink, he drank a glass of water and gazed out the window to the backyard. He imagined playing catch or watching a child play. He thought about getting a swing set and planned to do some research right away.

He grabbed his backpack from the back porch. He'd not put anything away since coming home on Saturday. He wanted to put the clock that Lauren had given him in the spare bedroom. He'd decided to use the Scooby bedding, too. He liked how it said "kid!" and not "adult guest". He could always switch out the bedding if it wasn't right for a kid or guest.

He put the uneaten granola bars away and threw the picnic blanket into a laundry basket in the basement near the washer and dryer.

Upstairs, he went to the spare bedroom and sat on the bed. He looked around and felt the room was ready. Placing the clock on the nightstand, he smiled. Lauren had been so sweet to give it to him. He wondered what she was really thinking about. Was she wondering why he'd put kids' bedding in the room?

He thought about how he was going to tell Lauren about his dream to foster. He wanted to tell her. He had to tell her now that it was taking up a lot of his evening hours, but he worried that she wouldn't react well. There was no commitment between them. Heck, other than the hiking excursion, they hadn't even been on a real date.

And now she'd just asked him out. She'd asked him out! Shows how bold and confident she was. A modern woman, taking things into her own hands. He was thrilled that she'd asked and disappointed that he'd had to turn her down. He hadn't frightened her away with his kiss on Saturday.

He thought about that kiss again. He'd played it back in his mind one hundred times since. Each time he imagined it, he felt a spike of adrenaline. It was as intoxicating and addicting as anything he could imagine.

Tonight's training was about communicating with the kids. Being as honest as possible while being upbeat and positive. Showing empathy. Trying to understand what they were going through. Could he use this training to talk to Lauren? He wasn't sure, but he hoped it would help.

CHAPTER TWENTY-ONE

HAWK CARRIED THE tray with their food to the picnic table where Lauren was sitting. After three hours running around and picking up stuff for the fundraiser, they were both ready for lunch.

Lauren said she had a taste for root beer, and Hawk had brought her to the hot dog stand south of town. It was less than a quarter mile from the airport, and they could see the runway from their picnic table.

A flight took off a few minutes after they arrived. Lauren worried that their conversation would be drowned out by the noise, but other than a few small charter planes, there wasn't a lot of flight traffic or noise.

"Hope you're hungry," Hawk said, putting the tray on the table.

Lauren looked over the tray. Three chili dogs, onion rings, french fries, and two root beer floats. "I am. Where's yours?"

Hawk's head tilted back as he barked out a laugh. "Let's see where we get with this and then decide if we need more." Sitting down across from her, he picked up one of the large floats from the tray. "Haven't had one of these in years. Good call."

"Me either."

They ate quietly for a few minutes. A small plane flew low overhead, coming in for a landing. They both looked up.

"Wow, I could see the pilot! He was wearing a blue hat," Hawk said.

"I saw that. It's a shame you don't like to fly. Besides getting somewhere quickly, there's a thrill in soaring like a bird."

"Well, you're the adventurous one. I'll take your word for it."

"What would it take to get you on an airplane?"

"I don't know. I don't understand how it works, so it makes me nervous. I like to understand what I'm doing, what the risks are. Kind of like assessing the exits when I walk into a place. One thing I know—you don't take the plane's exit when it's in flight."

Lauren laughed. "You're right. You don't do that."

Hawk changed the subject. "Hey, I wanted to talk to you about why I couldn't go out Wednesday."

Lauren was hoping this would come up today. It had been a worry all week. "I'm listening."

He took a deep breath. This couldn't be good. "I'm in training. Every Monday, Wednesday, and Friday for the next four weeks."

Oh, training. That's cool. Must be for work. "What's the training for?" she asked, taking a bite of an onion ring dipped in ketchup.

He hesitated. Strange. Finally, he continued, "I've applied to be a foster parent. The training is part of the process to become certified. It's been a dream of mine for a while."

Lauren paused between bites; the onion ring did a somersault in her stomach. She blinked at him, feeling like she was seeing him for the first time. "Foster? But you're not married."

He gave that slight smile, but this time it seemed pained. "I'm not. You don't have to be. But I want to help. I see a lot of kids at the community center in tough situations. A few of the boys I've coached have been in foster homes. The need is great. And it's something I can do—and I want to do it."

Lauren pushed the onion rings over to Hawk's side of the table. "That's interesting." Gosh, he was a sweetheart. A real softie. He was going to make some lady very happy someday. Her stomach flipped again. She hoped she wouldn't get sick. This was not the type of lunch to be eating before getting a shock like this. A foster parent? What single guy would want to do that? Well, one that had a house, was settled, was a good coach. A great guy. A prince charming. Back-peddling out of this situation was not going to be easy. Why couldn't she have met him in the future? Once she was done with grad school and established in a career. Why did she have to meet him now?

"What are you thinking right now?" he asked. A deep crease had formed between his eyebrows.

"That you are an incredible person—"

"And?" he prompted when she hesitated.

"That I worry we've met at the wrong time in our lives." She looked down at her food. There was no way she was finishing this chili dog with onions and cheese. She held back bile.

"Hey. I disagree," he said, reaching across and clasping her hand. "I'm so happy I met you now. In a few more months, you'll move away, and I might never have met you."

"There's the baptism for Trevor and Paige's baby."

Hawk looked stunned. "Paige is pregnant?"

"No. I meant in the future. We are tied together because of mutual friends. I'm sure our paths will cross again."

"That sounds ominous. Like you're not going to see me again before you move."

"I didn't say that. This is just a lot to take in. I'm shocked."

"I know. I should have mentioned it sooner. But I wasn't committed to doing it until recently. Once I applied, things started moving a little quicker than I expected. I don't mean to scare you off. I'm not asking you to take this on with me."

"How soon?"

"What do you mean?"

"How soon until you might be asked to care for a kid?"

"I have four weeks of training. I have to complete that first, then there are a few other verification steps. There's no way to know at this point."

Of course, it would be unknown, but Lauren wasn't used to living life that way. She planned. She executed. She reevaluated and then she planned again. Life was a journey. You had to plan for that journey. Prepare for it. She even had kids on her journey map, two of them before turning thirty. That was the plan.

"I see. It's great." Lauren was proud of her response. This is the way you did it. Never let them see you freak out. Maintain control. In a courtroom, in a meeting, in a family gathering. Her parents had taught her well.

"Thanks. I think so, too. But I know this has to be a shock to you."

"It is. But if it's what you want, I think it's great that you're going for it."

"Lauren." He stood and came around the picnic table, straddling the bench next to her and sitting so he faced her squarely. He rubbed her back lightly. She wanted to lean over into him. To feel comforted. To see if his touch would help her understand. "Look at me, please." His voice was soft, pleading.

Lauren turned and attempted a smile. He shook his head slowly. "You don't have to pretend with me, Lauren. I know this is hard to comprehend, coming out of the blue. It doesn't have to change anything between us. It's something *I'm* doing," he stressed. "I would never put this on you. I just ask for your understanding."

He put his forehead down on her shoulder. She liked the idea of him literally leaning on her. She tilted her head to rest on his. The top of his hair was warmed from the sun.

Hawk sighed. "I didn't finish my fries."

She moved her head, smiling as he raised his. He was trying to lighten the mood. "I think they may be cool by now."

"Yeah, probably. Don't get weirded out by my announcement, Lauren. I really like you, and I love spending time with you."

"As do I. I just…" It was her turn to sigh. "I am not used to surprises. I like to have a plan. A plan that has been thoroughly debated, pros and cons weighed out. Alternate choices considered. Then I make a decision. And up to this point in my life, I've made my own decisions. For me. Well, or for my parents." She didn't want to think about that too much. "I'm not used to someone else's decisions impacting me."

"I like that about you. I'm the same way. I have deliberated over this decision for a long time. It wasn't an easy one to make. In some ways, I worry I won't be enough as a single foster parent. Kids need a mom figure. But I am going to give it my all. I'll be there to help, support, hug, and love them with everything I got. No holding back."

"I can see that in you."

"Good. And though plans are good, sometimes you have to roll the dice and take a risk."

"Like flying?" she teased.

"Hey, let's not go that far."

She considered his words. Roll the dice. Bet on lady luck. It was such a foreign idea.

He pushed her hair behind her ear and leaned in for a quick kiss on the cheek. "Don't write me off yet."

She nodded gently. He stood and walked back around the picnic table. "What are you doing tomorrow? It's supposed to be great weather. And I'm not coaching basketball because of Spring Break. I thought we could take the top off the Jeep and take a little road trip. We'll bring Goldie. She loves an open-air ride."

"Is that safe?"

"Safe enough. I have a harness to secure her. What do you say?"

Lauren had planned to rewrite her Organizational Strategy class paper. Maybe this one time, she could roll the dice and turn in the paper she'd spent hours writing already. She knew it was good, but she'd had plans to make it perfect. Perhaps a day spent driving with Hawk and Goldie would be more perfect.

"Sure. I'm in."

CHAPTER TWENTY-TWO

*H*AWK WAS STANDING beside the Jeep petting Goldie, who was in the backseat. The top was off the Jeep, and Lauren thought it looked like freedom.

She'd spent Saturday evening reading for school, and she'd taken a break to write down her thoughts about Hawk's announcement. She struggled with a feeling of hurt that he had this other path in life that didn't include her. But of course he did. They'd only known each other for a few months. She decided she was lucky enough that he was single and interested in her; she wasn't going to waste time worrying about what she didn't have.

"Look who's coming with us today, Goldie!"

The dog barked.

"She approves." Hawk wrapped an arm around Lauren and pulled her close. She put her hands around his back and squeezed. Closing her eyes, she smiled into his chest. His familiar smell enveloped her in comfort and excitement. She was ready for whatever adventure Hawk had planned for them. At this moment, she was ready for anything, and marveled at the feeling of not being the one in charge.

Hawk brought his hand to her chin and raised her face to look at him. "Hey," he said.

"Hi."

He lowered his mouth to hers, and a passing truck honked. He pulled back and winked at her. "Guess it's too early in the day for making out on the street. You ready to go?"

She didn't want to let go of him or for that kiss to end. "I suppose we should."

He opened her door and gave her a hand as she climbed in.

"So, where are we going today?" she asked.

"To one of the places I mentioned to you when we talked about road trips before. And to somewhere else that we didn't talk about but I'm guessing you haven't been to."

"Where?"

"All surprises."

After a quick coffee stop, he drove for thirty minutes. They talked about work, school, and Paige and Trevor's upcoming wedding—everything except foster care.

He headed south on I-55, then took exit 140 for Atlanta. Lauren seemed to recall him mentioning Atlanta, Illinois in conversation but she couldn't remember why. A few turns and a few minutes later, their destination towered over her. They parked on the street and took in the nineteen-foot-tall statue called "Paul Bunyon" (not Bunyan), holding a hot dog.

Lauren laughed. "Wow. That is something."

Hawk grinned. "We have to take a selfie."

"Agreed."

He unhooked Goldie from the backseat and put her on a leash to stretch her legs. There was no traffic, so they jaywalked across the street. Goldie relieved herself beside the statue giant's shoe.

"Oops. Should have taken her to do her business first. Sorry, Mr. Bunyon," Hawk said, glancing up at the statue.

"I don't think he minds. But there may be a city ordinance— keep an eye out for the cops."

"Cops? It's Sunday morning, and the town has a population

of sixteen hundred. I think it's against the law to have a cop on duty under those circumstances."

Laughing, Lauren moved closer for the selfie. Hawk laid his arm across her shoulders and pulled her tight against his side. He lifted the cell phone and positioned it downward, angling it to get in both them and the statue towering above them. He clicked, and Lauren told him to send her the picture. She was excited that she'd have another photo of them together.

"I think Goldie feels left out," Hawk said with a frown.

"Really? Want me to get a picture of the two of you?"

"No, let's see if someone can get a family photo—I mean, group photo—of us."

Lauren smiled at the slip. Even if he didn't mean it, it was nice to hear it. Hawk glanced up and down the sidewalk.

"It's crickets," he said. "We may be waiting a while."

"Got anywhere better to be?"

"Than with you? No. Wait, I hear a vehicle." He looked left and waved at the pickup truck coming toward them. The driver pulled over and lowered his passenger window.

"Can I help you?" the man asked.

"Would you mind hopping out and taking a picture of the three of us?" Hawk asked. "Well, four, if you're counting the statue."

The man obliged, and they posed for the picture.

As their photographer drove off, Lauren turned to Hawk. "Please send me that picture, too."

"Of course," he replied, clicking on his phone. "Let's take Goldie for a stroll before getting back in the car. The next leg of our trip will take a little longer."

"Oh, yeah? Where are we headed?"

"Still a surprise."

They got to the corner and turned right. Lauren glanced around at the businesses and houses as they walked, marveling at the small town.

Hawk reached for her hand, and she was thrilled by his touch. "Hawk, what are your plans for Memorial Day? I was thinking about inviting you up to Chicago. We always do this huge cookout in Grant Park—our official summer launch."

"Oh, no, I can't. That sounds fantastic, though. But my brother and I have a trip to northern Wisconsin planned for that weekend. We leave the Thursday before and come back the Wednesday after. A little fishing, a little hiking, a whole lot of camping. I would back out if I could, but we have a campsite booked and we've been planning it for months."

"It's fine," she said. "It was just an idea."

"You can't wait for school to be out and for summer to get here, can you?"

"You're right. I'm looking forward to summer break, but then I'll be throwing myself right back into school in the fall. Ugh. I'm beginning to feel like a professional student. I really can't wait to have a real, full-time job with benefits. To be making my own money and not have to rely on my parents for so much." She sighed.

"Plans can change, you know. You could take a gap year."

"Ha! Tell that to my parents. As much as I would love to take a gap year to travel, it's not happening. I floated that idea out to my parents once, and it was a big fat no-go."

"Bummer," he said. "A year traveling sounds pretty good."

"Did it take you long to find a job out of college?"

"No. I was interviewing before I graduated and had a couple of offers. Right skills at the right time. I took three weeks off after graduation to catch up on sleep and take care of a few things I'd been putting off. I also moved into a new apartment before starting my new job."

"And you're happy at your job?"

"I am. Great company. My manager respects me, and I respect her. I'm good at what I do, and I enjoy it. The money is good, I've been able to buy my house, and I'm saving for a rainy day and retirement. I have what I need and am content. Other than the family thing, I'm in a great place."

Lauren had so many questions about the family thing, but she didn't want to go there today. He'd bring up fostering, and she wasn't ready to go deeper into that conversation. "Your company sounds like a great fit for you. I hope I'm lucky enough to find that when I start looking."

"I'm sure you will. Any company would be lucky to have you. You will have to weigh your options and pick the one that feels best to you. But remember, it's a job offer, not a lifetime commitment. If a job isn't right for you, you can always leave and go somewhere else."

"I hate the thought of quitting anything." She'd feel like a failure.

"Doesn't make sense to lock yourself into a job that you don't enjoy. It will bring down your mental health and then your physical health. Though I guess sometimes it could be in the other order. But regardless, no one expects you to stay at a job for forty years and get the gold watch."

"A gold watch?"

Hawk laughed. "You've not heard that? Back in the day, people used to work for a company their whole career and then retire and get a gold watch. No one really does that anymore."

They had returned to the street where the Jeep was parked. Hawk asked if she needed anything before they got on the road. They both agreed they needed a bathroom break and a coffee refill. Hawk said the next drive would take a couple of hours and Lauren was intrigued.

HAWK LOVED THE drive. The day was warm, the top was off the Jeep, and the air was that early spring, earthy kind of fresh. And most importantly, Lauren was sitting next to him, laughing, joking, and enjoying herself. It was great to see her relaxed, not worried about school, her parents, or anything else. As far as he could tell, this was the most relaxed she'd been in a while.

After dropping the foster care news on her yesterday, he had been worried that she would back away from him and take some time to process the news. When she agreed to this day, he knew he had to make it memorable. The statue of a giant and a hot dog was a great way to start the day, but he was taking her to St. Louis, and he couldn't wait to walk underneath The Arch with her.

It was almost noon by the time The Arch came into view. He heard Lauren gasp in delight. The road signs had told her where they were headed—he wasn't going to blindfold the woman for two hours.

"Pretty exciting, isn't it?" he asked her, daring a glance at her as he managed traffic.

"Yes! I've never been to St. Louis. Or anywhere in Missouri."

"Never? Wow."

"Nope. I always thought it was so far away."

"Well, sure, maybe from Chicago. But for us it was six in one hand."

"Huh?"

He shook his head. "Six in one hand, half a dozen in the other. Another expression you've missed out on. Anyway, there it is." He nodded toward the landmark. "The gateway to the west."

"Are we stopping?"

"Yes, but not just yet. First, we're going to another Route 66 landmark. The Donut Drive-in."

"OK, but does it have a name?"

"That's its name. Donut Drive-in. I find when a place doesn't have a fancy name, it has better food. We have to stop there first, as it closes at two. We'll get some donuts to go and have them for dessert. Before dessert, we'll stop for lunch. I found a dog-friendly pub online. Can't leave Goldie in the car; someone might grab her."

"Right. You've thought of everything."

"I tried."

Donuts bought and secured on the floorboard between Lauren's feet, they backtracked to the pub. They took a table on the outdoor patio and studied the menu. When the server came, they ordered soft drinks and food.

"I didn't realize how hungry I was until now," Hawk said.

"I agree."

"Hey, did you put sunscreen on? You're looking a little red across your nose."

"I did, but I'm so pale, I probably need to reapply. Thanks for the reminder."

"No problem. So, what do you think so far?"

"I'm having the best day. Thank you. I am starting to see the allure of the road trip."

Hawk tilted his head back and laughed. "I told you, nothing better. And here we're only exploring a small slice of Route 66. Maybe someday…"

He trailed off, and the server appeared with their drinks and a bowl of water for Goldie. *Thank goodness for the interruption.* He'd almost suggested that they make the whole trip, but to do that right would take weeks. A real *family* vacation. He smiled, thinking about whining kids in the backseat, earbuds in, watching movies on tablets. Lauren in the front seat reading a book or sneaking work in though they were on vacation. He could barely contain the joy and pride that swelled in his chest at the daydream.

Lauren had bent over to pet Goldie, and he took a moment to compose himself. If he blurted out half of what he wanted to say to her, she'd run screaming. Been there, got the T-shirt. He'd ruined more than one relationship by falling too soon.

To put a damper on his emotions, he thought about Lauren leaving for grad school. She hadn't been clear on when she was leaving, the beginning of summer or the end. Shoot, she hadn't even told him where she was going, if she'd made a decision yet. He pictured her waving goodbye, pulling off the curb in her Mini Cooper, a moving van loaded with her stuff pulling out behind her. The image put a damper on the joy he'd been feeling.

"Right, Hawk?" she asked.

"I'm sorry. I missed that."

"I told Goldie that maybe you'd order a little something for her. She was giving me the 'I'm hungry' look."

"She's always hungry."

It was the way he was feeling looking at Lauren—hungry for a future that wasn't promised to them. Certainly, wasn't promised to him. He could see her married to a rich professional. Probably a lawyer like her parents. He could picture her holding her own at a fancy dinner party. She wasn't made for backyard bar-beques and roadside picnics. He needed to figure out how to fall for the right woman, the right one for him, specifically. He sighed.

"You feel all right?" Lauren asked, laying a hand on his arm.

He smiled. "Yes, I'm fine. I'm just happy. Content. Glad to be here. With you." That had taken a serious tone he hadn't intended.

She gave him a slight grin. "With me and Goldie, right?"

"Yes. This is pure perfection."

He knew it: this was perfection. He hoped it was for her, too. She was always striving for perfection. Making and attacking her goals. He just wished her life goals, or rather love goals, were more in line with his. He could dream.

CHAPTER TWENTY-THREE

THE FOLLOWING SUNDAY, Lauren wished it were another Sunday Funday spent with Hawk, but she had to buckle down on homework today, so she had to decline his suggestion to go bowling. She had admitted that she'd never been bowling, and he could not get over the very idea. He wanted to remedy that at once.

She was reviewing and updating her weekly planner, sitting at the kitchen counter drinking a cup of coffee, when her phone rang.

It was her mom on the other end this morning. "Your dad had to run and pick up his dry cleaning. We're going to a matinee this afternoon and have dinner plans with your father's partner tonight, so it's a very busy Sunday. What are you doing today, Lauren?"

"Wow. You really have packed it in today, haven't you?"

"No rest for us today, that's for sure."

"Don't you get tired of it, Mom?"

"Of what?"

"The rat race. Overachieving at work, doing everything society expects of you. Don't you ever want to dial it back a little bit?"

Lauren's heart rate ticked up, like she'd run up the three flights of stairs to her apartment carrying six bags of groceries.

"Don't be silly. We set the pace for the race." Nicole laughed uproariously at her own statement. Lauren didn't find it funny. "You'll see, dear. There's no greater high than hitting the achievements you set out for yourself. Like you and your 4.0 grade point average. You are always setting a high bar for yourself, and you execute perfectly. Get the accolades. Get the awards. You won't regret it. Now, what are your top three goals for this week?"

Of course, she'd said grade point average, not the abbreviation. Lauren rolled her eyes. She felt again like she was providing a status report to her supervisor, not having a conversation or getting real support from her mom. She sighed. "I have a test in business law on Wednesday and a paper due Friday. On Saturday, Hawk and I will be doing more prep work for the fundraiser. Creating bid sheets, grouping a few of the donations together to get higher bids, that kind of thing. The fundraiser and charity auction are less than a month away."

"That's great. Do you need any help prepping for your law exam?"

Lauren heard the wistfulness in her mother's voice. Her parents were still disappointed that she'd chosen not to follow them into law. "No, I got it. I have a prep session with the leading student in the class on Tuesday. He's got all the material in hand and will help me with a couple of concepts. I'm sure I'll nail the test."

"He? Who is it? A potential suitor?"

Her mom was so formal. "No. Mom, I told you I'm dating Hawk. One person at a time is enough."

Oddly, she couldn't say 'boyfriend'. She wondered if Hawk considered her a girlfriend.

"Hmm. Well, if I can't help you with your test, is there anything else you need from me or your dad?"

"There is one thing. I was thinking about taking a trip to Greece the week of Memorial Day. The summer is going to be busy. Do you have any problems with that?"

"You'll miss the annual picnic!"

"I know, but it's the best week for me to go."

Hawk would be gone Memorial Day Weekend, too, so it was the best time to go.

"Well, I understand. You're a busy girl. Do you need money? Actually, strike that. A trip to Greece sounds like an excellent graduation gift."

"Really? That would be fantastic!"

"Is your friend Hawk going with you?"

"No, unfortunately." Lauren took a breath; she didn't want the next words to be hurtful to Hawk, even though he wasn't listening. "He's never flown before and says he doesn't have plans to."

"He's afraid to fly?" Her mother sounded alarmed; Lauren regretted telling her.

"Well, yes, I guess. But he doesn't seem upset about it. He's happy traveling by car."

"You know, I had a coworker once who was afraid to fly. You know what his wife did? She bought him flight lessons. Found that once he understood how it worked, he wasn't afraid anymore."

"Really? Wow." Now that she thought about it, Hawk had said something about not understanding the logistics of flight.

"Yes. He loved traveling afterwards. Never bothered him again."

"Huh. Interesting." Lauren jotted in her planner, "check out flight school for Hawk".

"Back to the trip idea. Do you have a plan?"

"I was looking at a hosted trip. Rick Steves has one that week with availability."

"Send me the details, dear. I'll talk to your dad about it tonight."

"Okay. Thanks, Mom. I need to go. Do you have anything else for me?"

"No. Good luck with school this week. Can't wait to talk to you next Sunday. I'll text you about the trip when I talk to your dad."

"Sounds good. Love you."

"Love you more."

Lauren put the phone down on the counter and pulled her laptop close. She searched for flight schools in the area. There was one in town, and the cost for a lesson and a flight wasn't too terrible. It was a pretty big gift for someone she'd just started to date, but Lauren wasn't afraid to go big. She put the charge on her personal credit card; she didn't want to have to explain this gift to her parents.

HAWK TYPED UP a few more notes on his tablet. In was Monday night and he was sitting in his foster training class. This evening's class had been full of incredible information on parenting a child.

Cara, the instructor, spoke passionately about the need to just be there. Spending time with the kids while they played or colored was critical. Especially when they were new to your home. They needed stability and the knowledge that you weren't there to judge them. You showed them love by spending time with them.

She stressed the criticality of providing them with the basic needs first: shelter, food, clothing, and emotional support. Some kids would arrive with a few items thrown quickly into a garbage bag, if they were lucky.

Hawk thought of the analogy of being a rock. Being unmovable, strong, steadfast. He could do that. He could be that.

He remembered the cop who had helped turn him around when his world had crumbled after his dad left. Brad Lankford had taken him to the community center and included him in pickup basketball games. The nights sweating it out on the court with the older players helped him cast off the anger and resentment he had at his dad's sudden departure from the family home.

It took that and some therapy in his early twenties to deal with the trauma of his broken home. Hawk felt that therapy helped him finally release the anger and resentment that he'd had for so long. He believed it had prepared him for the challenges that were going to come when kids were placed with him.

It didn't matter what came his way. He was ready. And if there were circumstances that he wasn't ready for, he knew how to ask for help. Asking for help is what got him out of trouble when he was a kid and prevented trouble when he could have made bad decisions as a young adult.

Some of the case studies that Cara discussed tonight were shocking. It broke his heart to hear about kids leaving one bad situation and landing in another. As heartbreaking as those stories were, they firmed his resolve. He knew becoming a foster parent was the right thing for him to do.

The knowledge that he'd possibly have a child to care for in a few months helped ease his angst over Lauren leaving for grad school just a little bit.

Cara ended the training session and Hawk stood to leave. Some of the others in class were going out for a drink, but Hawk declined. He needed to get home to let Goldie out.

LAUREN WAS WORKING at In Bloom Thursday afternoon when a man who looked familiar entered.

"How's it going?" he asked, as he looked around.

"Great." Lauren stepped out from behind the register. "What can I help you with today?"

He ducked his head slightly. "I'm hoping Anna Lee remembered that it's my anniversary and got some flowers in for me."

Lauren laughed at his sheepish attitude. "Well, we have lots of flowers. We usually do. Is there a particular kind you're looking for?"

"Yes!" he cried. "Calla lilies—they're the flowers my wife carried down the aisle on our wedding day, and I always get them for our anniversary. I forgot to order them ahead of time. I'm hoping Anna Lee might have remembered."

"Oh, you're right. We don't stock those all the time. I can check in the back and with her. What's your name?"

"Cal Ekman."

"Oh, wait. You're a musician, right?"

"Yes, I am."

"I saw you a few weeks ago. It was a fantastic show."

"Thank you so much. I'm glad to hear that you enjoyed it."

"I did! Wait here a moment and I'll check on those flowers for you."

Lauren smiled as she left the retail space. She couldn't wait until she could tell Hawk about Cal Ekman coming into the store.

At the door to the consultation room, she knocked softly. She heard Anna Lee call her in.

"Hi, sorry to interrupt you. Cal Ekman is here asking about calla lilies for his anniversary. I didn't see any in the front or the back."

Anna Lee smiled. "Tell Cal I got his back. They are in the back walk-in cooler. They're already wrapped; that's why you didn't notice them. Look for the vase with gold and purple wrapping. Lower shelf. You can't miss it."

"Wow. You're good." Lauren said.

"I take care of my regulars." Anna Lee turned back to the young blonde sitting in front of her. They were working on the young woman's wedding plan. Lauren heard Anna Lee mention lilies as she closed the door behind her.

She walked to the back and found the wrapped flowers right where Anna Lee had said they'd be. She took them to the front and set them on the register.

"You're in luck. Anna Lee had them all ready to go." She peered over the top of the wrap and smiled when she saw the bouquet of tall, slender calla lilies nestled in a lush array of thin, airy fern leaves. "And they're beautiful." She tilted the vase over so he could see them.

Calla lilies were her grandmother Kate's favorite flowers and Lauren always felt a rush of sweet memories looking at them. They had become her favorite too.

He nodded as he pulled out his wallet. "Sweet. Did you know the word calla means beautiful?"

"Really?" Lauren shrugged. "I had no idea."

"Yes." He signed the receipt. "We found that out after my wife chose them for our wedding. It's appropriate. My wife is beautiful inside and out. She'll be thrilled with this bouquet. Anna Lee is amazing. This is the fifth year in a row that she's had them ready without me ordering ahead of time."

"She knows what she's doing, that's for sure."

"You mean Anna Lee, right? Not my wife."

"Oh, yes. I'm sure your wife knows what she's doing, too." She laughed. "But I was talking about Anna Lee. It's so cool you came in today. I can't wait to tell my friends I met you in person. They are going to be jealous."

"I hope to see you at an upcoming show. I play around town a lot."

Lauren added that as one more thing she was going to miss when she moved away. "I hope so. Thank you for coming in today, and happy anniversary to you and your wife."

After he left, she pulled out her phone and texted Hawk. She wished she'd asked for a picture with Cal to prove she'd met him. *I'll have to go up to him next time we see him perform.* She hoped she would get the opportunity before she left.

CHAPTER TWENTY-FOUR

*L*AUREN DROVE TO Hawk's house on Saturday to work on the fundraiser. She arrived with two Avanti's Gondola sandwiches and bags of chips.

Hawk and Goldie met her in the driveway as she pulled in. They had just come back from a walk.

"Hello, beautiful," Hawk said as she got out of the car.

"Hi, yourself," she replied. She wanted to say "Hi, handsome" but refrained. "Got the sandwiches you requested."

"Great! I'm ready to eat, and then we can get busy."

Inside, he let Goldie off the leash and gave her fresh water. After begging a few moments for the ham from their sandwiches, Goldie curled up on the couch in the living room.

"What do you want to drink?" Hawk asked.

"Water's fine."

Hawk took two glasses out of an upper cabinet and filled them at the sink. "So, it's been almost two weeks since I've seen you. How are things going?"

"School's good. Prepping for finals next week."

"I'm shocked you're here, to be honest."

"I have a plan—"

"Of course." He smiled as he set her glass down.

"I have a plan, with down time included. I'm helping with this today, and playing pickleball with Nica, Grady, and Trevor tomorrow."

"Pickleball, really?"

"Yep. I checked out a rule book from the library and everything."

"You do prepare for everything."

"I try. I wish you were going with us."

"Well, you don't need a fifth player. Besides, I've got coaching in the morning and am helping my brother out in the afternoon. That kid always needs help."

"I hope I get to meet your mysterious brother someday."

Hawk grunted and took a bite of his sandwich, chewing aggressively. "Someday."

"Oh, Mr. Springer," she teased. "Is your brother even cuter than you?"

"Heck no. I'm much better looking. But I'm in no rush for you to meet him. Let's change the subject. Back to pickleball. Have you played before?"

"No. That's why I got the book, to understand the general rules. I'll figure it out tomorrow."

"I bet you're competitive."

She laughed. "Yes, you could say that. Now, what do we need to do today for the charity auction?"

Hawk pulled up a list on his tablet and read off his goals for their afternoon.

"Well, we better get started." Lauren crumpled up her sandwich wrapper and stood to toss it in the garbage. "I can't believe it's only three weeks away."

Hawk refilled his water glass. "It's crazy to think what the next three weeks will bring. Your graduation and the fundraiser are back-to-back Saturdays. It's exciting."

"Do you think you might come to my graduation?" Lauren asked.

"I wouldn't miss it."

She did a little dance of joy. Hawk laughed. Lauren thought about introducing him to her parents, which put a little damper on her joy, but she wasn't going to let that dim her excitement.

Hawk returned to the table and set his glass down. He turned towards Lauren and shimmied with her; she thought he looked ridiculous and adorable at the same time.

He reached for her hand, pulled her to him and began to slow dance with no music playing. "Ah, this is better," he said.

"We're not getting our work done like this."

"There's a time for all things. A time for work and a time for dancing with a beautiful lady."

"That's the second time today you called me beautiful."

"Only two? Not nearly enough."

"Hey, you know what I learned recently?"

"What?"

"Calla lilies come from the Greek word 'calla' meaning beautiful."

"How did you learn that?"

"Well, I work in a florist, for starters. But remember when I texted you that Cal Ekman came into the store to get flowers for his wife on their anniversary?"

"How could I forget?"

"The bouquet was calla lilies. He told me it meant beautiful, and I researched a little more and found it came from the Greek word. I was especially curious because lilies were my grandmother's favorite flowers and they've become my favorite too."

"You are a very curious person, aren't you?"

"I am."

"One of the many things I like about you."

He kissed her then. A slow, lazy day kind of kiss. Lauren had been ready to get started on the tasks ahead, but this was so much better. He raised his hands and cupped her cheeks. She realized that they had stopped swaying. She wanted to bottle this kiss. To memorize every detail. The way his strong fingers made slow circles in her hair. The firm confidence of his kiss. She ran her hands across his back, cataloging all the muscles, his shoulder blades, and the way he tensed when her hands slid toward his waist. She liked having some impact on him. He was making every nerve in her body hum with just his lips and his hands.

She broke away from the kiss and put her head on his shoulder. Hawk sighed and wrapped his arms around her. "I think I could do that all day," he murmured.

"I agree. But there's work to do."

Besides, she had a heart to protect.

They got to work and tackled everything on Hawk's list.

"Wow. We are whipping through this!" he said, clapping his hands when he checked off the last "to-do" item on the list.

"I'm impressed with us," Lauren said. "I hate to finish everything we meant to do and run, but I have to get ready for finals next week."

"And part of your plan included studying tonight?" he asked, with a lifted eyebrow.

"You know it. Hey, before I go, I have something for you. A little gift. But!" she paused. "You can't open it until I'm gone."

"What? Really? Why don't you want me to see it while you're here?"

"It's just—I don't know. I'm worried you won't like it, and I don't want to see that."

"Now I'm worried."

She lifted her tote bag and pulled out a slender box, slightly larger than a business envelope. "Here. Open it after I've gone."

"Again, you're being ominous. But, thank you." His voice rose. "I think."

She smiled and swung the tote bag up on her shoulder, pulling her keys out of her pocket. "Call me tomorrow night?"

"Definitely. Good luck studying. And good luck with your exams next week. I probably won't see you until the weekend."

"Right. Saturday is Paige's shower, and Sunday I'm vegging out. I want to stay in my pjs all day and read a pile of novels."

"Sounds like a perfect day. Would you be up for company?"

"Maybe. We'll see."

She gave Goldie a few pats as she passed by. Hawk followed her and opened the door. "I'll let you know when I open the gift. Thank you again."

"No hurry. Bye." She leaned into him and kissed him. He embraced her in a quick hug and let her go.

HAWK WATCHED UNTIL she pulled out of the driveway. Closing the door, he checked the time on his watch. He'd text her in fifteen minutes to make sure she'd made it home safely.

He walked through the living room and shook his head at Goldie, who had already fallen back to sleep on the couch.

The house felt too quiet without Lauren. He thought it strange that he'd lived alone for over four years, and he'd never felt the loneliness he now felt whenever she left. He reminded himself that he would have these feelings when foster kids left, too, but he was prepared for that. That was the purpose of fostering; it was a short-term arrangement while the children's home life was straightened out. Everyone hoped for the kids to be returned to loving family members. If their parents couldn't provide for them, the goal was to find a close family member or family friend to take in, love, and raise the kids.

He knew some foster situations were longer term, and he was prepared for that, too. But he wasn't prepared for Lauren to leave. He could see a future with her. Married and with their own kids someday. Not only did she check all the boxes, but she had also reignited his desire for marriage. Before Lauren, he'd almost given up hope. Several failed relationships had sent him into relationship hibernation, but Lauren had brought him out of hiding.

In the dining room, Hawk glanced at the skinny box she'd given him. A part of him didn't want to open it. If she didn't want to watch him open it, it couldn't be good. Alarm bells were clanging in his head.

The box was wrapped in robin's-egg-blue paper with small, yellow flower buds on it. Very springy and very sweet. Very deceptive.

His curiosity drove him to pick it up and give it a shake. Something slid back and forth, so he shook it again. It sounded as if there were two things sliding—one further than the other. He tapped it on his hand, debating.

Curiosity won, and he pulled at the wrapping paper. Once it fell away, he saw a plain white box. He lifted the lid to discover a folded paper and a small coin. He picked up the coin first. On one side was an image of a woman in an elaborate hat and robe. Written on it were the words "Lady of Loreto". On the other side were the words, "Protect us in our travels; keep us safe in our air travel and in our journeys".

"Hmm, interesting," Hawk muttered aloud. "She knows I don't fly."

Next, he picked up the paper and unfolded it. "Avion Flight Academy" was written across the top. It was a gift certificate for a three-hour introduction to flight "discovery" class. In that time, he'd be able to go up in a plane with a pilot. If he wanted, he could even fly the plane briefly with instruction from the pilot.

"No way. This must have cost a small fortune. Why did she do this? This sounds like immersion therapy."

He grabbed a beer from the fridge and walked to the living room.

He sat on the opposite end of the couch from Goldie, checking his watch. Lauren should be home in a few minutes.

He searched for the flight school on his phone. He saw that there would be a two-hour session first to explain flight concepts and then an hour flight with a pilot.

There was a part of him that thought it was the sweetest gift ever, but another part of him felt like this was her way of giving him wings, even as she planned to leave him for grad school. Did she think the gift of flight would be a replacement for her?

CHAPTER TWENTY-FIVE

"GET OUT OF the kitchen, Grady!" Trevor called across the pickleball court.

"You like saying that, don't you?" Lauren said to her partner.

"You bet." Trevor nodded. "I like giving the big bad banker a hard time whenever I can."

Nica tossed the ball across the court, and Lauren stepped back to serve. The ball sailed perfectly crosscourt, and Grady returned it. Trevor stepped up to hit when *he* overstepped into the kitchen.

"Who's in the kitchen now, Trev?" Grady yelled.

Nica caught Lauren's eye. "Boys."

Nica served and scored, as Lauren forgot to wait for the ball to bounce before returning the serve. That point ended their second game.

"I need a drink!" Nica called.

"Little early for drinking, Nic," Trevor responded as he moved towards the courtside bench where they'd put their extra gear and the cooler.

"I'll take one of those muffins," Grady said. "I've worked up an appetite."

Nica rolled her eyes. "You always have an appetite. Here, Lauren and Trevor, Izzy made these lemon poppy seed muffins this morning. They may still be warm."

"Sounds delicious," Trevor replied.

Lauren listened to the men chat about a new housing development that was being built near Trevor's place. Lauren had no interest in hearing what they speculated new houses would go for in this market. She would remain a renter for a few more years, at least.

"Will Paige move back into your apartment when she returns this week?" Lauren asked Nica, opening a bottle of cold water.

"Yes. She'll stay with us until they get married."

"That's good. Will you look for a new roommate then?"

Nica turned her head quickly. "Why? Are you interested? Thinking about sticking around?"

"No," Lauren replied slowly. "I'm still moving. I just don't know when or where."

Nica raised an eyebrow. "Is a certain dark-haired, handsome man making that decision even harder, *chica*?"

"He's not a deciding factor. I'm trying to figure out which school and city will be the best fit for me personally. I'm looking at businesses in those cities, cultural things like museums and theaters, and the like. Trying to make the best decision I can."

"But what about Hawk and your feelings for him?" Nica pushed.

"I don't think we're meant to be together. We have different goals in life. He's ready to start a family. I want a career first. If things were to work out between us, he'd expect me to settle down. He doesn't like to travel—well, he doesn't like to fly—and I do. I don't want to be stuck here and only go where I can get to in a car."

"Well, I get that you want to do that, but have you talked to him? You have to find compromises. Look at Grady and me. We are always compromising."

Overhearing her, Grady butted in with, "And by compromising, she means arguing. But it's okay. We are respectful when we argue. Arguing brings us to the best option, not my option or her option. Together we make it better."

"I mostly agree with that statement," Nica added.

Trevor chimed in. "Figuring out how to discuss issues and disagree without getting nasty is one of the most important things in a relationship."

"I can't imagine you and Paige arguing about anything," Nica said.

"You're right," Trevor responded. "I just do whatever she tells me to do."

Everyone laughed, knowing that wasn't true. Lauren thought about how sweet Trevor and Paige's wedding was going to be.

Lauren asked, "Will you be at the wedding shower on Saturday, Trevor?"

"Heck no. That's Paige's shower. I want all the love and good wishes showered on her."

"Yes!" Nica said, "We'll do our best."

Lauren turned to Nica. "Have you gotten a shower gift yet?"

"No. I still need to shop."

"I do, too. Want to go this afternoon?"

"Sure. I'd love that. Grady," she said, turning to her boyfriend, "we didn't have plans this afternoon, did we?"

"No. Go on ahead, Spicy. Have fun."

Lauren loved how he called Nica "Spicy". So sweet to be in a relationship and have pet names for each other. She hoped she'd have that someday.

"Hey, you can come hang out with me, Grady," Trevor added. "We can watch the final round of golf."

"Well, as boring as that sounds, I really should catch up on work this afternoon, instead."

Trevor threw a fake punch at Grady. "You're the biggest geek." He glanced back at the court. "Should we play another game? I think we're finally getting the hang of this sport."

CHAPTER TWENTY-SIX

WHAT A WEEK! The last round of finals for her undergraduate degree were behind her. Lauren was confident the results would be what she expected and that's what she would report to her parents when talking to them on Sunday.

But today was Saturday and Paige's wedding shower.

Entering the restaurant, Lauren asked the hostess where to find the bridal party and was directed to a lovely private room.

The tables were set with lavender tablecloths and vases of beautiful pink and white peonies. Of course, they were beautiful; they came from In Bloom. Lauren and Nica had helped Anna Lee make them that morning.

"Lauren!" Paige exclaimed. "I'm so glad you're here!"

"Where else would I be?

"Did you see the gorgeous flowers?"

"Yes, three hours ago when I helped arrange them," Lauren teased. "They look even prettier in here. What a beautiful room."

Anna Lee had said the arrangements would be unique and she wasn't joking. Lauren had seen the arrangements as they left In Bloom, but they were further transformed here. The elegant glass bowls that they used to hold the flowers were sitting atop stacks of antique books. A perfect display for Paige.

Anna Lee walked over, wearing a long, bright-pink dress with pink daisies scattered over it. Her short gray hair was pinned back from her face, making her dark brown eyes pop.

"Fancy seeing you here, Lauren." Anna Lee said. "Long time no see."

Lauren laughed. "Right back at ya. Where are you sitting, Anna Lee? Can I sit with you?"

"Over here." Anna Lee led the way to a table next to the one where Paige and her family sat. "Are you sure you're not supposed to sit with Paige? You're in the wedding party."

Lauren shook her head. "No, Paige told me to sit anywhere."

"Great. Then sit with me. Nica and Izzy are sitting here, too."

"Anna Lee, we never got to talk about John's daughter's wedding. How did it go?"

A server walked by with a tray of appetizers. Anna Lee took a napkin and four mini sandwiches. "I'm hungry! I've only had coffee today," she said in response to Lauren's raised eyebrow.

Lauren smiled and took one mini sandwich for herself.

Anna Lee munched for a moment. "Ah, that's better. Anyhoo, the wedding was sublime. Absolutely perfect. Beautiful. Grand. The bride was stunning. The details were on point. It was just perfection."

"And the flowers were pretty good, too. Right?"

"Of course! I can't wait to bring in pictures of the tables and the wedding party with their bouquets and boutonnières. I outdid myself, and I appreciate the hard work everyone put in pulling it off."

"It was a pleasure to help as always." Lauren looked away, fearing she'd shed a tear if she looked at Anna Lee as she said, "I'm going to miss working at In Bloom so much. Of course, the work is fun and creative. But it's working with you and the others that makes it so special. I can't imagine ever again being in such a warm, supportive work environment. I know I won't find that in a large corporation."

"Lauren, dear. You might not find it, but you can bring it. Be a leader that demands that kind of environment wherever you work. And if you don't find it and can't make it, then leave. Move on. Life's much too short to work in a mind-sucking, soul-crushing, worry-inducing place. My greatest wish is that every person that works for me takes the beauty of the flowers and the joy of In Bloom with them wherever they go when they leave. I look at my legacy as being not only the flowers that I sell and the arrangements I create. More than that, it is nurturing the young people that work for me so that they can spread love, joy, and beauty wherever they go."

"Wow." Lauren teared up. "That's beautiful. Just like you. And I will do my best to take that forward with me. Someone has to bring that to corporate America. Why not me?"

"Why not you? Indeed!" Anna Lee nodded her head vigorously.

Other guests were coming in, and they had to shuffle around to get out of the way. Paige brought her mother and two sisters-in-law to meet Anna Lee and Lauren. Paige's mom wore a long, flowing dress covered in a subdued floral print. Sue Bell and Anna Lee embraced each other and admired their similar dresses. Sue pronounced them spirit sisters and pulled Anna Lee aside to chat.

Lauren sat at a table and noticed confetti sprinkled about the settings—tiny pink books and light blue plumber's wrenches. Adorable.

Sitting on top of her place setting was a pink organza bag with a bar of soap inside. A tag attached to the bag said, "From Paige's Shower to Yours!" Again, adorable.

"Do you know who made the party favors?" she asked Anna Lee.

Anna Lee plopped into her chair and picked up the gift. "I heard Macey made them. How cute!" She brought the soap to her nose. "Smells like lemon and lavender. Very nice. So, Lauren, you graduate next weekend. Then what?"

Lauren admired Anna Lee's bluntness. "Well, I'm taking a trip to Greece at the end of the month. I put in a vacation request this morning. I hope it won't be a problem."

"Shouldn't be." Anna Lee picked up her water glass and took a long drink. "I'm really curious about when you're leaving for good. I am going to have to hire more help once you and Paige move on to bigger, better things."

"That's the burning question—when I'm leaving. I have until the end of this month to decide if I want to extend my lease for a month or two. My current lease is up June thirtieth. There are good reasons for moving in the middle of the summer. One is that I can get settled in well before school starts. But I'm not ready to leave."

"Because you have the greatest boss you'll ever have right now!" Anna Lee declared, laughing at her statement.

"Well, I think that may be true. There are some other reasons, too."

"Like?"

"Well, I'm seeing someone, and it pains me to think about leaving him."

"Ah. Interesting. I thought you had a new glow about you. Tell me more."

"His name is Hawk." His name was a comfort to say out loud. "He's in the wedding party, too. One of the groomsmen. I met him at Paige and Trevor's bridal party get-together. He's great. Good-looking, smart, caring, kind, funny. All the things. But there are two downsides. First, he doesn't like to travel, and second, he's thinking about being a foster parent. He's in training now. I feel we are too different to make it work in the long-term. But I really like him."

"Oh, hon." Anna Lee shook her head slowly. "You talk about decisions a lot. I know you like to weigh your decisions and debate the pros and cons until the cows come home. That's the intellectual approach. However, when it comes to matters of the heart and who we love, there's only so much analyzing you can do. It is one of the most important decisions in your life. And I've found that letting logic rule the heart can end in loneliness and heartache. Take it from me, when you find a good man, who gets you, understands you, and loves you anyway, it might be a good time to throw logic out the window."

Macey tapped on a water glass with a bread knife and asked everyone to take their seats, as lunch was about to be served. Lauren introduced herself to the two ladies who joined their table; they were friends of Paige's from high school.

As the servers walked around delivering salad plates, Lauren thought about Anna Lee's advice. She wanted to let go of her reliance on logic, but it had served her well up to this point.

LAUREN WAS SO committed to her day of "vegging out" that she texted her parents on Sunday morning and said she wouldn't be able to chat. She suggested they call if they needed to check in with her before coming to town for her graduation on Saturday. Her dad texted back, "Fine. Congrats on finals. Enjoy your week. We hope you have decided on grad school before your graduation ceremony."

She moaned as she read the message. She wanted to relax and not think about anything serious today. She had stocked up on snacks; she planned to have a twelve-hour charcuterie board to nibble on all day. She had even splurged on chocolate-covered almonds and gourmet ginger snaps.

Sitting on the couch with a coffee mug in hand, she planned out her day, making a list on a piece of pretty stationery that she had been given on her last birthday by her Grandma Evie. There was a row of bluebirds at the top of the cream-colored page. Lauren used the beautiful paper to write to her grandmother once a month. She wondered briefly if she'd get new stationery on her next birthday.

On today's list she wrote "facial mask", "self-manicure", "review Greece itinerary", "watch a movie", and "read". She had three new suspense novels downloaded on her e-reader. She refused to write down anything on her list that had to do with Hawk, grad school, or moving. Those were concerns for another day.

Around eleven, her intercom buzzed, and the doorman informed her there was a package waiting for her in the lobby.

She grumbled. She'd have to throw on more clothes to go downstairs; her sleep shorts and the tank would not be appropriate.

Dressed, she grabbed her keys and left the apartment.

In the lobby, her eyes were drawn to the tall vase filled with white calla lilies and pink stargazer lilies, framed by green leaves. It was breathtaking.

"Are those for me?" she asked, hoping they were.

"Are you Lauren Largent?" the weekend doorman asked.

"I am."

"Then, yes, those are yours. Along with this box." He pointed at a large cardboard box on his desk. "Think you can get both in one trip?"

"Hmm, I'd better not. I'll take the flowers first."

She rode up in the elevator, enjoying the sweet aroma of the flowers. In her apartment, she put them on the kitchen counter, strategically placing them where she could see them from the kitchen, living room, and bed. Before going back down for the box, she opened the card. It read, Congrats on finishing exams and senior year! Yours, Hawk.

She clutched the card to her heart. So sweet. Now she was curious as to what was in the box.

Another ride down and back up in the elevator and the box was secured. She placed it on the coffee table and went to the kitchen for a utility knife to open it.

She slit through the packing tape and opened the flaps. There was a piece of folded paper on top. She flipped it open and read, Enjoy your day of "vegging" out!! Call me if you want company, Hawk.

Lauren smiled at the note. Intrigued, she pulled a layer of tissue paper out of the box. Inside, she saw a wicker handle. She grabbed it and pulled a veggie basket. There were green peppers, red peppers, cucumbers, a head of lettuce, a bunch of carrots, a zucchini, a head of broccoli, and sweet potatoes. She laughed out loud as she moved the basket to the kitchen counter. She set it next to the vase of flowers and texted a picture to Paige and her cousin Delia.

To Paige she wrote, "Hawk is a YAM"

Her text to Delia said, "This guy knows the way to a girl's heart. Jealous?"

Not waiting for their responses, she left the phone on the counter and moved the basket into the kitchen. She put away the veggies that needed refrigeration and cut up the cucumber and a red pepper to add to her charcuterie board.

She mulled over how she was going to respond to Hawk. She thought about inviting him over, but she didn't want the pressure. Today was about relaxing, not putting on makeup, not putting extra time into her clothing choices; she just wanted to unwind and destress.

Refilling her water bottle, she took it to the living room. The cardboard box was still sitting on the coffee table. Assuming it was empty, she picked it up to put it by the door, so to take down to the recycling dumpster in the basement later. However, it didn't feel empty. She glanced into the box. At the bottom was something wrapped in a map. *Odd.* She lifted the package out and opened it. Inside was a book called *Route 66: Fun for the Whole Family.* She flipped the cover open. Inside, Hawk had inscribed, Let me know when I can plan our first road trip, H.

He's persistent and consistent, she thought as she put the book on the coffee table. She grabbed her phone and called him.

Hawk answered, sounding short of breath. "Hey, you."

"Hi. I just got an amazing delivery."

"Oh, yeah?"

"Thank you, Hawk. The flowers, the veggies, the book. I feel…" she paused. "Spoiled."

"I hope they brought a smile to your face."

"Absolutely. The flowers really brighten up the space, and I've already started eating the veggies. What are you up to—working out?"

"Glad to hear that. And no, not working out. I'm at Trevor's. He's got a dead tree in the backyard, and he asked me to come and help take it down and chop it up. He's worried that with a strong thunderstorm, the tree could fall on the house."

"Smart to deal with it before that happens."

"Right. And I get a load of firewood out of it, so bonus!"

Lauren chuckled at his enthusiasm.

"So," Hawk continued. "Want company later?"

"After you're sweaty from chopping wood all day? No, thanks."

"Ha, ha. You know I'd shower first."

"I know. Just teasing. I'm not up for company today. Nothing personal."

"Of course, of course. I get it. You wanted to "just veg". I can respect that. Well, if you change your mind, let me know. I could bring dinner. If you get lonely and want to call me later, do that. I hope you have lots of relaxation today."

"Thanks. Be careful with the tree. Don't get hurt."

"Yes, ma'am."

Hawk hung up and Lauren decided to take the cardboard box down right now; seeing it there, out of place, would not help her relax.

CHAPTER TWENTY-SEVEN

*L*AUREN WAS READY to tear off the cap and gown but knew her parents would want to take copious pictures first. They'd agreed to meet up on the north side of the arena after the ceremony. Lauren stood on the top step and scanned the crowd for her parents, Paige, Trevor, and Hawk.

She spotted her parents first. They were both dressed in navy suits; her dad wore a red tie, and her mom wore a red scarf around her neck. They were standing near a tree about thirty feet beyond the stairs. She waved and got her dad's attention. He waved back.

Shifting her weight onto her heels, her eyes swept the area again. This time she spotted Paige's pretty auburn hair, then the others. She waved wildly to get Paige's attention and pointed toward the tree.

Rushing forward, she found her parents and gave them hugs. "Finally! Can you believe it? I've graduated!"

"Congratulations, darling," Nicole said, air kissing Lauren's cheek so as not to smudge any makeup.

"Yes, congrats, Lauren. We knew you'd sail through." Her dad looked at his gold watch. "Will your friends be here soon? We have a reservation at eight."

"Yes, I saw them." Lauren turned her head and saw Hawk approaching. "Here they are."

Hawk picked her up and twirled her around. "Woo hoo, Lauren! Congrats!"

Paige's arms were around her as soon as Hawk set her down. "We did it! We've graduated. Well, mostly graduated. I'm done for now." She winked at Lauren as she pulled back.

Trevor hugged her as well.

Lauren introduced everyone and noticed her dad giving Hawk a thorough once over.

Nicole took charge next. "Let's get a few pictures now. We want evidence to send to the family. This will be our holiday card photo. Who's a good photographer?" She pulled an SLR camera from its case.

Lauren wanted to roll her eyes but didn't. Trevor stepped forward. "I'll take a few shots, and you can check them out."

"Perfect," Nicole responded. "I thought this hedge over here would make a nice backdrop. Lauren, Bob. Here. Lauren, you stand in the middle." Nicole fluffed Lauren's graduation gown and straightened her hat.

The three lined up, and Trevor took a couple of photos before handing the camera back to Nicole.

She reviewed the photos with a slight frown. "Hm. These are fine, but they need something. Something more interesting in the background. We are all wearing dark, somber colors. Any ideas?"

Paige raised her hand. Lauren wanted to tease her and remind her that she wasn't in class, but she understood her intense parents could have that effect on people.

"Yes?" Nicole pointed at Paige, just as a professor would.

"The restaurant that we're going to has a beautiful indoor waterfall feature wall," Paige replied. "It would be an amazing background."

"Really?" Nicole tilted her head and pursed her lips.

"Absolutely!" Paige's enthusiasm was infectious, and Lauren smiled.

"Well, that sounds like the perfect solution." Nicole turned to Lauren. "Is this everyone that's going to dinner with us? I thought you said seven."

"Anna Lee is meeting us there," Lauren answered. "She had no desire to sit for a couple hours through the ceremony."

"Can't say I blame her; it's painful," Bob said.

"Thanks, Dad."

"But," he added, throwing his arm around Lauren, "it's not every day your only daughter graduates from college. I'd be happy to sit all day to watch you walk across that stage. Let's go to dinner. I'm ready for a stiff drink."

"Okay. See everyone there," Nicole said. "Lauren, are you riding with us?"

"Yes." Lauren looked at Hawk quickly. She wanted to ride with him, but her parents were only in town for one night. He smiled and nodded back at her.

"We'll meet you there," Hawk said.

Luckily, the ride to the restaurant was quick. Her parents grilled her about her friends and Anna Lee. They wanted to know as much as they could before dinner, so they could be respectful and help guide the conversation.

After a few Instagram and Christmas card-worthy pictures in front of the water feature, they were seated and settled in. Anna Lee was waiting at the restaurant when they arrived. She had asked to be seated ahead of the rest of the party and had a glass of wine and a cup of coffee in front of her when the others joined her.

Lauren sat between her mom and Anna Lee; Hawk was directly across from her at the large, round table. They had been put in a back room and were fortunate to be the only occupied table, so the conversation was lively, inclusive, and easy to follow.

Once the dinner plates were taken away, Paige declared it was time for Lauren's graduation gifts.

Nicole looked confused. "I thought you graduated as well, Paige. Shouldn't there be gifts for you too?"

"My graduation ceremony was last night and we," Paige glanced around at her friends, "celebrated last night. They were all very generous," she added.

"Oh, and what was your major, Paige?" Bob Largent asked.

"English," Paige replied. "My graduation was with the College of Arts, Science, and Humanities." She reached under her seat and picked up her present for Lauren. "This is from Trevor and me. I hope you like it."

Lauren thanked her as she took the gift. She tore off the wrapping paper to find a leather-bound collection of essays written by women leaders. "This is fantastic, Paige. Thank you so much."

"My turn!" Anna Lee said, handing Lauren a rectangular package. She opened it to find a cross-stitch wall hanging of a green vase holding white, pink, and burgundy calla lilies. Underneath the vase was a quote that read, "It is good to have an end to journey towards, but it is the journey that matters in the end."- Ursula K. Le Guin".

"Wow, this is beautiful, Anna Lee!" Lauren choked up. The quote really hit home. She was guilty of focusing on endings, goals, and accomplishments. She forgot to appreciate the day-to-day beauty and joy that was life. "You know me so well." Lauren leaned her head on Anna Lee's shoulder.

Anna Lee put her arm around Lauren and handed her a napkin. "Here. Save those tears for later," Anna Lee whispered to her.

Lauren laughed softly and nodded. She dabbed at her eyes and willed herself to stop leaking moisture from her eyes.

Lauren's mom asked to take a closer look at the cross-stitch, and Lauren handed it over. "Oh my!" Nicole exclaimed. "This must have taken hours. It's beautiful. What a wonderful memory to take with you from your time working at a florist."

Lauren cringed. Working with Anna Lee was so much more than that. Her mother would never be able to understand what she was taking away from the experience. The guidance, love, and support that she'd received from Anna Lee were precious. She realized that only now, looking backward, could she appreciate the experience for what it really was. It wasn't just a part-time job to earn some money and work with flowers. It was a blessing.

"My turn!" Hawk called, passing a small box off to his left. It made its way around to Lauren quickly.

He'd used the same map paper that he'd wrapped the Route 66 book in. She unwrapped it and found a silver bangle bracelet with two charms on it. One charm was a compass with "Never lose your way" engraved on the back. The second charm was shaped like the state of Illinois, and there was a red, heart-shaped gemstone in the middle of the state where Bloomington/Normal was located.

"This is so cute! I love it!" Lauren said, slipping it on her wrist and holding up her arm for everyone to see.

"It's so you don't get lost and don't forget us," Hawk said. By "us" it was clear he meant him.

"Thank you," Lauren added, feeling a swell of emotions trying to overcome her. All the gifts were so thoughtful, and so caring. How could she ever forget these amazing people, her college years, or her time spent here, no matter where she went in the future?

"The compass is a perfect lead-in to our present," Nicole declared. Lauren glanced at her mom. She already knew what her parents were getting her; she hadn't thought they would bring anything tonight.

Bob pulled an envelope out of his suit pocket and handed it to her. She opened it quickly. Inside was a piece of paper, the receipt for the Rick Steves tour to Greece, as she expected. Inside the fold of paper was cash, a lot of cash.

"Whoa, thank you!" Lauren didn't want to be disappointed

or unappreciative. It was a very generous gift, but it hurt that they hadn't put a lot of thought into it, like her friends around the table had.

"What is it, Lauren?" Paige asked.

"A trip to Greece with a hosted tour. I've been wanting to go to Greece since my trip to Europe last summer."

"Amazing!" Paige said. "That will be so fun. When do you go?"

Lauren felt Hawk's intense gaze on her. "The week of Memorial Day."

She dared a glance at Hawk, he smiled at her, but there seemed to be a hesitation in his eyes. "That's great, Lauren. Have a wonderful trip. Don't forget your compass." He nodded toward her wrist.

"I won't."

Nicole signaled to their server. "We're ready for cake and coffee," she said once he approached. Turning to Lauren, she added, "We asked the restaurant to bake a cake for you."

Once dessert had been served and enjoyed, Bob asked for the check. Anna Lee reached for her purse and asked what her share came to. Lauren worried they would get into an argument when Nicole protested, "We have this. We are honored that Lauren's close friends could join us in her celebration this evening."

Anna Lee grumbled under her breath as she put her wallet away. "Well," she said looking at Bob and Nicole, "thank you for dinner and your hospitality. Lauren is a beautiful young lady with a heart of gold. Ya done good raisin' her."

"Thank you, Anna Lee," Lauren said, squeezing Anna Lee's hand. "I'm so glad you could come to dinner with us."

"Wouldn't have missed it." Anna Lee snapped her purse closed. "Sorry I missed the ceremony, but...but nothing. I can't stand sitting through hours-long ceremonies. I've seen people get diplomas before."

Lauren laughed. "No need to apologize. I get it."

Anna Lee stood and leaned over to hug Lauren. "My ride should be here. So, I have to run." She shook hands with Bob and Nicole and said good night to the rest before exiting the room.

"Well," Bob said, standing. Everyone else followed suit. "I'm ready to call it a night myself. Lauren, would you mind taking an Uber back to your apartment? Our hotel is right across the street."

"No, of course not," she responded.

"I'll take you home," Hawk said, stepping closer. "It was nice to meet you, Mr. and Mrs. Largent. Thank you for dinner."

Lauren hugged her parents and thanked them for the dinner. She knew they would leave for home early in the morning.

Paige, Trevor, and Hawk lingered with Lauren as she gathered her gifts. They walked together to the parking lot. Paige and Trevor gave her hugs and suggested brunch on Sunday. Paige planned to include her roommates, Izzy and Nica, and said she would invite Tilly as well.

"Sounds good," Lauren said. "Would you like to join us, Hawk?"

"Sorry, can't. After I coach in the morning, I'm helping my stepdad with their basement remodel tomorrow. Hanging drywall. I said I'd be there at one."

Trevor gave him a light punch. "I don't envy you. But if you need help, *after noon*," he stressed, "call me. I'm going to brunch with the ladies."

Lauren gave Page and Trevor hugs and waved goodbye as she climbed into Hawk's Jeep. She put the book and wall hanging at her feet.

Hawk got in and started the vehicle. Before putting it in gear, he turned toward her. "Congrats again on your graduation. We may not have known each other long, but I'm very proud of you. I think what Anna Lee said tonight was spot on—that you are a beautiful person with a heart of gold. I'm so glad we got to work together and to know each other better."

"Thank you. For everything. I love the bracelet. It's perfect."

"Just like you."

"No, I'm not perfect. Let me count all the ways."

"No. Stop. You don't get to berate yourself on your graduation night." He squeezed her knee and put the car in gear.

As Hawk drove, Lauren leaned her head back on the seat. There were so many thoughts rushing through her mind. She'd graduated. She was going to Greece in just a couple of weeks. She had to figure out her feelings for Hawk. If it weren't for grad school and his plan to foster, she thought they could have had a path forward together. Like a compass reading, a true north. But their goals were so different. She didn't know where her compass was taking her.

When they arrived at her apartment building ten minutes later, Lauren asked him up for a celebratory drink, but Hawk declined.

"I have a nine-a.m. start tomorrow," he reminded her.

"Right. Well, don't work the boys to hard at practice and I hope the remodel work is easy and there are no injuries."

"Thanks," he said, putting the car in park. "Thank you for including me in your celebration tonight. It was great to meet your parents. I'll see you up to your apartment."

Lauren nodded at the night door person as they entered the lobby. In the elevator, she turned to Hawk. "Thanks for seeing me up. It's very sweet."

"I think it's the least a person could do. Safety first."

At her apartment, she unlocked the door. "You sure you don't want to come in?"

"I would like to, but..."

"I know. Thanks again for bringing me home."

"Good night, Lauren." He leaned over and kissed her on the cheek.

"Night."

He left and she entered the apartment, flipping on all the lights as she made her way to the bathroom. She washed her face and applied moisturizer. She wasn't ready to brush her teeth, as she was having a celebratory drink, even if she was drinking alone.

She put on her pajamas and got a glass of wine. Curling up on the couch, she sent a text to Paige thanking her again for the gift and for coming to dinner. She grabbed her planner and wrote, "buy thank-you notes" on her Sunday to-do list.

Debating whether to text Hawk, she looked at the time. He should be home by now.

> **LAUREN:** Thank you again. I have a little more time on my hands now. Let me know if you're free to have some fun before the fundraiser on Saturday.

She put the phone down and picked up the television remote. Clicking the guide until she found *Singing in the Rain* was playing, she clicked over to it and waited for Hawk's reply. An hour later, no reply from Hawk meant she went to bed wondering if he'd made it home and fallen asleep before her text.

CHAPTER TWENTY-EIGHT

AWK WAS GRATEFUL for the busy week. The remodel work at his mom and stepdad's house on Sunday had taken all afternoon, and he volunteered to go back to continue helping after work during the week. He was glad they had a fenced backyard so he could bring Goldie and let her run around while he helped. By Thursday night, they were done.

As he was leaving, his mom pulled him aside. "I've seen you all week, but don't feel like I really know what's going on with you."

"You didn't figure that out with all the hammering, mudding, and painting in the basement?" He chuckled.

"Other than to feed you, I really haven't seen you. Are you okay? Any news on the fostering front?"

"I'm fully approved," he answered, smiling. He felt proud and excited. "Now, it could be a month, or several months, before I get a call."

"That's wonderful," Marilyn said, patting his arm. "Let me know how I can help."

"I will, Mom," he replied, giving her a hug. "Keep your eyes peeled for kid clothes on sale. All sizes, either gender. I want to have a small stockpile ready in an emergency."

"Will do. And how's the love life?"

Ouch. He hated it when she poked that bear.

"Not much of one. I'll keep you posted on that front, too."

He put Goldie on her leash and left.

He had hoped that staying busy would help keep his mind off Lauren. The reality that she would be leaving for grad school sometime this summer had come into focus after her graduation on Saturday.

He'd known it was coming but knowing and accepting had been separate concepts until Saturday night. To see those closest to Lauren wishing her well in the next chapter of her life confirmed to him that she would not be part of his.

Thinking about the fundraiser this coming Saturday was another welcome distraction. They were ready; every detail had been planned and validated and rehearsed. He was confident that it would go off without a hitch.

After missing Lauren's late-night text after her graduation dinner, he'd kept her informed about what he was doing and regretted that he didn't have more time to spend with her. He was comforted by the fact that she was getting ready for her trip to Greece. Seeing the look on her face when she'd opened the envelope from her parents had tweaked something in his heart. It reaffirmed that her passion was to see the world. She was comfortable getting on those planes and leaving for brighter destinations.

His feet were better off planted on the ground. He'd looked over the flight class she'd given him half a dozen times. He'd even called to check on how long he had to redeem it. But he still couldn't bring himself to sign up.

At home, he took Goldie for a short walk before going in. It was late, and he wanted to shower and go to bed.

He had just gotten in the front door and let Goldie off the leash when his phone rang. He looked at the caller ID. It was Anita Ryan, the caseworker from DCFS.

"Hello?" he answered on the second ring.

"Hello, Hawk. It's Anita. I have a child that needs emergency placement. I wanted to see if you could take him in tonight."

"Tonight?"

"Yes, tonight. I can bring him by in about an hour. We have a few more things to sort through before I can leave with him. I wanted to see if you were available."

"Absolutely, I'm available." A surge of adrenaline rushed through him. He forgot about the shower and bed. "Just one child, you said? How old is he?"

"Yes. A boy. He's six years old. I'll introduce you when I bring him. His mother was arrested tonight. We're searching for next of kin but haven't been able to connect with anyone yet. This could be a short-term placement; we're not sure."

"Of course. I understand. I'm here. I'm home. If you'll be a little bit, I'm going to take a quick shower. I was just going to do that when you called."

"That's fine. Like I said, about an hour."

She hung up, and Hawk did the same. He stood staring at his phone; his feet were frozen in place. He thought about work tomorrow and the fundraiser on Saturday. He was in a good place at work; he could take a last-minute PTO day. He'd have time to figure out what to do about the fundraiser. For now, all his thoughts turned to the child who would be staying with him and arriving very soon.

CHAPTER TWENTY-NINE

*L*AUREN WAS STILL mulling over Hawk's cryptic text message from Friday. It had said he wouldn't be able to meet for last minute prep that night like they'd planned, and he said he'd explain on Saturday. He added that he knew they were well prepared, and he expected nothing to go wrong with the fundraiser.

Lauren wished she had his confidence. She tried on three different outfits, finally settling on a sleeveless, floor-length teal gown with a high neck. She was glad it was long enough to cover her shoes, as she'd decided to wear a pair of almost-matching teal sneakers. She was going to be on her feet for hours and didn't want to get distracted by blisters or foot pain.

Thirty minutes before she and Hawk had agreed to meet, she was at the venue directing the workers on table placement. Two of their volunteers arrived shortly after the tables were set up and began putting out the silent auction items. Lauren followed behind laying out the corresponding bid sheets.

She glanced at her watch and saw that Hawk was officially late. She took a deep breath and chanted a few times to herself, *He'll be here. He'll be here.*

She was placing the last bid sheet when she heard one of the volunteers call out to Hawk. She turned and looked toward the main door. Her heart skipped a beat when she saw him. He'd gotten a hair trim and wore a black tuxedo. "Wow!" She couldn't keep the exclamation under her breath, and the venue coordinator laughed.

"He's a hottie!" the other woman exclaimed.

"Indeed." Lauren excused herself and made her way to where Hawk was putting a large box on an empty table. She did a double take when she saw a small child in a matching tuxedo, carrying a smaller box, walk in behind him.

As she got closer, she heard Hawk say, "Put your box on this table, Jameson. We'll grab a cart to get the rest from the car."

Lauren neared them with confusion. Who was the kid, and why was he in a tux?

"Hi, Hawk!" She called out as she approached. He looked up, and she nearly melted at the sight of his eyes. He looked tired, but she could tell he was playing through the pain, so to speak. He put on a wide smile and said hello. She was self-conscious at the sight of him. He had been so busy all week helping his parents that she hadn't seen him since the night of her graduation party. She suddenly wondered if it had just been the work, or if he'd been avoiding her.

"Hey, Lauren!" Hawk called. He put his hand on the shoulder of the boy beside him. "There is someone I want you to meet. This is Jameson. He's staying with me for a while."

Hawk gave her a look—a look that said *Don't ask a lot of questions*. She understood. A kid that needed foster care. This must be what had kept Hawk busy all week. She was crushed that he hadn't been truthful with her. She knew this was something he wanted; why didn't he just come out and tell her that this was why he'd been too busy to see her?

"Hi, Jameson. It's lovely to meet you," she said, holding her hand out to the young boy.

His dark brown eyes shifted around, looking everywhere but at her. "Hi," Jameson said in a very soft voice.

"I love your tuxedo," she said, trying to make the boy comfortable.

"Thanks," was his short reply.

"Aren't they great?" Hawk chimed in. "We got them this morning. Luckily, they had one in Jameson's size, and they matched us up with our ties and vests. I think we look like two sharply dressed dudes. Right, Jameson?"

"Yeah."

Hawk met Lauren's eyes again. "We're going to run out and get the rest of the stuff from the *van*."

Lauren smiled. "No Jeep today?"

"No. Had to rent a van with all the gear we needed to bring. Let's go, Jameson. We're on the hunt for a cart. We saw a few in the hotel lobby. Want to go with us?" he asked Lauren.

"Sure."

Once the cart was secured and loaded, Lauren noticed Hawk grab a backpack from the backseat of the van. He tossed it onto one shoulder as he pushed the cart filled with boxes of auction items.

Lauren tried to make small talk with Jameson; she asked him about school and his favorite cartoons. He gave her short, direct answers but didn't offer up any additional details.

Hawk enthusiastically directed everyone in the setup. He had Jameson help with a few simple tasks, but after a little while, he found a table where the boy could sit down and have some fun. Lauren noticed that Hawk's backpack was full of coloring books, crayons, books, and a couple of puzzles. There were even snacks and a water bottle.

She caught Hawk at the podium and pulled him aside. "Wow. You're really fostering. That's great. When did this happen?"

"Late Thursday night. I'd just gotten home from helping my stepdad when I got the call. I took yesterday off to help get Jameson settled."

"Oh. What timing! Right on top of this event."

"I know. I talked to him about it. I asked if he wanted to come with me—I told him that I could get my mom to stay with him today—but he wanted to come. The tuxedo was a little miracle to pull off."

"He doesn't talk a lot."

"No. That may change once he gets more familiar with me and has a chance to process what's happened with his family."

"Does this change your camping trip to Wisconsin next week?"

"I don't think so. I need to talk to the case worker and Jameson, but I think it'll be all right. I haven't brought it up to him yet, so don't mention it in front of him. I don't want to overload the kid."

Hawk smiled, and Lauren saw the exhaustion and the caring in his face. He was clearly excited about this responsibility, but he was also very tired.

"Is there anything I can do to help?" she asked.

"No, I got this. Hey, I see Ellen over there. I want to check in with her. I'm ready to see all our work finally pay off. I hope we raise more money for the community center than last year."

"I do, too."

He hurried off, and Lauren kept an eye on Jameson, even though Hawk hadn't asked her to.

Several minutes later, Hawk returned with a tall woman on his arm. "Lauren. I'd like to introduce you to one of my oldest friends. This is Sharon Tuttle, she's the program director for the community center. Sharon, this is Lauren Largent. The woman I've been talking your ear off about."

He gave his full smile to Lauren and she felt her knees get weak. She shook Sharon's hand. "I take it he meant long-term friend, not old. It's a pleasure to meet you, Sharon."

"Nice to meet you and put a face to a name. I'd love to share some stories with you." Sharon nudged Hawk with her elbow. "Make sure you have all the facts about this guy before you make any rash decisions."

Hawk shook his head. "I knew this was a bad idea. Sharon, stay away from her."

Sharon laughed and excused herself, saying she needed to talk to Ellen.

Once the attendees started to make their way into the ballroom, the evening flew by. Lauren monitored the silent auction tables, answering questions, bumping up bids on a few items she wouldn't mind buying, and straightening out displays manhandled by guests.

She even bid on the picnic basket filled with goodies she'd picked up from Annabelle's Chocolates. If she won it, she would give it to Hawk, she thought he could take Jameson for a fun outing with it.

She saw Nica and Tilly walk in together; she was thrilled they had bought tickets to the event. Anna Lee and her beau, John, arrived moments later and Lauren directed all four of them to a table near the front so they would have a good view during the live auction. The move paid off later when John got in a bidding war for a spa day package. He finally won it and said it was a gift for Anna Lee, the hardest working lady he knew. Everyone in the room let out a collective sigh.

She was thankful she was wearing comfortable shoes because by her estimate, she walked over six miles during the auction.

She got a chance to sit briefly with Hawk, Ellen, and Jameson when dinner was served. She managed to eat a few bites of the stuffed chicken dinner while talking with Hawk and Ellen about how the event was going. She gave her dinner roll and dessert to Jameson, who seemed to have an unending appetite. Hawk noticed and gave her an appreciative smile.

Throughout the rest of the evening, Lauren kept glancing at both Hawk and Jameson. She noticed that the pair were keeping an eye on each other as well. When Hawk was speaking and facilitating the live auction, if he were quiet for more than a few seconds, Jameson would look up and make sure he was still at the podium. It crushed Lauren's spirit to realize the heart-wrenching reality of Jameson's situation. To be taken away from family and put in the care of a stranger had to be devastating for any child, no matter the situation they were coming from.

When the event was finally over, Lauren plopped down at their table to get off her feet for a few moments before they packed up their remaining items. Jameson had fallen asleep at the table, his head resting on his forearms. Hawk finished a conversation with Ellen and Sharon, then motioned Lauren to the podium.

"We did it," he said, pulling her into a hug. "Can you believe it? Are you as exhausted as I am?"

"Maybe. But it's not a competition."

"Right."

"Did you see Jameson fell asleep about thirty minutes ago?"

They both looked toward the kid as Hawk nodded. "I'm not surprised. I know he hasn't slept well at my place, new environment and all. But he does love that Scooby-Doo clock...and the bedding," he added, puffing out his chest and raising his chin.

Lauren laughed. "You are proud of that bedding. Well, I'm going to box up the stuff left on the silent auction tables. Should I put it on your cart?"

"Yes, please do."

"Oh, by the way, I won one of the silent auction items and I want to give it to you. Hold on." She went to the side table and retrieved the picnic basket. She brought it back and handed it to Hawk. "Here. I thought you could take Jameson for a fun excursion with this picnic basket. But save the bottle of wine for another day."

He laughed. "I'll save it for us. Thank you so much. I think he'd love a picnic at the park."

She smiled. "Good. Let me know if you need help this week with the aftermath of the fundraiser."

"I think it's under control, but I'll let you know if I need help. My main priority will be Jameson. I want to make sure he's settling in and getting comfortable with me. He's got a couple more weeks of school, and I want to make sure he finishes strong."

"You're a good guy, Hawk Springer." She leaned forward and kissed him on his cheek. There were still people milling around, and she didn't want to become a source of entertainment.

"Thanks, Lauren. For that and for all the help with this event. I couldn't have done it without you."

CHAPTER THIRTY

IN THE UBER on the way to the airport, Lauren checked her phone again. Once her flight took off for Greece, she didn't expect to have a lot of interaction with friends and family for the next eight days.

The driver asked too many questions about where she was going and how long she would be gone. She was glad she'd had him pick her up from the Starbucks a block away from her parents' apartment.

She ignored the driver's latest question and pretended she was texting someone on her phone. She'd not heard from Hawk all week, and while she knew he was busy with Jameson, it didn't ease the hurt and disappointment she was feeling.

Since she was flying out of Chicago's O'Hare Airport, she'd stayed with her parents Wednesday night, and her mom had asked about Hawk. Nicole said she could feel a connection between him and Lauren at graduation. It surprised Lauren because her mom never talked about personal relationships like that. Her parents pressured her on the grad school decision, and she told them she would decide while she was on the trip to Greece. She had already told the landlord that she was going to stay until the end of August. She couldn't imagine leaving this summer. Even though Hawk currently had his hands full with fostering, she hoped there would be opportunities for them to do things together over the summer.

Ever since the fundraiser, all Lauren could think about was how off their timing was. Like Hawk, she couldn't wait to have a family and she understood his desire to be a foster parent. She regretted that the time wasn't right for her to support him. She imagined that in just a couple of years, they could be married and foster together. But she couldn't take that on right now. It would be better to get through grad school and start her career first.

Once she settled on the flight, she texted her parents to let them know she was taking off. She considered texting Hawk, but decided she'd wait until she was back. She took out the travel guide to Greece that she'd bought for the trip and poured over the pages, thinking about the sights she would see and the history and culture she would learn about over the next week. She hoped the excitement for travel would help ease the loneliness she was feeling. Traveling alone had never bothered her before, but this time she couldn't help but wish Hawk were sitting in the seat next to her.

WADE HAMMERED THE last stake into the second tent. He would sleep alone in the smaller tent, and Hawk and Jameson would sleep in the larger one.

"Tents are up!" Wade exclaimed, proud of his effort.

Jameson hauled sleeping bags into the larger tent with Hawk's direction. "I'd really hate to sleep outside," Jameson noted.

Hawk thought the kid shivered. He smiled and tried to reassure him. "It's okay, Jameson. We're lucky there are a lot of people camping in this park this weekend. There are lots of people looking out for each other."

"And we'll have a fire going most of the night to keep the animals away," Wade added. On the drive up, Jameson had asked several questions about what kind of wild animals they might see while camping.

"Jameson, will you help me gather some deadfall for our fire?"

"Deadfall?" Jameson asked, stepping out of the tent.

"Sticks," Hawk answered. "Twigs that've fallen and dried out."

"But we bought campfire logs."

"Yes, we did, but smaller sticks will help the fire get started."

They gathered the needed kindling, and Wade made the fire while Hawk and Jameson finished unloading their gear and food.

When their work was finished, they sat around the campfire to enjoy its smell and the warmth of the crackling flames. Once the fire stopped smoking, they decided to make s'mores.

Jameson dropped his first two marshmallows in the fire but was successful on the third try. He sat at the picnic table enjoying the treat and looked up at the stars.

"Oh, wow! The sky is so cool!"

Hawk and Wade glanced up as well. "Yes, it is. That's why we love to get out in the woods and camp." Wade smashed his latest marshmallow between graham crackers and a peanut butter cup. "You can't see the stars like this in town."

"What's that?" Jameson asked, pointing northeast. "It's blinking."

Hawk looked up. "That's an airplane."

Jameson nodded. "Wonder where they're going."

Hawk shrugged. "There is no telling."

"I can't wait to fly in a plane! It has to be the best thing. Way up there, higher than birds can fly. Going wherever you want to go,"

Jameson said. Hawk noticed how his eyes lit up as he marveled at the flashing lights and the freedom of flight.

He thought about Lauren taking off in a plane for Greece yesterday. He'd been too busy this week to connect with her, and he regretted it. He feared that his time with Jameson was just adding to Lauren's long list of reasons not to date him. Kids, flying—he'd given her so many reasons to run.

Jameson yawned.

Hawk noticed. "Ready for bed, kiddo?"

"I guess."

"We'll walk to the restroom and brush our teeth. Grab your small case with your toothbrush."

Ten minutes later, they were in the tent and in their sleeping bags.

Hawk thought Jameson had fallen asleep as soon as he lay down, as he was breathing calmly and steadily, but a few minutes later, Jameson whispered, "Hawk?"

"Yeah, J?"

"Can I scoot closer? I think I heard something walking next to the tent."

Hawk smiled in the dark, but dropped the smile before answering so Jameson knew he was taking him seriously. "Certainly. Hold on." Hawk grabbed the boy's sleeping bag and dragged both bag and boy closer. He felt Jameson wiggle even closer. The kid's shoulder and leg were pressed up against him, the two sleeping bags between them.

"Night, Hawk."

"Night, Jameson."

Hawk closed his eyes, but sleep was elusive. His thoughts flipped between Lauren and Jameson so fast, it was as if they were spinning around on a merry-go-round. For both of these important people in his life, Hawk was consumed by what-ifs.

What if Lauren asked him to move to wherever she went to grad school? What if she didn't? What if Jameson was with him a long time? What if he wasn't? What if Jameson got hurt on his watch? What if Jameson wandered away in the woods and got lost? What if Jameson got sick? What if Jameson hated camping?

So many what-ifs and so much time to lie awake and worry.

CHAPTER THIRTY-ONE

FTER THREE DAYS of touring, eating, and exploring Athens and the Delphi region, Lauren was getting to know many of her tour companions.

As she drank coffee and ate breakfast with Gwendolyn Sisk-Boudreau, she learned Gwen was the CEO of a large importer of Greek olives and olive oil, dates, and other foods. Gwen had singled Lauren out and taken an interest in her, as another single woman traveling alone.

Lauren loved talking to the elegant woman in her late sixties, who was having a professional resurgence. Gwen said she'd considered retiring at sixty-five, but when she hit that milestone, she felt fine and decided to carry on. Lauren admired her drive and passion for her company.

Gwen had asked Lauren about her future and was thrilled to learn that Lauren was driven to find a leadership role in a great corporation. They talked extensively about Gwen's business and company.

Lauren had thought a lot about her discussion with Anna Lee at Paige's shower and questioned Gwen about her company's culture.

Gwen suggested that Lauren consider getting her foot in the door of a company *while* she pursued an MBA degree, not after.

Gwen took a drink of her espresso and looked out at the Parnassus Mountains. She sighed. "Lauren, do you know I never got a master's degree?"

"Really? I assumed all CEOs had one."

"Well, I know a number that do not. Now, if you have the way, means, and desire to get it, go for it. I just think you should know that it's not a prerequisite. As a matter of fact, we have a Senior Manager position opening and we don't have many internal candidates. I would love it if you considered it. The company leadership is amazing." She winked at Lauren. "I'd love to mentor you personally. With your GPA and drive, I know you'd hit the ground running."

This had never been part of Lauren's plan, and she couldn't imagine having *that* conversation with her parents, but the more she talked to Gwen, the more the prospect excited her.

Lauren asked Gwen about the pay structure, benefits, and travel requirements. She was thrilled to learn that all leaders were expected to travel to Greece at least once a year. What a perk!

"You know, I haven't worked in a corporate environment yet," Lauren said, putting her coffee cup back in its saucer, "and maybe the hiring manager won't like me, but I would be honored to apply. Please tell me what the next step is."

"As soon as you get home," Gwen answered, "send me your résumé and I'll pass it along to the hiring manager, along with my wholehearted recommendation." She took a small case out of her purse and pulled out a business card. "Here. My card with email address and phone numbers. Call me if you don't hear anything within two days of sending me that résumé."

"I will. Thank you so much for the idea and the opportunity. I will do my best to present well in the interviews."

"I know you will, my dear." Gwen nodded and smiled warmly. "And I hope you're a member of our team by the fourth of July."

Whoa, that would be fast. How would she explain this to her parents? They had stressed the necessity to go from undergrad directly to grad school since she was five. They said they'd seen so many of their friends put grad school on hold and never get back to it. The allure of making a nice paycheck, and then becoming beholden to a paycheck and a certain lifestyle ended the idea of grad school. They argued that gap years turned into gap decades.

But all Lauren could think of was the opportunity to start real-world learning right away. Getting her foot in the door of a good company would teach her so much more than a textbook could. And she was self-motivated enough to get the MBA degree, despite her parents' fears. Gwen had mentioned tuition reimbursement as a company benefit. It seemed like a win-win to Lauren.

The tour director announced that it was time to board the bus for the drive to Olympia.

Lauren grabbed her tote bag and put on her hat. She followed Gwen out the door of the hotel's restaurant and onto the bus.

Gwen pulled a printed document out of her bag and settled in to read during the bus ride. Lauren was thankful she got the window seat so she could look at the view along the drive.

Lauren took the opportunity to think more about the idea of getting a full-time job instead of going to grad school. She was mentally listing all the benefits, so she could prepare herself before speaking to her parents.

Twenty minutes into their drive, Lauren noticed her reflection in the window. She had a grin on her face. She'd been thinking about Hawk and hoped that when she told him about living in Chicago, he'd be as excited as she was.

Ten minutes before they were scheduled to stop, Gwen put the report back into her bag and shifted toward Lauren. "You've been quiet."

"I didn't want to bother you while you were reading."

"I need an excuse to distract me from work."

Lauren laughed. "You're on a tour—a vacation tour. Isn't that enough of an excuse?"

"You are right." Gwen pulled a lip balm out of her bag and applied it before continuing. "But duty calls. Did you come up with any other questions for me while you were sightseeing?"

"I am curious," Lauren began, "if you have children, and how you managed work with young kids."

"I do. I did. And quite well. It helps to have a partner that is as committed to child-rearing as you are. They say it takes a village, but I think it at least starts with having a true partnership at home. Sure, sure, lots of people raise kids alone and do a tremendous job. But I can't imagine how I would have done that and been able to advance in my career like I wanted. When you are on the same page as your partner about how to love your kids, how to raise them, and what values to teach them, it makes things easier. Not that there aren't challenges along the way. Of course, there are. And, in retrospect, if I'd had to give up my career for my kids, I would have done that in a heartbeat. They are my greatest legacy, not my career. I hope it doesn't happen and I don't foresee it happening, but if my company were dissolved next year, my kids and their kids and their kids will go on. My bloodline is more important than any bottom line."

Lauren nodded and considered Gwen's words as the bus came to a stop. Hawk would be that type of partner, devoted to raising kids. From what she knew about him, she felt they were aligned in their philosophies on raising kids, but she knew they needed further discussion. Her biggest concern was whether he would be willing to fly for vacations. She wanted to show her kids the world, not just their small slice of it. It would be a showstopper for her if Hawk didn't feel the same way.

She shook the bracelet he'd given her, jingling the two charms. She rubbed the tiny compass, thinking about the different directions that life could take her. She knew the Illinois charm held the right path for her and she visualized the Route 66 map from Chicago to Normal—from home to the heart of Illinois, where her heart had found its home with Hawk.

HAWK STOOD STARING at the phone in his hand. Anita Ryan told him that they had found a family member to take Jameson—his maternal grandmother. She had been caring for a sick aunt on the east coast and couldn't take Jameson until she returned.

Hawk was happy for Jameson, but disappointed that his first foster placement had only lasted two weeks. He was going to miss helping with homework, putting puzzles together, and hanging out with Jameson. His favorite part of the day had been turning off Jameson's bedroom light after tucking him in. Leaving the young boy to fall asleep in a safe and calm environment filled him with joy.

Anita would pick up Jameson in an hour, so Hawk decided to take the boy for ice cream. Yes, it was before dinner, but that kid would have no problem eating a hamburger after ice cream; he was always hungry.

"Jameson, would you like to go for some ice cream?" Hawk pulled the keys off the hook, feeling confident he knew what Jameson's answer would be.

"Ice cream?" The boy looked up from the coloring book and put down a blue crayon.

"Yes, let's talk and drive."

In the car, Hawk told him that he was going to stay with his grandmother, and Jameson seemed relieved.

"Good, I like Grandma's house."

"Great! I'm so glad to hear that," Hawk said. "I'm going to miss you. It has been a blast having you stay with me."

"Okay."

Hawk smiled. Nothing like a six-year-old to put you in your place.

They went inside to order their ice cream but went back outside to eat it. They sat at the same picnic table Hawk and Lauren had used weeks before. Hawk looked at the tall fencing around the airport as he enjoyed his root beer float.

"Hey, J, there's a plane taking off. Look!" Hawk pointed to where a mid-size plane was beginning to taxi.

"Wow. So cool. Have you ever been on a plane, Hawk?" Jameson asked, loading his spoon up with the ice cream, caramel syrup, and whipped cream in his sundae.

"No. I haven't."

"I'd go to Disney, if I could fly."

"You can get there in a car, too."

"That takes too long. Boring."

Hawk laughed. Maybe the boy was right. Twenty-plus hours in a car would probably be a nightmare with kids.

He thought about the flight school gift certificate Lauren had given him. Maybe it was time for him to conquer his fear and give it a try.

"Should we get a hamburger or a hot dog once we're done with our ice cream?" Hawk asked, stirring the slowly melting ice cream in his root beer.

"Yes!"

"All right. I have to make a phone call. Keep eating."

Hawk picked up his phone, thankful he'd saved the number for the flight school. He dialed and asked if they had an opening on Saturday. They did, and he booked his time slot.

Turning back to Jameson, he mused, "Maybe it's time I got comfortable flying, J. What do you say?"

"Do it, Hawk!" Jameson replied.

Hawk nodded, content. Booking the class gave him something to look forward to. He was still nervous but willing to give it a try. Having this to look forward to would ease a little of the heartache he knew he'd experience once Ms. Ryan took Jameson to his grandmother.

He glanced at the time. "We'd better get those sandwiches to go. We'll have to get all your stuff ready before Ms. Ryan comes."

Hawk was sending the clothes and toys he'd bought specifically for Jameson with him; he'd also bought a new backpack and a wheeled suitcase. He'd done all he could to help ease this transition period for Jameson.

Later that night, once Jameson had left and he and Goldie went for their last walk of the evening, Hawk took out his phone. He wanted to text Lauren just to say hi, but he wasn't sure if there would be astronomical roaming rates, with her traveling in Greece, so he didn't. He went to bed with her and Jameson on his mind. He said a little prayer, wishing both of them safe journeys and smooth transitions home.

CHAPTER THIRTY-TWO

EFORE HER FLIGHT home, Lauren had mentioned to Gwen that she would be in Chicago on Monday and Tuesday visiting her parents and hinted that if there was a chance she could interview then, it would work nicely but of course, if it were too much of a hassle, she'd understand.

Gwen got a gleam in her eye and said, "Way to go, Lauren. I knew you were a go-getter. Email me your résumé as soon as you can, and I'll talk to the hiring manager on Monday."

That worked. Lauren got a call on Monday for interviews on Tuesday. It was a relief her parents were working; she was able to get ready and leave for the appointment after they'd left home. She hadn't told them about the discussions with Gwen and the possibility of a job. When she returned from her trip and they asked about grad school, she asked for a few more days before deciding. She hoped the decision would be about a job offer and not grad school.

The interviews went well. She met with the hiring manager, his leader, and a Human Resources director. She was confident she'd nailed the interviews, but worried that the lack of experience would hurt her chances.

She left for Bloomington right after the interviews and was happy she wouldn't be home when her parents got home from work to answer their "What did you do today?" questions.

She had made plans to meet Paige for dinner and pulled into the restaurant five minutes early.

Inside, she found Paige waiting at the bar.

"Hey, Paige. Want to get a drink, or take our table?" she asked, giving her friend a hug.

"Let's get a table. I'm hungry!"

They settled in and studied the menu for a minute. Paige quickly put hers down. "I'm getting a chicken Caesar salad. Don't let me get anything else. My wedding is in four days! Eek!"

Lauren smiled at her. "I'll get that too, so you're not tempted by a greasy burger or shrimp scampi."

Paige's eyes rolled back, "Oh, scampi. Wish my honeymoon would hurry up and get here. I'm going to pig out!"

"I bet. Are you all ready? Need any help the next few days?" Lauren took a sip of her ice water.

"No." Paige picked up a roll from the breadbasket, sighed, and put it on her little plate. "Everything is ready to go. Are you working at Anna Lee's on Friday?"

"Yes, I think everyone is. I'm relieved Nica and Tilly have things covered on Saturday."

"Yes, we'll be getting pampered Saturday morning. I can't wait. I'm nervous, excited, and so thrilled. Everything is coming together. Now, please get my mind off my wedding. Tell me about your trip!"

"It was fantastic."

"I admire you for traveling solo. Did you meet anyone?" Paige wiggled her eyebrows.

"I did. But not in a romantic way. I met the CEO of an importing company and—" She paused for drama. "I interviewed with her company today. That's why I'm in the suit."

"Oh, I wondered. I thought maybe you were just stepping up your apparel game. But if you interviewed, what does that mean for your MBA and grad school?"

"If I'm offered the job, I will postpone grad school. The company has a fantastic tuition reimbursement program, and I think by working first, I'll get even more out of an MBA degree."

"How do you think the interview went?" The server put their salads down, and Paige picked up the knife to butter her roll.

"Interviews. Three of them. I think they went well."

"What do your parents say?"

Lauren cut the large pieces of lettuce in her salad. "I haven't told them. They are expecting an answer on grad school soon. I hope I get a job offer quickly. It will be a shift, but I think they'll come around."

Paige had finished one roll and was buttering the next one. "And what about Hawk? What does he think of these plans?"

"I haven't talked to him since I got back."

"Really? Nothing?"

"Just a text asking if I landed okay Sunday night. I told him I had, and then—crickets. I told him I was staying in Chicago for a couple days, so maybe he wanted to give me time with my family or he's just really busy with Jameson."

"Hmm, seems odd. I can ask Trevor if he knows what's going on."

"No. Don't bother. I'll see him this weekend."

"Yes, Friday at the rehearsal, if not before."

"Yes, the rehearsal. What time are we meeting again? Jet lag." Lauren wanted to move Paige off the topic of Hawk. She just assumed he was busy with Jameson, and she understood that. His attention should be on Jameson, not on worrying about her.

"Six at the park. The officiant will be there to walk us through our entrances and the ceremony. Then off to dinner. Can't wait!"

"Me either."

Lauren really couldn't wait. Hopefully, it would be her chance to talk to Hawk and let him know a change in her plans. She'd thought a lot about work and kids and Hawk while on her trip. She was ready to help him in his calling. If he'd let her.

"HAWK. WHAT'S UP?" Trevor asked when Hawk answered his call.

Hawk stared out the window of his office and contemplated the question. "I'm finishing up my workday."

"Do you and Jameson want to come over tonight and chase lightning bugs?"

Hawk put his phone on speaker and set it on the desk. "Sounds fun. But." He let out a sigh. "Jameson's no longer with me. A family member took him in last week."

"Oh, man. I can tell you're bummed. I'm sorry."

"I am, but it's okay. It's the best thing for Jameson. That's what counts."

Trevor paused. "Right. Well, no lightning bugs. Want to go grab a drink?"

Hawk considered. He'd wanted to stop by Lauren's tonight to try to catch her at home. He had a lot to talk to her about but didn't want to do it over the phone, and with the wedding coming up this weekend, things were just going to get more challenging. But this was one of his best friends, who was on the verge of getting married and probably needed a distraction. "Sure, I'll meet you. I just need to finish up a few things here. Give me an hour?"

"No problem. Let's meet at High Jinks."

"I'll see you there."

Hawk hung up and opened the lid of his personal laptop. With a few keystrokes, he bought two plane tickets to Boston. He was still nervous contemplating his first real flight, but the thought of Lauren there beside him made the nerves worth it.

Next, he searched for fun things to do in Boston and Cambridge on the weekend. He found a walking tour of downtown Boston, an amphibious vehicle tour that went from land to water, and a ghost tour in Cambridge. He searched for a few restaurant recommendations, but he wanted Lauren to have input into the trip and where they ate.

Now, how to present this trip to her. He decided he needed a little help from his friends. He sent Paige a text message.

> **HAWK:** Hey. Do you think you could stealthily get Lauren's shoe size for me?

He didn't have to wait long for her response.

> **PAIGE:** Easy peasy. We're the same—size 9.

He asked that she keep the question to herself and said he'd see her on Friday.

He glanced at the time. If he hustled, he would have enough time to purchase the other part of Lauren's surprise before meeting Trevor. The shoe store he needed was across the street from High Jinks.

CHAPTER THIRTY-THREE

IT HAD ALREADY been an exciting day and Lauren still had the rehearsal dinner coming up. She'd received a job offer from Gwen's company first thing that morning. She managed to hold all her shouts of joy until she was off the phone. But once she hung up, she turned on a pop music playlist and danced round her living room.

The day before, she had written down several questions that she would ask if they offered the position, so she was prepared for the phone call.

After her questions were answered, she accepted the position and received an email from Gwen an hour later, welcoming her to the organization.

Lauren had to wait until lunch time to call her parents. She called her mom first, who immediately conferenced her dad into the call.

It took twenty minutes to answer their questions and, in the end, she felt they were onboard with her decision. She explained to them that Hawk had become a factor in her decision making and they said they'd like the opportunity to get to know him better. Though they were disappointed she was putting off grad school—for now—they were excited to have her back in Chicago.

After parking at the Latimer Greens Park, Lauren grabbed the box containing mini practice bouquets from the front seat. Anna Lee had sent them with Lauren when she'd left In Bloom that morning.

Getting out of the car, she scanned the parking lot to see if she recognized any of the other members of the wedding party. Nope. She hoped she wasn't late and hurried toward the open-air pavilion.

She found the group milling about.

Paige was the first to see her and waved. "Lauren!"

"Hi, I made it."

Paige wore a pale green dress that made her eyes sparkle. Lauren put the box down and hugged her friend.

"We're waiting for Tricia and then we'll get started. Mingle. Macey has a question for you about jewelry." Paige floated over to the officiant, who was speaking with Paige's parents.

Lauren looked around for Macey and felt her breath catch when she saw Hawk. He was talking to Chase and hadn't noticed her yet. He was wearing dark slacks and a blue-checkered, short-sleeved button-down shirt.

She smoothed out her cream-colored pants and flagged Macey down. They were agreeing to wear silver jewelry for the ceremony when Hawk approached. Macey quickly excused herself.

"Ms. Largent," he said in a serious tone, "it's good to see you. It's been too long."

She took a moment to take him in. His warm eyes, his inviting lips. It had been much too long. She gave him a quick hug.

"Hello," she began. She glanced around. "Where's Jameson? Have a sitter tonight?"

Hawk blinked slowly, a pinched smile on his face. "He's with his grandma. Permanently. I miss him, but I'm happy for him."

"Oh, Hawk." She put her hand on his arm. "I'm so sorry. When?"

"Last week."

"Oh." She didn't know what to say; she'd assumed he'd been busy caring for Jameson, and that was why she hadn't heard from him. His feelings for her must have cooled.

"I'm all right. Now, I can't wait to hear about your trip."

A gong sounded. A real gong. Lauren swung around at the sound. Paige's brother Brian was standing behind her with a smaller version of the instrument in one hand and a mallet in the other.

"Let's bring it in, everyone!" he yelled.

Everyone laughed and Lauren looked at Hawk. "Guess it's time to get this rehearsal going."

"Indeed." He placed his hand on her lower back as they moved to the front of the pavilion.

Lauren listened to the instructions intently, but never lost track of where Hawk was. She felt she had homing pigeon instincts.

At the end of the rehearsal, Trevor told everyone that they were running ahead of schedule and had to fill forty-five minutes before their reservation at the restaurant. He directed everyone to join them at the restaurant's bar.

"Lauren, before we head over, I have something for you. Do you mind stopping by my Jeep?"

"You do? I'm intrigued." She thought about the backgammon set she'd bought for Hawk in Greece. It was at her apartment. This weekend, she wanted to focus on Paige and Trevor's wedding.

He walked to the passenger side and opened the door, pulling out a large dark blue gift bag with strands of white curling ribbon hanging from the handle.

He handed it to her. "Open it."

She pulled out the tissue paper and laid it on the seat, then leaned over to look in the bag. Reaching in, she pulled out a pair of dark brown hiking boots.

"Boots, huh? Planning another hike?"

"Absolutely. Now look in the boot."

Expecting to see socks, she was surprised to see an envelope. She set the boots on the seat and pulled out the envelope. She turned to him with a quizzical expression.

"Money for socks?" she teased.

He lip twitched up in that half smile of his. "Open it."

She opened the envelope and found two sheets of paper. The first sheet was a printed itinerary with a list of sightseeing tours in Boston and Cambridge. The second was a confirmation email for two airline tickets to Boston.

"Hawk…," she drawled, "what's this for?"

"Well, I've been thinking about the grad school decision you've been struggling with. Wait, you haven't made that decision yet, have you?" He paused, waiting for her response.

"No…"

"Good. So, I thought we'd take a quick weekend trip to see Harvard. Walk around, take a few tours. I have an itinerary started as you can see. I know you like planned tours. So, we'll call it 'Hawk's Exciting and Adventurous Tour of Boston and Cambridge'. It will be a blast."

"But—but you don't fly. And this is a confirmation email for two airline tickets, one for you and one for me." She pointed to the second sheet of paper.

"Well, it'll be my first real flight. I took that flying class you gave me. Thank you again for that. It was incredibly generous and incredibly thoughtful. Now, I'm not saying I won't throw up, but I'm willing to try. Lauren, I don't know what's ahead of us and I know it's not going to be easy. But whether we're hiking in the woods or taking a flight somewhere, I want to be by your side." He paused and took her hand in his. "I know the long-distance thing will be tough, but if we both give one hundred percent, I think we can do it."

"I'm so glad you took the class and are willing to try to fly. That means a lot to me." She took a deep breath. "And I care an awful lot about you. You have come to mean so much to me. I think about you all the time. I wonder what you would think about a news report I hear, or an article I read, or a TV show I watch. When you're not by my side, I feel unmoored, like I'm bouncing along in the ocean on a floatie." She raised the corner of her lip in a half-smile. "And, about the school thing…I have some news to share."

"What news? I thought you hadn't decided."

"I'm not going to grad school this fall."

"You're not?"

"No. I've accepted a job offer in Chicago. It'll still be a long-distance relationship, but not as long as Boston or Stanford. If you're willing to give it a go, I am, too."

Hawk picked her up and swung her around. "One hundred and ten percent."

Lauren laughed. "A hundred and twenty percent!"

Hawk laughed, too. "A hundred and thirty. Hey, leave your car here. Ride with me. I think we have a lot of catching up to do after dinner. Plus, Goldie misses you."

"She is missable."

"As are you."

"I can't, though. The bridesmaids are staying with Paige tonight. To keep her company and help settle her nerves. Rain check?"

He hadn't let her go since he'd spun her around; his arms still wrapped around her body. "Rain check—how about Sunday Funday? Ready to break in those hiking boots?"

"Yes! Let's do it."

CHAPTER THIRTY-FOUR

AFTER A COUPLE of hours hiking in the Singing Woods Nature Preserve in Edelstein, fifteen miles north of Peoria, Lauren's boots were dirty and appeared to be broken in. This Sunday Funday had started with Hawk bringing her a bouquet of white calla lilies, "just because", and stopping for a big greasy breakfast at Max's Coffee Shop before the drive to the nature preserve.

During the hike, they laughed about what a whirlwind the previous thirty-six hours had been. They talked in depth about Paige and Trevor's wedding the day before. There were so many fun memories and highlights for them to share with each other. Hawk said the only disappointing aspect of the wedding for him was that he and Lauren did not get to walk down the aisle together. But his disappointment was tempered by the fact that they had treated the wedding as a date. They danced every slow dance together and stayed together for most of the evening.

"Ready to head back?" Hawk asked, as they came out of the woods and saw the parking lot.

"Yes, I think I need a shower," Lauren replied.

"And a tick check."

"Gross. But yes. That too."

They approached the Jeep and Hawk tossed his backpack into the backseat and strapped it down. It was a gorgeous day, and he'd left the vehicle's top off.

As he settled into the driver's seat, he laughed to see Lauren peel off her boots and socks.

She shook her head. "My feet need to be aired out. Don't make fun."

"Good thing we have plenty of *fresh* air," he said as he started the Jeep.

"Ha, ha," she said in a monotone voice.

"So, the boots worked out all right?"

"Perfect!" She smiled at him. "Thanks again." She buckled in and laid her head back on the seat for a moment. "What a glorious day and a wonderful hike! This may be my new favorite thing to do."

"Spending time with me?" Hawk asked playfully.

"That's a given. And you introduced me to hiking. I appreciate it."

Hawk thought about what she'd introduced him to—flying. After the lesson and short flight, he felt better about the idea and would feel even better after their first trip. They were scheduled to go in two weeks, just before Lauren started her new job in Chicago.

He was thrilled she'd be so close. It wasn't close enough, but it would do for now. They'd talked all morning about how they were going to make the mid-distance relationship work. They would speak on the phone every evening and see each other every weekend. He was thankful he wouldn't have to take a flight to see her.

"So, ideas for dinner?" he asked, backing out of the parking spot.

"Can we order a pizza?"

"You bet! Are you ready to try out the backgammon set when we get back?"

"Yes, I am. Before we do that, I want to call my parents and make sure they're ok with me moving back home. I didn't think to ask when we spoke before. It would be great to build up some savings before looking for my own place."

"Right. And who knows, maybe there will be other factors in play before you choose a new place. Like me. And Goldie."

She nodded. "Absolutely! No major decisions without consulting each other first. We're a team."

"Yes, we are. We're a dream team." He picked up her hand and kissed the back of it.

He had a pretty good idea of what the future had in store for them. He was filled with excitement and anticipation.

His phone rang, and he glanced at the caller ID. Ms. Ryan.

"Whoa! I'm going to pull over." He spotted a gas station ahead and turned in.

Putting the car in park, he hit the answer button and put the call on speaker. "Hi, Anita."

"Hawk," she said, briskly. "I know it's Sunday afternoon, but I have an emergency. Are you home?"

"I'm not." He looked at Lauren to see her reaction; she seemed calm and curious. "But I will be in about an hour. What's up?"

"I have an eight-year-old that needs placement. It's summer, so she won't be in school. You'll need daycare. Will that be a problem?"

"I don't think so. But can I call you back in a few minutes? This is a major decision, and I need to check in with my support team."

"Five minutes? Fine. Call me back." She hung up.

Hawk turned to Lauren. Before he could say anything, she was nodding her head.

"You should do it, Hawk. I can help over the next two weeks."

"What about our trip?"

"Refundable tickets, right?"

"Yes."

"We'll go another time. This is more important."

Hawk sighed. This was why they were a dream team. "When I call back, I'll make sure we have some time before she brings the child over, so you can call your parents. But I recommend not telling them I'm fostering right away. Ease them into that."

Lauren smiled. "Good call. Hey, I haven't told you, but I started looking into foster care myself—to understand it better so I can support you. Like you said, major decisions will take both of us."

Hawk leaned over and hugged her. "Lauren, I can't tell you how happy that makes me. How happy you make me." He pulled back and noticed tears in her eyes.

"Ditto," she said. "Now call Ms. Ryan back. There's a kid that needs you."

"Right." He pulled up Anita's number and hit send, smiling at Lauren. "Ms. Ryan," he said when she answered, "we got this. We'll make it work."

Lauren squeezed his hand and smiled. "Dream Team," she mouthed.

Yes, the Dream Team. They would make it work.

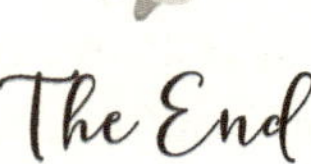

The End

EPILOGUE

One Year Later

LAUREN SQUEEZED HAWK'S hand. "Are you ready?" His Adam's apple bobbed as he swallowed, and he squeezed her hand in response. "Yep," he said between tight lips.

"I'm here if you need me."

"Yep."

Lauren looked out the window of the Boeing 787 and bit her lip to keep from smiling. *This is going to be a long flight*, she thought. She let go of his hand and leaned down to grab her tote bag, taking out the backgammon set that she'd bought Hawk during her trip to Greece last year.

"Are you ready for me to kick your butt?" she asked, hoping to distract him. She knew appealing to his competitive nature would help.

"You brought backgammon?" he asked. "On our honeymoon?"

Lauren smiled. "I thought it might come in handy in times like this. As a distraction."

"Hmm, won't we take off soon?"

"It'll take a little while to board everyone. We can get a game in."

The flight attendant stopped. "Would you like a glass of bubbly? A little birdie told me it's your honeymoon."

233

Hawk laughed. "And by little birdie, do you mean my wife's t-shirt?"

Lauren was wearing a black, long-sleeved T-shirt with *BRIDE* emblazoned in hot pink sparkly letters four inches high across the front.

"Well," the attendant answered, "that was my first clue."

Lauren laughed. "It's a little cheesy. But I love it! And yes, we'd love a glass of champagne. It might help calm our nerves." She rolled her eyes in Hawk's direction.

"Ah, yes." The attendant winked at Lauren. "Coming right up."

Hawk twisted in his seat and put his hand over Lauren's. "Let's hold off on the game. I'm all right. I'd rather talk about the wedding or what we're going to see in Paris. *Anything* but the flight."

"All right." She put the backgammon set back in the tote. "We have a lot to talk about. Like everything we have to do when we get home. Closing on our new house. Packing up your house. Moving all our stuff into the new place. Submitting a joint application to foster. There's so much to do—my brain hurts thinking about all of it."

"Hey, slow down, sweetie. Take a deep breath. Your nervousness will amp up my anxiety. And we don't want that, do we?"

Lauren chuckled. "No, we don't. Okay. Let's talk about the wedding. Again. Was it everything you wanted it to be?"

"It was fan-flipping-tastic! Everything I wanted. But if we had eloped like you suggested, I would have loved that, too. The only thing that mattered to me is that you were standing by my side when the officiant pronounced us husband and wife. Everything else was a bonus. Was it everything you wanted it to be?"

The flight attendant returned with glasses of champagne. "Compliments of the crew. Congratulations on your marriage."

Lauren was glad she'd said marriage and not wedding. She agreed with Hawk. The wedding wasn't the important part. The marriage was. That her parents had let her and Hawk arrange and coordinate their wedding on their own terms was the icing on the cake. The ceremony had taken place outdoors and it had been a glorious June Saturday. The altar sat at the edge of a small lake that featured a water fountain in the middle of it. Anna Lee had draped the white trellis with the most extravagant blanket of white calla lilies, soft burgundy roses and lush greens. She'd used the same flowers in the bouquets and the centerpieces.

Since Lauren's parents insisted on paying for the wedding, she made sure the flowers were one of the most expensive items, right behind food and drink.

They kept their guest list down to eighty people. Having the wedding in Central Illinois helped keep the count low; her parents' Chicago-based law partners and acquaintances wouldn't have made the two to three-hour trip.

Lauren's mom was very supportive and not controlling, as Lauren had feared. She offered advice and opinions but did not dictate any aspect of the wedding. Lauren felt as if something had shifted between herself and her parents. Moving back home and having daily interactions instead of a weekly check-in phone call had helped. Lauren's hard work and rave reviews from her new boss helped her parents see she was forging the right path for herself.

Getting back to Hawk's question after a sip of champagne, Lauren said, "Yes. The wedding ceremony and reception were everything I had hoped for. But you, Hawk Springer, are everything I ever wanted. I am so excited about beginning our life together. I know it won't always be champagne and roses. We'll have our share of hard times, but I think we've proven to each other that together we can conquer anything."

"Even a fear of flying."

Lauren laughed. "Cheers to that! I'm so thankful you took that flight class and opened yourself up to the possibility of flying. I'm sure the couple of short flights we took prepared you for this one."

Hawk raised an eyebrow. "I'm not feeling as confident as you are, but with you beside me, I know it'll be all right. Now, back to the wedding. What were your top three favorite memories of the reception?"

Lauren paused for a moment. "Top three. Hmm. Number one was our first dance as husband and wife. Such a special moment, and I hope someday we'll be that couple that wins the longest marriage dance. It was sweet when your great-aunt and uncle were the last ones dancing. Wow, to be married sixty-two years, just beautiful."

Hawk nodded. "That was great, and I agree, our first dance was my favorite memory, too. Now, what's your second favorite?"

"Second would be cutting the cake. Thank you for not shoving cake in my face."

"Wouldn't dream of it. And your third?"

"Third, the bouquet toss. Did you see Tilly standing there with her arms crossed before I tossed it?"

"Yeah, that was comical. It was even better once those flowers were in the air. She ended up leaping for them."

"The look on her date's face was priceless. I guess they're just friends, but I don't know. There might be more there than either of them wants to admit. I saw them slow dancing, and it looked more than friendly to me."

"Well, maybe when we get back, you can ask her about it. Maybe our wedding will be the catalyst for another beautiful relationship."

Lauren smiled. "I would love that. Now, what were your favorite memories from the reception?"

"My first was the same as yours, the first dance. Second, my brother's toast as best man. He killed it. I was so proud of him. And third was mingling with everyone and accepting their congratulations. What a moment—to be surrounded by so many people who were there to witness our marriage and to wish us well. It was just an incredible day. I feel so blessed to have had the perfect day, the perfect ceremony, and the most perfect bride in the universe."

"Oh, Hawk. You've already got me. You can cut the flattery."

"It's not flattery. It's the truth." He put his arm across her shoulders and pulled her close.

A voice came over the PA system announcing that the flight crew would be shutting the doors and the plane would be taking off in a few minutes. Lauren felt a ripple flow through Hawk. "Hey, you got this," she said.

"I know," he agreed. "With you, I do. We're a dream team."

"That we are, Mr. Springer."

"That we are, Mrs. Springer."

Hearing him say her married name sent tingles down her spine. They had so much to look forward to—their honeymoon, their new home, future foster kids, and someday, a few kids of their own.

BONUS SCENE

NOTE: This scene takes place *during* the events of *Lilies for Lauren*. This scene is from Anna Lee's point of view, and it occurs the day after Anna Lee's boyfriend's daughter, Deana's, wedding. Lauren asked Anna Lee about it at Paige's bridal shower.

SALTY JUMPED ON Anna Lee's chest for the third time. She opened one eye and looked at the bedside clock. Ten a.m. *No wonder the cat is hounding me*, she thought.

She threw back the bedcovers and slowly sat up. "I know you're hungry, Salty. It's very late. Hold onto your britches and I'll get your kitty kibble in a minute."

Anna Lee rubbed her eyes and picked up her glasses. She pushed off the bed with a grunt. Too much dancing the day before and she was feeling it in every muscle in her body—except maybe her eyelids.

Salty sat at the end of the bed, watching every movement. When Anna Lee started for the door, Salty flung himself off the bed and landed with the grace of a cat half his age.

A few minutes later, Anna Lee rambled into the kitchen with Salty dancing around her ankles. She poured a scoop of food into his bowl and scratched him between the ears.

She shuffled to the stove to put the kettle on for tea. While she waited for the water to heat, she sat at the dinette and looked through the window to the backyard where she watched a couple of robins hop around, searching for worms and bugs.

She pulled her personal journal close to her and picked up a pen.

April 23 - Thank goodness it's Sunday! A day of rest and more rest for my old bones. Deana's (John's daughter) wedding was yesterday and I'm exhausted.

Deana was absolutely gorgeous. Her dress, hair, and makeup were divine. She asked me to create a flower crown for her and it was the most spectacular one I've ever made! I used white and pale pink miniature roses, ivy, and clear crystal beads. It sparkled when the light hit it just right.

The ceremony was touching. I saw Ed shed a few tears. And I'll admit it—I cried a little bit myself to see John walk his daughter down that aisle. I declare. I couldn't help but think about an alternate universe where my Gene had survived Vietnam and walked our daughter down the aisle. I wonder if our daughter ever married and if her adopted father walked her down the aisle. I hope so. Shoot, maybe she's even had children of her own who've gotten married. Oh, I'd love to know how her life turned out. I just want to know she's ok and that my giving her up didn't ruin her life.

Well, I digress. Back to the present, or at least yesterday. The ceremony was beautiful; the reception was spectacular. Funniest memory—the bouquet toss. Someone tried to push me out onto the floor, but I grabbed a hold of a table and wouldn't let go! No, sir-ee. But that wasn't the funniest part. When Deana tossed that bouquet, Tara and another girl jumped at the same time for it. Tara won! Maybe John will walk another daughter down the aisle before long. But the funny part was, when she came down, she broke the heel off her shoe and had to limp around. Didn't take her long to go barefoot. What a sight.

John managed the wedding fairly well. I know he missed his wife. She'd been alive when their first daughter married so this was the first wedding she'd missed. I was no stand-in, but I think John appreciated me being there.

I'm sure he'll call later this morning. He suggested going to lunch, but I'll decline. I'm not leaving my house today. I need to recharge for the workweek. Lots to look forward to this spring. Next weekend is the fundraiser Lauren is helping with, and the weekend after that is Paige's wedding shower, and then both of them will be graduated and likely moving on. I hate to see them go, but they got their lives to live. I hope they don't forget me and come back to visit.

Now, that Tilly. She's a puzzle. She's sweet, but she drives me crazy. Sometimes I want to throttle that kid. She's always asking questions and wants to know everything. Never meets a stranger. She's going to make a good therapist someday. Or maybe a flower shop owner. Ha-ha.

Well, Salty is meowing at the door, wanting on the back porch to watch the birdies. I think I'll get a cup of tea and join him out there.

WHAT'S NEXT?

I hope you enjoyed *Lilies for Lauren* and are rooting for all the In Bloom ladies. If you were disappointed that Paige's wedding was not included in this story, be on the lookout for *Tulips for Tilly*—Paige's wedding kicks it off. After Paige's wedding, there are lots of surprises awaiting both Tilly and Anna Lee, you won't want to miss them.

If you enjoyed this story, I hope will consider leaving a review. A review helps a story get discovered and helps other readers know if a book is right for them. Leave a review wherever you normally do—Amazon, Goodreads, Barnes & Noble, The StoryGraph, etc.

In case you've missed the first two books in the series…

Peonies for Paige—Paige is planning to go to New York for a summer internship, but what happens when the internship falls through and she meets a handsome plumber at In Bloom? The e-book is in Kindle Unlimited on Amazon. https://www.amazon.com/dp/B0B8GD3H1K. There are also paperback and hardback versions available on Amazon, Barnes & Noble, Bookshop.org, and other book retailers.

Book two is *Dahlias for Dominica* and tells Nica's story. She dreams of flipping houses, and the sparks and stars align when she meets her handsome landlord, Grady. It, too, is available in Kindle Unlimited on Amazon www.amazon.com/dp/B0B9T6GN61.

There are also paperback and hardback versions available on Amazon, Barnes & Noble, Bookshop.org, and other book retailers.

Tulips for Tilly will be released in the summer of 2023. You can preorder the e-book on Amazon now while it's on sale! https://www.amazon.com/gp/product/B0BTMVP1PM

ACKNOWLEDGEMENTS

First, I want to thank my husband, Tim, for supporting my writing dream. Thank you for being my sounding board, my inspiration, and my champion. I don't know what I would do without you. I love you!

Family is everything, and I owe a sincere thank you to my siblings, siblings-in-law, aunts, uncles, cousins, nieces, and nephews for all the encouragement. I love you infinitely.

A huge shout out to Marisa F, Rebecca E, and Camille D for beta reading—thank you for your kind words, constructive feedback, and brilliant ideas.

Thank you to the professionals that supported this project—Rebecca H for copy editing and Stacy U for editing and proofreading—thank you for your extra flexibility with dates this go around!

Stephanie and Melissa at Alt 19 Creative—thank you for the gorgeous book cover and interior formatting!

And a heartfelt thank you to you, dear reader, for taking a chance on this story.

ABOUT THE AUTHOR

Kasey Kennedy is an Illinois gal through and through. She grew up in Central Illinois, completed college at Southern Illinois University Carbondale and soon after, moved to Chicago. She's been in Chicago or the surrounding suburbs ever since.

Kasey is very happily married to her husband Tim and loves nothing more than spending time with him–especially when that involves live music! If not attending a live show, they are usually enjoying evenings on the deck, listening to music; visiting their large families; watching movies; or planning their next trip.

When not dreaming up new characters and new stories, Kasey is reading or planning what to read next. Occasionally, she pulls out the guitar that she has been trying to learn for 30+ years and strums enough to annoy her cat, Pepper.

Keep in touch:

FACEBOOK:

https://www.facebook.com/kaseykennedy8/

INSTAGRAM:

https://www.instagram.com/kaseykennedy8/

WEBSITE:

https://www.kasey-kennedy.com